DESERT CITY DIVA

DESERT CITY DIVA

Corey Lynn Fayman

This first world edition published 2015
in Great Britain and in the USA by
SEVERN HOUSE PUBLISHERS LTD of
19 Cedar Road, Sutton, Surrey, England, SM2 5DA.
Trade paperback edition first published 2016
in Great Britain and the USA by
SEVERN HOUSE PUBLISHERS LTD.

Fayman, Corey Lynn, author.
  Desert city diva.
  1. Private investigators–California–Fiction.
  2. Murder–Investigation–Fiction. 3. Cults–Fiction.
  4. Detective and mystery stories.
  I. Title
  813.6-dc23

ISBN-13: 978-0-7278-8548-7 (cased)
ISBN-13: 978-1-84751-657-2 (trade paper)
ISBN-13: 978-1-78010-711-0 (e-book)

All Severn House titles are printed on acid-free paper.

Severn House Publishers support the Forest Stewardship Council™ [FSC™], the
leading international forest certification organisation. All our titles that are printed
on FSC certified paper carry the FSC logo.

MIX
Paper from
responsible sources
FSC   FSC® C013056
www.fsc.org

Typeset by Palimpsest Book Production Ltd.,
Falkirk, Stirlingshire, Scotland.
Printed and bound in Great Britain by
TJ International, Padstow, Cornwall.

To Maria, for the roads we've travelled,
and the solitudes shared.

ONE

The Bite

I t was a bad idea to go out for Mexican food at 2:30 in the morning, but that hadn't prevented Rolly Waters from stopping by the Villa Cantina for a plate of machaca after his gig. It wasn't the machaca that was going to kill him, though. It was the bite on his leg. It was a whole string of bad ideas that had brought him to this wretched state, on the nauseous edge of mortality. Bad ideas, bad decisions, bad choices – whatever you wanted to call them – each one had inexorably led to the next. And each had led to this moment, as he barfed his guts out in the emergency room at the hospital. He didn't even know the name of the hospital. He didn't know the name of the town it was in. He only knew that he'd never felt this sick. He knew he was going to die.

Medical personnel dressed in grubby green scrubs gathered around him, thwarting his passage into oblivion, perhaps hastening it. One of them jabbed his left arm with a needle. Another wrapped his right arm in a blood pressure cuff. They pulled his pants off and inspected his ankle as the vital signs monitor beeped in his ear. His left leg felt like burning coals had been inserted under his skin. A woman made him swallow two pills. She gave him a shot glass of liquid that smelled like rotten eggs. Stomach acid swirled up in his throat. The doctors and nurses floated on a bilious green cloud. He lifted his head and leaned over the bucket. His stomach heaved but nothing came up. He closed his eyes and lay back on the bed. The air smelled like old fish. He surrendered to the vivid manifestations of an unsettled sleep.

Poisson. It was the French word for fish. One letter different from poison. There were no fish in the desert. There was no water. The aliens drank gold in their water. The people drank poison. The people couldn't breathe. They gasped for air like fish in the living room.

He opened his eyes. The harsh light of the emergency room

glowed with a creeping softness. A nurse came by and gave him two more pills. He laughed. Valium always made him loopy like this. If he was going to die, he would be defiant in death, laughing his way into the great darkness. There were worse ways to go. He would die laughing, with a smile on his face. Out of his mind. Definitely Valium. Over and out.

The man had a gift for him. The man was a bird. The bird sang a song. The song had gold notes. The girl had gold eyes.

He awoke. There was no one around. He watched with dull fascination as the blood pressure cuff on his right arm inflated again. It was going to blow up in his face. As it was about to crush his arm into fractured bits of bone gravel, the cuff exhaled and collapsed. He turned his head on the pillow and looked up at the ceiling. The tiles in the ceiling were damaged. Crumpled and stained. His left leg still burned, but less so than before. His stomach seemed steadier.

A nurse appeared next to him, acting like she wanted to take his temperature. He opened his mouth and took the plastic tip under his tongue. She checked the number, nodded and removed the thermometer.

'Coming down,' she said. She looked at the display on the blood pressure monitor. 'Blood pressure's down too.'

'I'm not gun' die?' Rolly said, nodding his head in affirmation.

'No. Doesn't look like you're going to die today,' the nurse said. She smiled at him. 'Of course, we'll need the doctor to confirm that. He's the one that gets to decide.'

The nurse was cute. Real cute. Macy Starr was cute, too. In a different way.

'How's your leg feeling?' the nurse asked.

'Bedder,' said Rolly. His mouth felt like it had been blasted with fine sand.

'Good. I'll check back in a little bit. It's going to be a couple more hours, to make sure you get down to normal.'

'Where am I?'

'Brawley General Hospital. Do you remember checking in?'

'I remember driving in a rocket ship. There were some blue lights. It smelled like fish.'

'That's Brawley, all right. It's the fertilizer that smells. I don't know what the rocket ship part's about.'

'Something bit me.'

'A black widow spider. Probably not a good idea to go tramping around barefoot in Slab City like your friends said you were doing.'

'My friends? Are they here?'

'I can check if you want. Do you feel ready to see people?'

'In a little while,' Rolly said, feeling sleepy again. The nurse closed the curtains and left. He lay back on the pillow.

He was sitting in a rowboat on a sandy hill. His father was there. They were in the same boat. His father shouted at him, giving orders. His father handed him a ukulele. He said there was a bomb in the boat. His father saluted, then jumped out of the boat and swam away.

Rolly opened his eyes. He remembered where he was. The Brawley General emergency ward was quieter now, last night's hubbub reduced to a muted hum. He wondered if the staff had forgotten about him and closed the place down, gone to lunch, or breakfast, or whatever meal it was time for.

The monitoring equipment they'd hooked him up to continued to beep at regular intervals, but it seemed less alarming now. The swelling in his leg had gone down, along with the pain. He felt almost normal. He felt ready to check out. That didn't count for much. He knew how it went in the emergency ward. Like Zeno's arrow, each minute got longer the closer you got to being discharged. He lay back on the bed, stared at the crumpled, stained tiles in the ceiling.

Three days ago, he'd gone out for Mexican food at 2:30 in the morning. That's when he'd met Macy Starr, at the Villa Cantina. If he'd gone home right after his gig, or just gone to the grocery store, he would never have taken her case. He wouldn't be lying in the hospital in the rotten fish city of Brawley with a black widow spider bite on his ankle. Things would get complicated with Macy now, accounting his hours, parsing them into the personal and the professional. Last night they'd had sex in the Tioga. The spider bite was a message. The message said he was an idiot.

Macy Starr had golden eyes.

TWO
The DJ

Macy Starr had golden eyes. She had strawberry-blonde hair. It hung down in dreadlocks that surrounded her tan, freckled face like a halo of soggy breadsticks. At this moment, she was drenched in sweat, the kind of sweat that pours off your body when you work a room with bright spotlights and poor ventilation. It was nightclub sweat, an affidavit of her vocation, and Rolly's, the sweat that blooms off the bodies of musicians, strippers and stand-up comedians. No amount of antiperspirant or hygienic preparation would hold it back.

Macy was a dance club DJ, cranking out beats until the early hours of morning. She'd just finished her gig at the club adjoining the Villa Cantina restaurant in downtown San Diego. Rolly had stopped in at the cantina after his own gig that night, bending guitar strings at Patrick's Pub six blocks away. Under normal conditions, an old-school guitar player like himself and a young beatmaker like Macy would have little to say to each other. They would not have crossed paths. Vera, the hostess, had introduced them. Macy needed help. She needed advice, the kind only a guitar-playing private detective could provide.

Macy had tattoos all over her thin muscular arms – geometric marks and mythical creatures, symbols of something. Rolly had no idea what. She was a small woman with the nervous energy of a flycatcher. Her eyes were amazing. They sparkled with bright flecks of gold that seemed to illuminate the dim light of the back corner booth. A bead of sweat dripped down Macy's neck and fell into her lovely jugular notch. She was at least twenty years younger than Rolly.

'Not much to look at down there,' she said, interrupting his gaze.

'Your shirt is, uh . . . kind of unusual,' said Rolly, raising his eyes from Macy's chest.

'You like Stoner Mickey?' she said, looking down at the front of her tank top, a rainbow-eyed Mickey Mouse wearing head-phones and smoking a king-sized joint.

'I assume that's not officially licensed?' said Rolly.

'It's a one-off. I made it myself. Disney's lawyers would tear this off my body in copyright-induced rage if they ever saw it. They're hardcore about branding. That's what I heard anyway. What do you think?'

'About Disney?'

'No, dumbass. About that guitar thing. You ever seen anything like it?'

The guitar thing in question wasn't really a guitar. It was a one-stringed instrument propped up on the booth in between them. It was well made, with a finely finished wood body, a gold-plated tuning peg and a vintage single-coil pickup. You could make some noise with it, but it lacked the refinements and playability of a real guitar.

'I'd call it a diddley bow,' said Rolly.

'Diddley what?'

'Diddley bow. They started in the South. Sharecroppers would attach a piece of wood to their house, drive in a couple of nails and stretch a wire between them so they could thump on it. Kind of a poor man's guitar. Homemade. Not usually this nice.'

'What about on the back?' said Macy.

Rolly grabbed the diddley bow and inspected the back. A photograph had been laminated on to it, a black-and-white photo-graph of a teenage girl and a young man in a baseball uniform. The man had his arm around the girl. Both of them were smiling. There were palm trees in the background. Their smiles looked genuine.

'You think this is your aunt?' Rolly said.

'I guess so. Daddy Joe called her Aunt Betty.'

'Who's Daddy Joe?'

'I'll get to that.'

'You don't know Aunt Betty's last name?'

'Not unless it was Harper. That's Daddy Joe's name.'

'And you think it was Daddy Joe that left this here for you?'

'Vera said the guy who left it was a big Indian.'

'The woman in this photo doesn't look Indian.'

'Because she's black?'

'Well, she does look more African-American than Indian, don't you think?'

'You're an expert on racial distinctions?'

'No. I just . . . Are you . . . Native American?'

'No. Not now that there's money on the line.'

'What's that?'

'Nothing. I don't care. I got out of that damn place. I don't need their money.'

'What money?'

'They built a casino. If you're part of the tribe, you get a share of the money. I ain't on that list.'

'Oh.'

'Yeah. DNA.'

'You mean your genes? They check your DNA?'

Macy pointed at three letters tattooed between her jugular notch and her left breast.

'This DNA stands for Do Not Ask,' she said. 'Get used to me saying it.'

Rolly nodded. 'OK,' he said. 'But I'm an investigator. I have to ask questions.'

'It's my personal credo,' said Macy. 'Do not ask. DNA. Just do what you want to do. But if I say DNA to you, that means I want you to shut up.'

'What about Daddy Joe?' Rolly said. 'Can I ask you about him?'

Macy stared at Rolly for a moment. He stared back. She broke first.

'OK, just give me a second,' she said, looking away. 'You can fantasize about what my little tits might look like or whatever else you want to think about this crazy bitch you just met. But don't ask me anything else until I say it's OK.'

Rolly nodded. He tried not to picture what enticements lay under Macy's shirt, but it was like trying not to think about pink elephants once somebody had mentioned them. He scraped at his plate, but there was nothing left worth eating. The refried beans had gone cold. He looked around the room. The cantina was busy. Staying open after last call had been good for business. At three in the morning, it became a refuge for the after-hours crowd with no place to go, for the leftovers who needed sustenance, a greasy ballast to diminish the hangovers they'd be nursing the next day.

'OK,' said Macy. 'I'm ready.'

Rolly nodded. He liked Macy. He liked her directness.

'So here's the deal,' she began. 'I was adopted. I think. Nobody ever explained a damn thing to me and I never cared much, I guess. You could say I've got some parental issues, if you wanna go all Doctor Phil on me. Anyway, I grew up on the Jincona Indian reservation. It's out east, in BF Egypt.'

'My band's playing at their casino tomorrow.'

'Yeah, great, whatever. Daddy Joe Harper and his wife were the ones that took care of me, until Mama Joe died. Then Kinnie took care of me. She's Daddy Joe's real daughter. Kinnie never liked me much. I don't blame her. Aunt Betty was there, for a little while, when I was a baby. To tell you the truth, I'm not sure I'd remember her if it wasn't for that picture there. Daddy Joe kept that diddley bow thing in his closet. He'd bring it out sometimes and tell me about Aunt Betty.'

'What'd he say?' said Rolly.

'DNA.'

'Sorry.'

'No questions right now. Not while I'm trying to get through this.'

Rolly nodded. Macy fingered the gold charm that hung from her neck. The charm was shaped like a tube. There was some sort of inscription on it.

'Anyway,' Macy continued, 'Daddy Joe always used to show me that photograph. He'd say "This is your Aunt Betty. She brought you to our house. She brought you here. We never want to forget her." He'd tell me that, and then one day I asked him, you know, "What happened to Aunt Betty? Where did she go?"'

Macy paused. Rolly waited. DNA.

'He said she went to be with her friends,' Macy said. 'That her friends had all gone away, so she felt lonely and sad. He said she took a walk in the stars.'

Rolly nodded again. 'Is it OK if I ask another question now?' he said.

'Yeah. I guess. If you can make anything out of all that.'

'Do you know who your birth mother was?'

'I knew you were going to ask me that. Seems like the obvious thing, doesn't it?'

'That Aunt Betty's your mother?'

'Yeah.'

'You think this baseball player might be your father?'

'That makes as much sense as you being my father. Less, even.'

'What do you mean?'

'Look at me. I've got lighter skin than either of them, and freckles. This blonde, kinky hair? There's no coloring. It's my natural hair. I mean, it wouldn't make sense, heredity-wise, if they were both my parents, right?'

'Yeah. I guess. I don't really know how that stuff works.'

'I did some reading. I'm a mutt, not a purebreed.'

'We're all mutts, in one way or the other.'

'What's your background?'

'Norwegian on my mom's side. My dad's more Scotch Irish.'

'Yeah, well, some of us are more mutty than others,' said Macy. She lifted her eyelids and stared at Rolly again. 'You ever seen anybody with eyes like these?'

'No,' said Rolly. 'I can't say I have.'

'Wolf Girl,' she said. 'That's what the kids on the rez used to call me. Because of my eyes. That and because I ran around in the hills by myself all the time.'

Rolly considered several things he could say about Macy's eyes but none of them seemed appropriate; nothing a portly, fortyish man could say to a woman her age without sounding desperate or foolish. He resisted the temptation. The reservation kids had it right, though. There was something like wolf light in Macy's eyes, a fierceness in her that stirred something inside him. He needed to stop it from stirring. He needed to keep his professional pants on.

'When was the last time you saw Daddy Joe?'

'Five years ago.'

'Have you talked to him?'

'Not since I left. There were some issues. We weren't really on speaking terms when I left.'

'What happened?'

'Just the usual teenager stuff. I had to get out of that place. DNA.'

'OK. You're sure it was him, though, that brought the diddley bow tonight?'

'I'm just going on what Vera said. A big guy. Older. Looked Indian. Daddy Joe's big, enough that you notice it. He used to be chief of tribal police.'

'Your Daddy Joe was a cop?'

'I wouldn't call the tribals real cops.'

'You don't get along with them, either?'

'DNA,' said Macy. 'Anyway, it must be something important, this diddley bow thing. I don't see Daddy Joe driving all the way down from the rez to give it to me otherwise.'

'Maybe you should call him tomorrow.'

'Can't go there. Too complicated. How is it with your dad?'

'My dad?'

'Yeah. How well do you get along with your dad?'

Rolly smiled. 'DNA,' he said.

Macy laughed. 'That bad, huh, Waters?'

Rolly nodded.

'Yeah, I get it,' said Macy. 'Thing is, I can't figure out how Daddy Joe found me here. He's retired. He just sits up there on the rez all the time, in his house, going over his old files.'

'Maybe he saw your name in the paper or something.'

Macy reached in her back pocket, pulled out a postcard-sized piece of paper and passed it to Rolly. 'That's my flyer,' she said. 'I post those around town.'

'DJ Crazy Macy?' said Rolly, reading the flyer. It had a photo of Macy, her dirty-blonde dreadlocks spread around her head, backlit into a luminescent corona.

'That's my stage name,' she said. 'One of 'em. Dubstep Blonde, Dizzy Gold Negra. It depends on what kind of mixes I'm playing. This weekend I'm Crazy Macy.'

Rolly resisted the impulse to make a smart remark. Macy looked like she expected one.

'You want to know about my necklace?' she said.

'Hmm?'

'You didn't notice it, did you?'

'Sure I noticed. It's gold, right?'

'Uh, yeah. And?'

'It's a tube. Looks like there's an engraving.'

'You know, Vera told me you were this hot shit detective guy, but I'm starting to wonder if she's smoked too many jalapeños.'

'It's late and I'm tired. I'll give you my card. We can talk tomorrow.'

'You still haven't noticed? Look at the damn picture again.'

Rolly looked at the photo on the back of the diddley bow. He noticed this time. He looked back at Macy. 'Aunt Betty's got the same necklace, hasn't she?'

'That's what it looks like to me.'

Macy undid her choker. She passed it to Rolly. 'Read it,' she said.

Rolly squinted his eyes. 'Eight, three . . .'

'Eight, three, six, eight, nine, two, nine, five, four,' said Macy, completing the number for him.

'What does that mean?'

'No idea,' said Macy.

Rolly flipped the gold tube around to look at the other side.

'The same numbers are on both sides,' said Macy. 'That's all there is.'

'Maybe it's a date?' he said.

'I thought that at first,' said Macy. 'But it doesn't make any sense as a date.'

Rolly tried several permutations of the number. He had to admit the date idea made no sense at all. It wasn't a phone number either; it was missing a digit.

'How long have you had this?' he asked.

'A little more than five years,' Macy said. 'Daddy Joe said it was mine.'

'He gave this to you?'

'He said he was going to. When I was of age.'

'Does he know what the number means?'

'I guess he might.'

'Don't you think you should ask him?'

'Like I said, me and Daddy Joe have some issues. He said he was going to give the necklace to me when I turned legal. Eighteen. He would have, I guess.'

'What's that mean? You guess?'

'I left the rez before I turned eighteen. I ran away. I took the necklace.'

'You mean you stole it?'

'Yeah, that's right, Waters. I stole it. I lived in the police chief's house and I stole his twenty-four-karat gold necklace.'

THREE
The Hospital

Alicia Waters sat in the waiting room at Mercy Hospital wearing a rumpled green sweatsuit. Her blonde wig was askew. Long streaks of black mascara ran from her eyes. Her pretty pink face looked puffy and red. It was the first time Rolly had seen his stepmom looking less than impeccable. She was usually a chubby bundle of smiling enthusiasm and spotless cosmetics, always tidy, bright-eyed and more than presentable for a night out at the officer's club. But Alicia hadn't had time to pick out an outfit or touch up her makeup after her husband, Rolly's father, had collapsed in their driveway, turning blue and clutching his chest.

'It's that damn Tioga,' she said, wiping her eyes.

'What's a Tioga?' said Rolly.

'He bought a mobile home. I never really liked the idea, but he got so excited about it. He even stopped drinking. Well, he was drinking less – you know, not like he does sometimes.'

'I'm sure that was nice,' said Rolly's real mother, Judith, who sat next to Alicia, providing Kleenex and sympathy. 'Did you have a trip planned?'

'Oh, I couldn't keep up with it. He kept coming up with new places,' said Alicia. 'First it was a week, then a month.' She shuddered. 'I mean, can you imagine me spending a whole month cooped up in that hideous thing?'

'You were leaving soon?'

'Next week,' said Alicia, dabbing at her eyes with the tissue Rolly's mother had provided.

'I guess that trip's off,' said Rolly. His mother glared at him.

'I went along with it,' said Alicia. 'I mean, I thought it would be nice to go somewhere – perhaps a long weekend to try out the whole thing. One of those nice campgrounds where there's lots of people to meet. I thought that would be enough, that maybe he'd get over it. He kept saying he wanted to see the country, like it used to be. To get out in nature or something.'

Alicia shuddered and blew her nose.

'Ugh,' she said, though it was unclear if she was referring to nature in general or the soggy tissue she clutched in her hand. Rolly's mother handed her another Kleenex.

'What happened?' said Rolly.

'He was working on the damn thing this morning. Early. Changing the oil or something, I don't know. He had these big wrenches. I went out to bring him some coffee. I knew something was wrong. His face was all purple. I made him sit down. I feel so guilty.'

'It's not your fault,' said Rolly.

'He was trying to fix it up nice for me so I'd be happy. He knew I didn't like it, the whole idea. We bought it used, you see. It needed some work. He spent a lot of time out there. It was too much for someone his age. I wish they'd tell us something.'

Rolly's mother looked over at him. 'Why don't you check again, dear,' she said. 'See if they've got any news.'

Rolly nodded. He turned and walked to the check-in station.

'Yes, sir,' said the clerk, without looking up. 'Can I help you?'

'I wanted to know if there's any news on my father. Dean Waters.'

'A doctor or nurse will come out to see you when he's ready.'

'He had a heart attack.'

The clerk nodded. 'Let me check his status,' she said. She tapped a few times on the computer then looked up at Rolly.

'He's still listed in resuscitation,' she said.

'What does that mean?'

'That's the most recent entry. He may have been moved by now, but there's no update.'

'When will we know something?'

'I'm sorry. I'm not able tell you that, sir. A doctor or nurse will speak to you when they're able to provide an update.'

'Thank you.' Rolly nodded. He walked back to his mother and Alicia.

'No news is good news, I guess,' he said. Alicia began crying again. Rolly's mother shot him an exasperated glance.

'Rolly,' she said, 'why don't you see if you can find the cafeteria, maybe bring something back for the rest of us?'

'I couldn't eat a thing,' said Alicia.

'Maybe some juice,' said Rolly's mother. 'You need to have something.'

Rolly's mother shot another glance at him. He didn't argue. He doubted they would know anything soon. An emergency room nurse he had dated told him the secret once. Take any time estimate given by the ER staff and multiply it by four. If someone said you'd be out in thirty minutes, it would be two hours. If they told you an hour, it would probably take four. It was the painstaking sluggishness at the heart of the beast. He'd been in enough emergency rooms to confirm it. He walked back to the check-in station. The clerk gave him directions to the cafeteria.

He went through the swinging doors and out of the ward, spotted an empty chair and slumped into it. His body felt heavy, weighed down with conflicted feelings. He hated his father for having a heart attack. He hated his father for being a drunk, for the way his father had treated his mother, but mostly he hated his father for being an arrogant son-of-a-bitch who was going to die without apologies. His father was an alcoholic bastard who'd never given Rolly anything, beyond a predilection for bottled spirits.

Rolly knew it was stupid to feel this way, like he'd been cheated. He was partly to blame. He'd kept his distance, never speaking his mind, reluctant to face his father straight on. Dean Waters had captained two naval warships, a wife and a son. He'd always been the man who gave orders, until the U.S. Navy demoted him and took away his command, until his wife and son abandoned their home. The old sailor had always worked too hard, too intensely. He'd always drunk too much, too, but he'd never learned to listen to anyone. He never cared what anyone said. Now he'd pressed his second wife into first-mate status for a landlocked cruise she never wanted to take, a low-rent re-enactment of his glory days on the high seas. Except this time they'd be making ports of call in a crummy old Tioga, docking in trailer parks.

Rolly rubbed his chest, confounded by the pain. His own heart would get him someday if he didn't start eating better. Other vices hadn't managed to do him in yet. Alcohol. Drugs. Angry husbands of women who didn't wear wedding rings. Car accidents. All had come close. He stood up and stretched. He wasn't dead yet. And neither was his father, as far as he knew. He walked down the hall and followed the signs.

The cafeteria was quiet when he arrived. The lunch hour had passed. He picked up an apple and a banana for his mother and a bottle of orange juice for Alicia. He paid the cashier, walked into the dining room and placed the tray with the large blueberry muffin and a cup of coffee he'd bought for himself on a table in the corner. He sat down and tried the muffin. It tasted like lemonized chemicals. The coffee hit his gut like pure acid. He finished both items anyway. He didn't want to go back to the emergency room.

He thought about Macy Starr, the woman he'd met the night before at the cantina. She'd agreed to let him borrow the diddley bow, the one-string guitar, so he could do some research. The diddley bow intrigued him – the quality of the work that had been put into something that was usually a rustic homemade instrument. He wanted to take it by Norwood's guitar shop if he got a chance, find out if Rob had seen one like it, if he could tell him anything about it.

He hadn't mentioned it to Macy, but he'd recognized the baseball player in the photograph laminated onto the back. He'd never seen the player in a minor-league uniform before, so he needed to be sure. He pulled his phone out of his pocket, searched through the directory and tapped on a name. There was a picture on the wall, drawn with crayons, of a hospital building with flowers and stick-figure children dancing around it.

'Hey,' said Max Gemeinhardt, answering the phone.

'Hey,' said Rolly. 'I've got a trivia question for you. Baseball. The hometown team.'

'Shoot,' said Max. Max was a baseball encyclopedia. You couldn't stump him.

'Eric Ozzie,' said Rolly. 'Did he play in the minors?'

'Of course he did. Wenfield's the only local guy who skipped the minors. Well, there was Naly and the first Dale Roberts, but neither of them stayed around long. And they both got sent down at some point.'

'Where'd he play? Ozzie, I mean. Did he ever suit up for a team called the Coconuts?'

'Sure. Hawaii. That was our Triple-A team back then. They're gone now. Why'd you want to know?'

'I've got a photo of him, in his Coconuts uniform. I think it's him, anyway.'

'Well, if it looks like him it probably is.'

'He looks pretty young.'

'Just out of high school, I imagine. He got called up halfway through his second year.'

'How long ago was that?'

'Geez, let me think. Not so good with dates anymore. I guess it'd be about twenty years ago, give or take.'

'The Sneaker.'

'He hates that nickname, you know.'

'Yeah. I'm sure that's why he based his whole business model around it.'

'The man's not stupid. The branding was there. So what's this photo you've got?'

'A client gave it to me. She's trying to identify a girl who's standing next to him. Ozzie's in his baseball uniform with his arm around the girl. It looks like it's after a game or something. My client doesn't know that it's him.'

'How old is the girl in the photograph?'

'I don't know. Fourteen, fifteen, sixteen.'

'You didn't tell your client it was Ozzie?'

'No.'

'You want to talk to him?'

'Well, it seems like that might be the easiest way to find out who the girl is.'

'If he remembers.'

'Yeah. If he remembers.'

'That's a long time ago.'

'My client says she was adopted.'

'This isn't some kind of paternity thing, is it?'

'My client's about the right age, but I don't think so. She seems more interested in the girl who's with Ozzie. She says it's her aunt but it might be her mother. That's what she's trying to find out.'

'Sounds a little squeegee to me.'

'That's why I didn't tell her who he was. I wanted to be sure.'

'You did the right thing. You want me to call him?'

'Hmm?'

'I did some legal work for Ozzie a few years back. It was a

medical thing. That quack doctor who prescribed the painkillers for him. We settled with the insurance guys, out of court.'

'So Ozzie owes you one?'

'Not really. I got my share of the money. It was a pretty good settlement, though. Helped him finance that first restaurant. He'll take a call from me.'

'Well,' said Rolly, 'if I try to call him I'll have to go through the front office and leave a dozen messages before he calls me back. You know how that is.'

'Let me call him. I'll get back to you.'

'Thanks.'

'Glad to do it. How's your mom?'

'She's OK.'

'Something wrong?'

Rolly looked at the picture on the wall again. Children and flowers – simple shapes drawn in crayon colors.

'I'm at the hospital. My dad had a heart attack.'

'Oh, man, sorry to hear that.'

'We're all here. At Mercy. Mom and Alicia and me. In the ER.'

Max didn't say anything for a moment. Neither did Rolly.

'Well,' said Max, 'I'd offer to come down, but it sounds like you got enough on your hands.'

'Yeah. Alicia's a mess. Mom's getting agitated.'

'And you're in the middle. As usual. You gonna be OK?'

'I don't know. It's mostly just weird right now. I guess I'm OK.'

'Well, I hope your dad pulls through. Give me a call if you need anything. I can find a way to distract your mother if you need some time to yourself.'

'Yeah. Call me if you hear something from Ozzie.'

'I will. Talk to you later.'

Rolly hung up. He checked the time on his phone. Moogus was picking him up around five. They were carpooling to tonight's gig, at the casino on the Jincona Reservation where Macy grew up. It was a longer drive than usual, through the winding roads of the East County mountains. He put the phone back in his pocket. He had hoped to get down to Norwood's today with the diddley bow. Depending on how things went with his father, he might still have a couple of hours. He picked up the apple, the banana and the bottle of orange juice, and headed back to the emergency ward.

FOUR
The Shop

Rob Norwood stood hunched over the back counter, looking at his laptop computer when Rolly entered the store on Tenth Avenue, a few blocks from the Villa Cantina. Rolly referred to the shop as Norwood's Mostly, as did most of his guitar-playing associates, but the official name for the place was Mostly Guitars. It was a miracle the shop still existed in its present location. Most of the neighborhood had been overtaken by high-rise condominiums and fancy coffee shops. Norwood's worn-down one-story anachronism blighted the block, but Rob remained stubborn in his devotion to staying there. He didn't pay rent. His moneyed wife had purchased the building for him years ago, before the present mania for urban living had revitalized the city center.

'You need something?' said Norwood, without looking up from his computer. 'Or is this just a social call?'

'Much as I enjoy our little heart-to-hearts on the issues affecting today's music industry, I can't dilly-dally,' said Rolly, pulling up to the counter.

'This won't be one of your "lemme try that one" marathons?'

'I'm in a hurry,' said Rolly. He pulled the diddley bow out of its case and placed it on the counter. 'What can you tell me about this?'

Norwood looked at the diddley bow, then over at Rolly. 'You want to sell it?' he said.

'Can't. It's not mine.'

'So why do you want to know about it?'

'I told a friend I'd look into it.'

'Does he want to sell it?'

'No. She doesn't. I don't think so.'

'I can get her good money for it.'

'How much?'

'A thousand bucks.'

'Really?'

'Well, it just so happens I had a guy in here yesterday looking for one.'

'Really?'

'Yeah. If it's what I think it is. This guy yesterday was looking for one just like it.'

'Really?'

Norwood sighed and rolled his eyes. 'That's three reallys in a row,' he said. 'Am I so . . . mistrusted?'

'No. I believe you. I'm just surprised.'

'Who's this chick you're asking for?'

'She's a client, that's all.'

'Uh huh.'

'She's more interested in the picture on the back.'

'Can I look?'

Rolly nodded. Norwood lifted the diddley bow, flipped it over and inspected the back.

'This is a fortuitous moment,' he said.

'What?'

'It's exactly the one he was looking for – the guy who came in.'

Norwood pointed at two small letters engraved just below the bottom right corner of the photograph. 'B-M,' he said. 'Buddy Meeks.'

'That name sounds familiar.'

'You should remember better than anybody. He worked in the Guitar Trader shop.'

'You mean the nerdy guy, right, with the big glasses? That Buddy?'

'That's the one,' said Norwood. 'I got to know him a little bit when I did commission sales up there. Strange dude. Awesome guitar tech, though.'

'I remember him now,' said Rolly. 'I wouldn't let anybody else work on my guitars.'

'Yeah, I remember that too. You used to piss off the other guys in the shop – the snotty teenage punk who insisted that he had to have Buddy work on his guitars, acting like the rest of them were incompetent peons.'

'I had very high standards.'

'Admit it. You were snotty.'

'Maybe. A little. That Buddy guy did great work, though, you gotta admit. You really think he made this thing?'

'That's what the guy told me. He was looking for a one-string guitar with Buddy's mark on the back. I was kind of thinking "good luck with that" and now here you are walking in with the very thing.'

'You think I could talk to this guy?'

'So you can go around me and sell it to him directly?'

'It's not for sale. Like I told you.'

'Maybe you should check with your girlfriend, see if she wants to sell it, now that you know it's worth something.'

'My client's not interested in how much it's worth. She wants to know about the photo on the back. Did the guy say anything about that?'

'No,' said Norwood, continuing his examination of the instrument. He looked at the photo. 'Who's it supposed to be, anyway?'

'That's what I'm trying to find out.'

'This baseball guy looks like he might be somebody.'

Rolly shrugged. Norwood would have to figure that out for himself.

'It's nice work,' said Norwood. 'But I don't see how the thing's worth a thousand bucks.'

'Surprised the hell out of me,' Rolly replied.

'Well, the guy said he was willing to pay if I could find it for him,' said Norwood. 'Maybe it's got sentimental value for him, too.'

'Are you going to tell me his name?'

'Only if your girlfriend's willing to give me a cut.'

'How much do you want?'

'Thirty percent.'

'Ten.'

'Twenty.'

'All right. She won't want to sell it, though. Now can you tell me the name?'

Norwood extended his hand. Rolly shook on the deal. Norwood placed the diddley bow back on the counter, peeked under his laptop and pulled out a business card.

'Randy Parker,' he said, handing the card to Rolly. 'That's the guy's name. He has a shop called Alien Artifacts over in City Heights. I looked it up on the Web.'

Rolly reviewed the information on the card. Gold stars and planets were embossed on a purple background.

'What does he sell?' he asked.

'Looked to me like it was UFO memorabilia. Science-fiction collectibles.'

'There's a market for that?'

'Apparently.' Norwood shrugged his shoulders.

'You think this has something to do with UFOs?' said Rolly, indicating the diddley bow.

'Your guess is as good as mine,' said Norwood. 'I remember Buddy was into some unusual stuff – theories about aliens, like that Chariots of the Gods stuff. I remember one time he was talking to me about how there were these unique musical frequencies, tunings, with special properties that resonated in our DNA. Too weird for me.'

'You know where I can find him?'

'Buddy? No idea. You could ask up at Guitar Trader. That was a long time ago, though. I doubt anybody up there remembers him. I think he started his own shop, somewhere in East County.'

Rolly pointed at the dots along the neck. 'What do you make of those inlays?' he said. 'They don't look correctly spaced for fret marks.'

'Yeah, I noticed that, too. I guess they're just decorative. You try plugging it in yet?'

'Nope. Too busy.'

'You want to try it now?'

'I gotta get going,' said Rolly.

'You might ask your girlfriend if she knows anything about an amplifier or something that's supposed to go with it. He wrote the name of the thing on the back of the card there.'

Rolly flipped the business card over, read the scrawled words. 'Astral Vibrator?'

Norwood laughed. 'Yeah, that's it. Maybe your girlfriend wants to keep that for herself too.'

'It's an amplifier?'

'I guess. This Randy guy said you plugged the diddley bow into it. He said it was a box, 'bout so high and so wide.' Norwood indicated the approximate dimensions of the Astral Vibrator with his hands.

'I'll ask her about it,' said Rolly. 'Let me know if you remember anything about Buddy.'

'OK. You need anything else?'

'I could use some guitar strings.'

'How many?'

'Two packs. You got any eights?'

'For your delicate little fingers?'

'I read somewhere that B.B. King plays eights.'

'Using eights won't make you sound like B.B. King,' said Norwood. He squatted down then opened the cabinet on the floor behind him. He pulled out two packs of guitar strings and returned to the counter.

'Ten dollars,' he said, tossing them on the countertop. Rolly pulled a twenty from his pocket. Norwood opened the register, tossed in the twenty and pulled out two fives.

'How's that Telecaster working for you?' he said, handing Rolly his change.

'All cleaned up and ready to go,' said Rolly. 'First public appearance tonight.'

'Where you playing?'

'At one of the reservations. Jincona.'

'You play there before?'

Rolly shook his head. 'First time at this one. I've played at all the others.'

'Kinda soul-sucking, isn't it?' said Norwood. 'All those people sitting there punching one-arm bandits and none of 'em paying any attention to you.'

'Money's good,' said Rolly. He slipped the guitar strings into his back pocket and wrapped the diddley bow up in its cloth. 'Once a month I guess it won't suck up too much of my soul.' His phone buzzed in his front pocket. He pulled it out and answered.

'Hey,' said Max. 'You at home?'

'I'm downtown.'

'Even better. You close to the ballpark?'

'Eight blocks or so.'

'I talked to Ozzie. He's down there, at the ballpark. Some kind of kids' event. Said you could stop by.'

'Great.'

'Just go to administrative office. Give 'em your name. How soon can you make it?'

'I don't know. Twenty minutes?'

'That'll work. I'll let him know.'

'Thanks.'

'You bet. Anything new on your dad?'

'They moved him out of emergency. Into intensive.'

'Well, I guess that's some kind of progress. Let me know if you need anything.'

'Thanks. I will.'

Rolly slipped his phone into his pocket.

'Who's in the hospital?' said Norwood.

'My dad had a heart attack.'

'The Captain?' said Norwood.

Rolly nodded. 'It's nothing,' he said.

'It's not negligible,' said Norwood.

'It doesn't mean he's not an asshole,' Rolly said. 'What were we talking about?'

'Well,' said Norwood. 'I gave you that guy's card. Randy Parker. I'm assuming you'll talk to him. You're going to tell him you talked to me and that you've got the guitar he was looking for. You get whatever information you need from the guy and then you talk to your girlfriend about selling the thing. Owes me twenty percent finder's fee if she does.'

'Right, right,' said Rolly. 'Except for one thing.'

'What's that?'

'She's not my girlfriend.'

FIVE

The Ballpark

R olly sat in the reception area of the downtown ballpark's business office, waiting for an administrative assistant to locate an employee who could usher him in to see Eric Ozzie. A poster-sized photograph of Ozzie in his baseball uniform hung on the wall, along with those of other well-known players. Ozzie's professional career had been cut short by injuries and a nagging addiction to pain pills, but he'd once come close to setting the team record for stolen bases in a single season. His down-home demeanor and occasional malapropisms had made him a fan favorite, but three straight years battling the Mendoza line had finally ended Eric Ozzie's summers in the big leagues. Within a few years of his retirement, he parlayed his personality and ambitions into a fast-food concession called Sneakers, a variation on the nickname given to him by the team's broadcast announcer. The Sneaker had always been quick on his feet, able to capitalize on opportunities.

The inner door opened. An earnest-looking young man stepped into the office, holding a clipboard and a cell phone.

'Mr Waters?' he said, approaching Rolly. They shook hands. 'I'm Jerry Kirby. I can escort you out to the field to meet Mr Ozzie now.'

'Thank you,' said Rolly.

'What's that you've got there?' the man asked, indicating the cloth case in Rolly's hand.

'It's a guitar,' said Rolly, 'A one-string guitar. It's got Mr Ozzie's picture on it.'

'It's a gift?'

'Not exactly. I'm a private investigator.'

'Oh. I see,' said Jerry. 'Well, follow me.'

Rolly followed Jerry through the door and down a long hallway.

'Eric's out on the field with the kids,' said Jerry as they walked down the hall. 'Big day today for them. We've got more than five hundred here from the various organizations.'

'What kind of organizations?'

'Oh, you know, representing our underserved population. Boys and Girls Clubs. St Vincent's. Eric loves doing these events. He's got his own foundation, you know. Free sneakers for all the kids.'

They passed through two additional doors and entered the clubhouse. Rolly had been in the locker room once, with Max, on a tour. During the off-season it was just a bunch of empty lockers in a big circle. He followed Jerry through the clubhouse and out to the field.

'Have a seat,' said Jerry, indicating the dugout bench. 'I'll let Eric know that you're here.'

Rolly took a seat and looked out at the baseball diamond. There were kids everywhere, organized into small groups around the various bases. There were more kids in the outfield, getting coached on the fundamentals. Tables had been set up near the visitor dugout. Adults stood behind the tables, handing out box lunches. Rolly recognized the look of the packaging. The boxes contained Ozzie's titular product, Sneakers, which were deepfried balls of cornmeal mush wrapped around various fillings: jalapeño cheese, Italian meatballs and pineapple cream. More than one person had joked that the product's name described its effect on one's digestive system.

Jerry waved to catch someone's attention. Eric Ozzie stepped out from behind the food service tables, wearing a white apron on top of black pants and a purple dress shirt. He still looked in playing shape. Rolly stood up as Ozzie walked into the dugout.

'Mr Waters?' said Ozzie, extending his hand. His grip was solid, just shy of crushing, a well-calibrated professional's grip.

'Thanks for seeing me,' said Rolly.

'No problem,' said Ozzie. 'Any friend of Mr Gemeinhardt is a friend of mine. He said you were a musician?'

'Yeah. I play guitar.'

'You were in that band The Creatures, right? Max told me. I remember when you guys used to play around town. Didn't you sing the anthem at one of the games?'

'Yeah. We did once,' Rolly said. He had a vague memory of standing with Matt, out near home plate, strumming chords while Matt belted out the melody. 'Did Max explain why I wanted to talk to you?'

'He said you're a private investigator now, something like that?'

Rolly nodded. He took a business card from his wallet and handed it to Ozzie.

'Quite a change from playing guitar, I imagine,' said Ozzie, inspecting the card.

'Less so than you might think. I still play guitar some.'

'That's good. Gotta keep up your skills. So what'd you wanna see me about?'

'It's this,' said Rolly, undoing the cloth wrapper from the diddley bow.

'What's that?' Ozzie asked.

'It's called a diddley bow.'

Ozzie grinned. 'Well, I heard of Bo Diddley, but not a diddley bow.'

'There's a photograph, on the back. I think it's you.'

Rolly flipped the diddley bow over and presented the back.

Ozzie squinted. 'Jerry?' he said. 'Can you get me my glasses? I think they're on one of the tables.'

Jerry scurried out of the dugout.

'Can I take a closer look?' said Ozzie, indicating the diddley bow. Rolly nodded and handed it to him.

Ozzie walked to the dugout steps, angled his position to catch the sunlight. 'The Hawaii Coconuts,' he said, reviewing the photograph. 'Man, that was a great place to start your career. Except for the plane flights.'

'How long were you there?'

'A year and a half. Moved up to the majors in August.'

'Do you recognize the girl in that picture?'

Ozzie stared at the picture a moment. 'No. I don't think so,' he said.

'You've never seen her before?'

'Not that I remember. Who is she?'

'That's what I'm trying to find out.'

'It was a long time ago, you know, playing in Hawaii. Look at those palm trees in the background. I think they only had about a thousand seats in that park. Pretty girl. Must've been a fan. Why are you looking for her?'

'My client gave that to me. She's looking for her aunt. That photograph is all she's got to go on. She remembers a woman who looked like that living with the family when she was very young.'

'What about the rest of the family? Wouldn't they know?'

'My client was adopted.'

'Oh.'

'She's estranged from her adopted family. They've got some issues, I guess.'

'Where'd she get this . . . what do you call it, diddley bow?'

'She's not really sure of that either. Someone left it for her. Possibly her adoptive father.'

'Did she say anything about me?'

'As far as I can tell, she doesn't know who you are. She didn't recognize you in the photo, anyway. She never mentioned your name. I didn't tell her – thought I should wait until I'd talked to you first.'

'I appreciate that. How old is this woman, your client?'

'Twenty-one, almost twenty-two. That's what she told me, anyway.'

Ozzie considered the photo for a moment, calculating his past. 'You say this girl in the photo is supposed to be her aunt?' he said.

'Aunt Betty. That's the name she remembers. As I said, she's not sure. She doesn't know her mother and father.'

'I guess I know where you're going with this,' said Ozzie. He looked out towards the field, then back at the photo, then over at Rolly. 'I'd be in a lot of trouble if I'd slept with this girl, don't you think?' he said. There was a slight modulation in Ozzie's voice as he spoke, the barest hint of vibrato. 'How old do you think she is here?'

Rolly shrugged. 'Somewhere between fourteen and eighteen, I'd guess.'

'I don't know about eighteen. She looks younger than that.'

'I hope you don't mind my asking.'

'Well, you haven't really asked yet. But I'll answer anyway. I appreciate you not telling your client about me in case she figures out who I am and gets ideas, but really, I don't remember this girl. I'm damn well sure I never went out with her or nothing.'

Ozzie stepped back into the dugout and handed the diddley bow back to Rolly.

'Thanks for your time,' said Rolly.

'No girls,' said Ozzie.

'What's that?' said Rolly.

'That was the last thing my momma said to me, before I went to Hawaii. No girls.'

Rolly smiled because he couldn't think of anything else to do.

'She made me promise,' said Ozzie. 'Like it was going to ruin my career if I started having sex. She thought those island wahines were gonna lead me into temptation, that I'd end up like my daddy. That first year, in Hawaii, I was good. I was all about baseball. She died around the time I got to the majors, my mom.'

'I'm sorry,' said Rolly.

'Well, she was pretty messed up. She got me as far as she could. I guess maybe I was the only thing she had any hope for in her life.'

'She must've taken pretty good care of you.'

'Not really,' said Ozzie. 'But that's a story for another time. I know you got work to do.'

'I don't mind,' said Rolly.

Jerry returned with the glasses. Ozzie put them on.

'Show me the picture again,' he said. Rolly showed him. Ozzie reviewed it, then took off his glasses. He tapped them against the palm of his hand, looking thoughtful.

'No,' he said. 'I don't remember her.'

'Thanks for taking another look,' Rolly said.

'We're trying new flavors today,' said Ozzie, 'with the kids. I always enjoy this event, having the kids in, giving back something. I spent some time in the shelters growing up. I know what it's like. You really remember days like this. It's something special. You carry it around for a while. It really does help.'

'I'm sure it does.'

'You're welcome to join us.'

'I probably should get going,' Rolly said. 'I've got a gig tonight.'

'Where you playing?'

'Out at one of the casinos.'

Ozzie looked thoughtful again, as if he might say something. But he didn't.

'Well, it was nice meeting you,' said Rolly, extending his hand. 'And getting to sit in the dugout.'

'Yes, nice to met you, too, Mr Waters,' said Ozzie. 'If you need anything else, just give me a call.' He reached in his pocket, pulled out some coupons and handed them to Rolly.

'Two for ones,' he said. 'Use 'em next time you and Max come to the ballpark.'

'Thanks.'

Ozzie stepped out on the field. Jerry led Rolly back towards the clubhouse.

'Hey,' someone called. Rolly turned. Ozzie had ducked his head back into the dugout.

'What is it?' said Rolly.

Ozzie waved Rolly's business card. 'I can call you, right, at this number, if I remember something?'

'Sure. Anytime.'

'I was thinking . . . I just wanted to make it clear. Just so you don't think I'm trying to get evasive or nothing.'

'OK.'

'You were in that band, right? You probably had girls hanging around, chasing after you?'

'Sure.'

'That stuff I said about being good, my first year in Hawaii, that was all true.'

'I believe you.'

'But later, you know, in the majors, that was, well, like they say, that was a whole 'nother ball game.'

'I understand,' said Rolly, not sure if Ozzie was confessing or bragging. He could only imagine how his own behavior might have been in the majors.

'My momma was gone. I had a lot of girlfriends in the majors. And, you probably know this, I guess, but I do have a couple of kids out there. I paid for 'em, though. I mean, I'm supporting them. They're good kids. I'm doing my part, doing right by their mamas, taking responsibility.'

'I appreciate your telling me.'

Ozzie stepped into the dugout and moved closer. 'I just want you to know that I'm not trying to evade anything,' he said. 'I don't remember that girl in the photo. But if you find out something, let me know. If there's a child out there that's mine, I'll take responsibility. That's all I'm trying to say.'

'Understood.'

'This girl, your client, what's her name?'

'I can't tell you, not without her permission.'

'Sure, well, I'd be willing to talk to her if you want, if she remembers anything else. I'd like to help, if there's anything I can do. That's all I'm saying.'

'I'll keep that in mind. Is it OK if I tell her it's you in the photo? I'll let her know I talked to you, that you don't know anything.'

Ozzie nodded. 'Sure. You tell her I hope she finds her aunt or her momma or whoever that girl is.'

'I will,' Rolly said. Ozzie shook his hand again and dashed back on to the field to take care of his kids. Rolly saw something when he shook hands with Ozzie, something he'd never noticed in any photos or on the TV ads. Eric Ozzie had flecks of gold in his eyes.

SIX
The Collection

The Alien Artifacts store on El Cajon Boulevard didn't look otherworldly. It looked like any other neighborhood storefront, except that the shades had been drawn, presumably to block the late afternoon sun.

'Looks closed,' said Moogus as he parked his truck in a metered spot half a block down the street. They had carpooled to save gas on their way to the casino engagement. Rolly had talked Moogus into taking a detour. The shop wasn't far from the freeway.

'Give me a minute,' said Rolly. He opened the passenger door. 'I wanta' take a look.'

'OK. Don't take too long.'

'We've got plenty of time.'

'You're the one who's always worrying about being late.'

'We'll be fine.'

'Whatever you say, boss.'

Rolly climbed down from the cab of Moogus' truck and walked down the sidewalk. The sign in the window of the store said it was closed. There was a light on inside. He tried the door. It opened. A bell tinkled above his head as he walked in. 'Hello?' he called.

'We're closed,' someone answered from in back.

'Yes. I'm sorry. I was looking for Randy Parker.'

A door in the back of the shop opened. A woman appeared. 'Randy's not here,' she said.

'I was hoping to talk to him. He gave me his card.'

The woman walked out towards Rolly. She wore a long purple dress with loose, translucent sleeves. Long white hair fell down past her shoulders. A barrette of gold stars kept the hair out of her face. She stared at Rolly for a moment, attempting to drill into his brain with her eyes. Rolly smiled and deflected her gaze, keeping his eyes impermeable. She turned her head and looked at something on the counter.

'Randy's gone for the weekend,' she said.

'Can I leave a message? I tried calling his phone.'

'That's his phone over there, I'm afraid,' she said, pointing at the counter.

'Is there any other way I can reach him?'

'He went to the desert. I don't know how long he'll be gone. Who are you?'

Rolly pulled one of his own cards from his wallet. 'Roland Waters,' he said. 'Rolly. I'm a private investigator.'

The woman took the card and adjusted her hair band as she read it. Her white hair made her seem older at first, but Rolly decided she might only be a few years older than he was.

'How did you meet Randy?' the woman said.

'I haven't met him yet. A friend of mine gave me his card. He thought I could help Mr Parker.'

'How so?'

'He was looking for something – Mr Parker was. Do you work here?'

'Yes. I'm Randy's full-time assistant. You can call me Dotty.'

'Nice to meet you, Dotty.'

'What was Randy looking for?' said Dotty.

'I'd like to leave a message, if I can.'

'Is it about that guitar?'

'You know about the guitar?'

'Oh, yes. It's an important artifact. From the Yoovits.'

'I don't know anything about the . . . what's it called?'

'The Yoovits. U-V-T, for Universal Vibration Technologies.'

'You're saying the guitar belonged to them?'

'Randy didn't tell you?'

'I didn't actually speak to Randy,' said Rolly, making a mental note to ask Norwood if Randy Parker had said anything about UVTs. 'Perhaps you could explain it to me.'

'Well, Mr Waters, I'm sure you've heard of the Annunaki theories, about the space travelers who arrived on our Earth from the planet Nubiru in 6000 B.C.?'

'Afraid not,' Rolly said. He pressed his lips together, feeling uneasy about the direction the conversation had taken. Norwood hadn't told him Randy Parker was nuts.

'Well, of course it's not true,' said Dotty. 'It's just one of the early alien theories. I simply use it as an example. The UVTs also believe that aliens are among us. We have interbred over the epochs of time, so we have alien DNA inside us – in varying proportions, of course.'

Rolly remembered the DNA tattoo Macy had inked under her jugular notch. *Do Not Ask*. A coincidental awareness. Perhaps.

'I see,' he said, debating how much longer he felt willing to listen. 'I still don't understand what this has to do with the guitar Mr Parker is looking for.'

'Oh, everything,' said Dotty. 'You see, the Universal Vibration Technologies began as a healing system, combining color vibrations and the ancient musical frequencies. It was discovered that these frequencies could release the alien energy within each human being. It was easier for some, of course – those who already had high levels of cross-pollination.'

'Uh huh,' Rolly said.

'You've heard of the chakras, of course?' said Dotty. 'The Kundalini?'

'Yes,' Rolly said, surprised he'd heard of anything the woman had to tell him. After the car accident, in his first year of recovery, his mother had insisted on teaching him meditation techniques, including the chakra vibrations. He'd gone along with it. He'd chanted the mantras. It hadn't stuck. As far as he knew, his mother still practiced her chants.

'There was a young man who lived among them, highly skilled in the craft of instrument making . . .'

'Do you mean Buddy Meeks?'

'Yes, that was the man's name. It was said that he had a strong alien component. He designed the instruments for the Conjoinment.'

'What's the Conjoinment?'

'In the astral year 4017, Saturn and Jupiter aligned. The Ancients approach the Earth at the peak of the alignment. This is known as the Conjoinment. The UVTs gathered together to signal them, so that they might be taken up.'

'You mean like in that movie, *Close Encounters*?'

'The Ancients do not need a physical spaceship. Their approach is more nebulous. There are portents. The Conjoinment occurs approximately every twenty years.'

'You seem to know a lot about this.'

'I am well versed in alien theories. As is Mr Parker. That's why he started this shop.'

Rolly looked around the room, scrutinizing the items on the tables and shelves. There were all sorts of strange things on display, from little green men to ray guns to models of spaceships.

'That's an *X-Files* lunchbox, isn't it?' he said.

'We buy and sell popular culture items, as well as more authentic artifacts of human interaction with the alien existence,' said Dotty.

'Very interesting,' said Rolly. 'Do you have any items related to the UVTs?'

'Oh, yes. Quite a few. Would you like to see them?'

'Definitely,' Rolly said. He wondered if Moogus was getting antsy yet, then decided not to worry. Moogus always got antsy before a gig.

Dotty led Rolly to the back corner of the shop. She stopped in front of two paintings that hung on the wall. In the top corners of the first painting were images of Saturn and Jupiter. Energy beams flowed out from the planets in orange and yellow bands, curving into the foreground where a pyramid shape enclosed a naked, sexless human form holding both palms outward.

'Very nice,' Rolly said, attempting to show his appreciation. The painting was amateurish, bordering on hideous.

'This is a representation of the Ancients,' Dolly said. 'They come from the Oort cloud, as it passes between Saturn and Jupiter.'

'Oh,' said Rolly, fairly confident there weren't any clouds passing between Saturn and Jupiter, but not entirely sure. He wasn't up on his astronomy. 'They look friendly.'

'The human form you see represented is referred to as a Gentling. We are all Gentlings, to one degree or another. The pure form of the Ancients is astronomical and terrifying to human beings. So they must appear to earthlings in Gentling form. The frequency waves you see are more like the Ancients' true nature, but even so, it is just an artistic representation of the forces within them.'

'You mentioned something earlier about vibrations.'

'You are very astute, Mr Waters. This represents the Universal Vibrations.'

'Uh huh. And this other painting? Is that the guitar Mr Parker is looking for?'

'Yes,' said Dot. 'That is the one.'

A man stood in the foreground of the second painting playing a one-string guitar, a diddley bow. The diddley bow was plugged into some kind of box. Orange and yellow bands of energy, similar to the ones in the first painting, flowed out from the box.

'What's that?' he asked, pointing at the box.

'It is known as the Astral Vibrator.'

'Is it an amplifier, for the guitar?'

'We have not divined its true use.'

'Isn't Mr Parker looking for one of those, too?'

'Yes. The UVTs were highly musical, you see. They were known for their euphonics. We have some CDs if you'd like to hear.'

Dotty pulled some CD cases off the shelf next to the paintings and handed them to Rolly. He flipped through the covers. *Intuition Modulations. Quantum Perceptions. Codon Transmutation.* The titles reminded him of some of the music his mother listened to, stultifying New Age drivel. He hated it. There were no blues notes, no rock and roll rhythms, no jazz harmonies. He handed the CDs back to Dotty.

'What's that?' he said, noticing something else on the shelf, next to the CDs.

'It is a representation of the Sachem,' said Dotty. She handed the doll to him. It was a baby doll, painted gold, with blonde hair and gold eyes.

'What's the Sachem?' said Rolly.

Before Dotty could answer, the bell tinkled on the front door and someone entered the shop. Rolly turned, expecting to see Moogus. The man who'd walked in saw Rolly and stopped. Overdeveloped biceps stretched the sleeves of the man's gray T-shirt. His hair was jet black. It looked unnatural, like a dye job or rug.

Dotty crossed in front of Rolly and walked towards the man. 'Randy,' she said, 'you left your phone here, didn't you?'

The man nodded. He kept his sunglasses on.

'This is Rolly Waters,' said Dotty. 'He's a private investigator. He says he can help us find the guitar.'

The man nodded again. Rolly joined them at the front of the store.

'Hello, Mr Parker,' he said, offering his hand. The man nodded again, then shook his hand. He had a strong, aggressive grip. There was a tattoo of a watch on the man's right wrist. The face on the watch had no hands.

'Rob Norwood gave me your card,' said Rolly.

'Who?' said the man.

'He's got a guitar shop downtown. You were there asking about a one-string guitar?'

'Yeah. That's right. What's his name again?'

'Rob Norwood. His shop's called Mostly Guitars. I think I might be able to locate this guitar you're looking for.'

'You know where it is?'

'I'm a private investigator.'

'You want money?'

'I have some questions about the guitar.'

'Like what?'

'It's not actually a guitar. It's called a diddley bow.'

Randy Parker didn't seem impressed with Rolly's knowledge of stringed instruments.

'What's your questions?' he said.

'Well,' said Rolly, 'I understand a man named Buddy Meeks might have built it. His mark should be on the back.'

'How'd you know that?'

'You told Mr Norwood that. He told me.'

'Yes. That's right.'

'Are there any other identifying marks you might describe to me?'

'Marks?'

'Well, anything unusual or distinctive.'

'No.'

'Nothing about the design or decoration?'

Randy Parker glanced over at Dotty. The sunglasses prevented Rolly from reading his eyes.

'What did you tell him?' Parker said to Dotty.

'We talked about the UVTs,' said Dotty. 'I showed him the paintings.'

Randy Parker returned his attention to Rolly. 'What else do you know?' he said.

The bell rang as the the front door opened. They all turned to see who had entered the store. It was Moogus.

'We're closed,' said Parker.

'I'm with him,' Moogus said, pointing at Rolly. 'We need to get going.'

'Yes,' Rolly said. 'We do.'

Whatever was going on, he didn't want to aggravate Randy Parker any further. He moved towards the door.

'Where're you going?' said Randy Parker.

'We've got to be somewhere. In East County.'

'We're rockin' the rez tonight,' said Moogus.

Randy Parker took a step towards them. 'What's that supposed to mean?' he said.

Dotty put a hand on his arm. Parker stopped.

'We've got a gig at one of the Indian casinos,' said Rolly.

'It was very nice to meet you, Mr Waters,' said Dotty. 'Please come back when you have more time to talk.'

'That OK with you, Mr Parker?' said Rolly. 'If I come back to talk sometime?'

Parker glanced over at Dotty. An unspoken agreement passed between them.

'Yeah,' Parker said. 'You come back anytime. Come back and we'll talk.'

'Let's go,' said Moogus.

Rolly followed Moogus out to the sidewalk. As the door closed behind him, he heard a sound like a handclap. His best guess was Dotty had slapped Randy. Or Randy had slapped Dotty. It could have gone either way. They were both telling stories. The stories weren't quite the same. Rolly followed Moogus back to the truck and climbed in.

'Nice rug on that guy, huh?' said Moogus.

'I thought maybe it was a dye job.'

'I'd lay odds he's a cue ball, covering up some head tats. Good thing for you I showed up.'

'He was getting a little agitated.'

'Yeah, well, when a guy like that gets agitated, he's likely to bite off your ear.'

'What?'

'EWMN. The T-shirt covered up part of the tattoo, but I knew what it was.'

'What does EWMN mean?'

'Evil, wicked, mean and nasty. Tattooed on the back of his neck. He's a jumpsuiter for sure.'

'You mean an ex-con? He was in prison?'

Moogus laughed. 'You should hire me, as a consultant or something.'

'Why is that?'

'Well, for a detective, you don't seem too sharp at identifying the criminal element.'

'No, I guess not,' said Rolly. He slumped into his seat. He hated dealing with the criminal element.

SEVEN

The Tower

'How much longer do you want to wait?' said Moogus.
'Just a couple more minutes,' said Rolly. 'Then we'll give up.'

It was 4:30 in the morning. They'd been sitting for over an hour, parked outside the locked entrance to Desert View Tower, a funky old tourist trap on the eastern edge of the mountains. During regular hours visitors could buy candy, postcards and other knick-knacks inside the tower. They could climb to the top of the circular staircase and gaze from the open balcony into the barren furnace of the Anza Borrego Desert, or explore the rock gardens nearby, where one of the owners had carved animal shapes out of the sandstone boulders. There was a buffalo, a hawk, a crocodile and some other animals Rolly couldn't remember. His mother had brought him here years ago, on one of the countless adventures she'd forced him to endure when he was a teenager.

'Is this what you call a stakeout?' said Moogus.

'I don't know what I'd call this,' said Rolly.

'I always thought it'd be cool to go on a stakeout.'

'This isn't a stakeout. The guy wants us to meet him here.'

'You're sure about that? It's been almost an hour.'

'I'm not sure about anything.'

'Who's this guy s'posed to be, anyway?'

'I don't know.'

'You think it's that ex-con from the shop?'

'I hope not.'

'Could be a trap,' said Moogus. 'He knew we were gonna be at the casino.'

'I expect something would have happened by now if it were a trap.'

'Yeah. I guess. That guy had it in for you, though. I could tell. After my time in the pen, I know an orange peeler with intent when I see one.'

'You were only in jail for two months. You're not allowed to use prison lingo unless you've done at least a full year.'

'Who made up that rule?'

'I did. Just now.'

'Hey, hard time is hard time.'

Rolly searched the area outside the car, considering what he should do next, if anything. A field of large boulders stood on either side of the road, casting long shadows as the full moon sank towards the western horizon. Someone had left a postcard of the Desert View Tower in his guitar case, sneaking it in during the band's last set at the casino. A cryptic message had been scrawled on the back of the card.

TEOTWAYKI

Golden Eyes Key

Arrive before sunrise

The first line meant nothing to him. It looked like an Indian word. But he couldn't help feeling the second line referred to his new client. The sender knew something about Macy Starr. The third line he interpreted as a command, that he should go to the place pictured on the postcard by the time indicated. He'd talked Moogus into going along with this stupid idea by promising to pay for a full tank of gas. If no one showed up at the Desert View Tower by sunrise, so be it. He would go home and sleep. He wouldn't charge Macy for the hours.

'You get horizontal with her yet?' said Moogus. 'This chick you're so worked up about?'

'I only met her last night.'

'Since when did that stop you?'

'She's my client. Besides, I'm old enough to be her father.'

'Is she legal age?'

'Yes.'

'I repeat my last query.'

'I'm pretty sure she's not interested in middle-aged guitar players.'

'How about a drummer who likes to think young?'

'Shut up,' said Rolly.

He stared out the window at the dirt road, the rocks and scraggly brush.

'Hey,' said Moogus.

'What?'

'You think the guy who left you the card lives in that tower thing?'

'It's possible, I guess.'

'Maybe we should sneak in, on foot, you know, stealthy-like, and case the joint.'

'Did you really say "case the joint"?'

'Yeah. Isn't that how you detective guys talk? We'll get the drop on him.'

Rolly sighed. His friends assumed his day job was like what they'd seen in the movies – muscle-headed thugs, gin joints and wisecracking dames. In reality, most of the cases he worked on were stupid arguments pitting dumb against dumber. He interviewed accident victims for insurance companies, took photos of deadbeat dads spending money that should go to their kids. He searched for absent wives and runaway teens. He didn't carry a gun. He didn't own one. Even thinking about carrying a gun made him queasy.

Still, he was glad to have Moogus with him. Moogus had actual biceps. He could handle himself in a fight. Moogus had been to prison, after all, if only for two months. He could act like a tough guy. He knew how to intimidate. Rolly was better at talking his way out of confrontations. Aside from playing guitar, it was the one thing he was good at.

They heard a sound from outside the truck. A bird call. Something clattered against the back window.

'What was that?' Moogus said, turning around.

'I don't know.'

They waited a moment. The bird called again. The rear window clattered.

'Somebody's throwing shit at us,' said Moogus. He reached for the door handle.

'Hold on,' said Rolly.

'For what?'

'I think I see him.'

'Where?'

Rolly pointed to a shadow moving through the scrubby bush. The shadow crouched down behind a scraggly shrub.

'There. You see him?'

As if in response, the figure rose up. They heard the bird call again. The shadow swiveled its right arm. A handful of sand and pebbles rattled the front window.

'I guess he wants to get our attention,' said Rolly.

'He's got mine,' said Moogus, rolling down his window.

'Hey jerkwad!' he shouted. 'Stop throwing crap at my truck.'

The shadow stood its ground. 'Who are you?' it asked.

'It doesn't matter who I am,' Moogus said. 'Don't throw shit at my truck.'

'You're the drummer.'

'Yeah. That's right.'

'I want the guitar player,' said the shadow.

'He's here with me. You the guy who left the postcard?'

'I must query him. The guitar player.'

'Why can't you talk to me?'

'Drummers are nincompoops. They cannot play the proper frequencies.'

Moogus turned to Rolly. 'Can you believe this guy?'

Another handful of dirt and rocks hit the windshield. Moogus opened his door and stepped out. He took a few threatening steps towards the shadow. 'I told you. Stop throwing that shit at my truck.'

The shadow retreated and moved farther up the hill. 'I want the guitar player,' said the shadow. 'I want the Waters.'

Rolly climbed out of the truck, circled around the front and walked up next to Moogus. 'I'm here,' he said. 'What do you want?'

'I will not speak, not with him. I wish to query the Waters.'

'We drove together. He gave me a ride.'

'The questions are for you,' said the shadow. 'Not the skin-beater.'

'What do you want me to do?' Rolly asked. The shadow disappeared. They heard rustling and scraping higher up in the rocks.

'Up here,' said the shadow from a different position. 'The skin-beater must return to the vehicle.'

Rolly and Moogus exchanged glances.

'This guy's a wack job,' said Moogus, under his breath.

'I don't think he's dangerous,' said Rolly. 'Go back to the truck.'

Moogus shrugged and retreated. He leaned back against the truck's cabin, folded his arms and stared up at the rocks, channeling his best badass.

'Over here,' said the shadow. 'I will speak from the orifice.'

Rolly stepped off the road and walked up the hill towards the boulder field. As he got closer he noticed a vertical line through the tallest boulder, an open fissure running from top to bottom.

'Hold,' the man said. Rolly halted, three feet from the fissure. The crack was wider at his end of the boulder and narrowed as it went back, amplifying the man's voice.

'Are you a gold drinker?' the man said.

'No,' Rolly said. 'Not that I know of.'

'Are you a Gentling?'

'Same answer, I guess.'

The man made a sound like a bird. 'Teotwayki! Teotwayki!'

'That's what you wrote on the postcard, isn't it?'

The bird call came back for an answer.

'Is it supposed to mean something to me?' Rolly asked. 'I don't understand.'

'Teotwayki. That is what it means.'

'What does the second line mean?' Rolly said. '"Golden eyes key?"'

'Golden Eyes has the key.'

'The key to what?'

'The Astral Vibrator.'

Rolly felt the hairs on the back of his neck stand up. Randy Parker was looking for the Astral Vibrator. It went with the diddley bow.

'Do you know where I can find the Astral Vibrator?' he said.

'It lives with the Gentlings. The Waters must practice the frequencies.'

Rolly had been part of many strange conversations in the early morning hours with drunks and drug addicts, all sorts of chemically impaired nightcrawlers who hung around on the street after closing time. They would stand on the sidewalk ruminating loudly on life's challenges while you packed up your equipment and tried to get away before they decided you were their best friend.

'What are these frequencies you want me to practice?' he said.

'The Waters must learn the Solfeggios.'

'I don't know what that is.'

'Golden Eyes has the key.'

'The diddley bow? The one-string guitar? Is that what you're talking about?'

'I am affirming.'

'I have a question for you, then. There's a photograph on the back, a man and a woman.'

'I am affirming.'

'Who is she, the woman? Do you know?'

'The Waters should ask the big Indian.'

'Daddy Joe? Is that who you mean? Is he the big Indian?'

There was no answer. Rolly cleared his throat. He looked up at the night sky. There were lots of stars but no flying saucers around – at least, none that he could see. Things were weird enough without any aliens.

'He is gone,' said the man in the rock.

'Daddy Joe?' said Rolly. 'Where'd he go?'

'The skin-beater. He's gone.'

'The skin . . . wait.'

Rolly turned and looked back towards the truck. Moogus had disappeared.

EIGHT
The Shocker

Rolly took two steps down the hill, searching the landscape.

'Moogus!' he called. 'Where are you?'

He heard scuffling sounds behind him. Someone screamed.

'Ayaaah!'

'I got you now!' said a voice. It was Moogus.

'Teotwayki!' the man called. 'Teotwayki!'

'I got him, Rolly!' said Moogus. 'I got . . . Hey! Who . . .?'

Rolly heard a strange sound, like an electric woodpecker tapping on rocks. Someone screamed.

'Aaagh!'

The electric woodpecker rattled again. The screamer screamed.

'Aaagh!'

The screamer sounded like Moogus. Rolly bolted up the hill and worked his way around the boulders. 'Moog?'

'I'm down here,' said Moogus. 'Shit damn. That smarts.'

Rolly spotted someone lying on the ground behind the big rock. He crept down the incline and squatted down beside Moogus. 'Are you OK?' he said.

'Boo-oof,' said Moogus. 'Just give me a minute, here.'

Moogus sat up and shook his head back and forth like a cartoon character clearing his brainpan. He put his left hand out, touching it against the rock for balance.

'What were you thinking?' said Rolly. 'I told you to stay by the truck.'

'There was somebody else. Up in the rocks. Creeping around.'

'Why didn't you tell me?'

'I don't know. I just had a feeling. I thought I could nab him.'

'What happened?'

'I got up there, where I thought the other guy was. I couldn't find anybody. Then I heard the guy that was talking to you. He was right down below me. So I jumped him.'

'You shouldn't have done that.'

'Next thing I know, someone's zapped my ass and I'm looking up at the stars.'

A cackle of laughter rolled down the hill and bounced off the boulders. 'Teotwayki!'

'I don't like this,' said Moogus.

Rolly stood up. 'Hey,' he called. 'Are you still there?'

'What do you call a drummer with half a brain?' said the voice.

'Seriously, Rolly . . .' said Moogus.

'Gifted,' came the unrequested answer.

'I'm going to kill that guy.'

'Just wait here,' said Rolly. 'I need to talk to him.'

'Be careful,' said Moogus. 'There's somebody else out here. With a taser or something.'

'Sounds to me like his bodyguard's better than mine.'

'Fuck you.'

Rolly turned back to the boulder field. 'Hey!' he shouted. 'Whoever you are. I still want to talk to you.'

No one answered.

'I need some answers,' said Rolly.

'Proceed!' called the voice. 'Find the crocodile.'

'What?'

'Proceed to the crocodile.'

'The crocodile?' said Moogus. 'What's he talking about?'

'There're these statues,' said Rolly. 'Animals somebody carved out of the rocks.'

'To the crocodile!' said the voice.

Rolly stepped forward.

'Don't do it,' said Moogus.

Rolly shushed him. 'Just sit tight,' he said. 'Don't screw things up anymore than you already have.'

Rolly took another step and lifted himself to the top of a small rise. He could see a dirt path curving down the back of the rise and up another hill, where it ran between two large boulders. The first hint of daylight pushed at the darkness. He left Moogus and trudged down the path. The trail rose and twisted. He passed another boulder then stopped in his tracks. A stone crocodile grinned at him in the dim light, baring its bas-relief teeth.

'OK,' Rolly said. 'I'm at the crocodile.'

'The skin-beater is impudent,' said the man. 'Unattuned to the stars.'

'He gets like that sometimes,' said Rolly. 'He won't bother you again.'

'The boogie man stuck him with the bad frequencies.'

'There's someone else out here?'

'I am affirming.'

'Is he a friend of yours?'

'I am denying. Not a friend.'

'He didn't come here with you?'

'I am denying.'

'Who is he then?'

'A villain. He brought the negative frequencies.'

Rolly didn't like the idea of any villain lurking about, let alone one with a stungun bringing negative frequencies. He needed to get out of here. But he needed to ask the man about Daddy Joe and the photograph first.

'The photograph, on the back of the diddley bow – who is it?'

'The big chief must tell you. That is agreed.'

'You mean Daddy Joe, don't you?'

'That is affirmed.'

'Why can't you tell me?'

'The Waters must practice,' said the voice. 'The Waters must read the diagram.'

'What diagram?' said Rolly. 'Does Daddy Joe have the diagram?'

'Daddy Joe is a dead man,' said another voice, from behind him. The electric woodpecker rattled. A negative frequency shot through Rolly's body and his brain exploded into a bright bolt of pain. He twisted away from the stinging woodpecker and collapsed, almost hitting his head on the crocodile.

'Teotwayki!' the bird called again. Soft footsteps padded away from him.

'Rolly!'

'Uhnn,' grunted Rolly. He pulled his head up and rested it on the crocodile's neck. A gob of drool fell from his mouth. He heard footsteps approaching, someone walking up from below.

'He got you too, didn't he?' said Moogus.

'Uhnn,' Rolly said.

'Take it easy,' said Moogus. He leaned down and lifted Rolly's head off the stone crocodile, slipped his shoulder in behind Rolly's back for support and helped him sit up. In the distance Rolly heard the sound of a car starting up.

'Someone . . .' said Rolly, '. . . gettin' away.'

'Yeah. I hear it.'

'Uhnn,' said Rolly.

'You'll be OK,' said Moogus. 'Might take a minute or two.'

'Uph,' Rolly said, waving his hand towards the sky.

'What's that?'

'Ged up. Look car.'

Moogus furrowed his brow as the sound of the car's engine floated through the rocks.

'Look, look, lithenth,' Rolly said. Moogus finally seemed to understand. He dropped Rolly against the crocodile and stood up.

'I see it,' he said. 'Over there. What the hell is that thing? It looks like a spaceship or something.'

The sound of the engine faded into the distance.

'He's gone.'

'Lithenth?'

'No license. I could only see the top half. It's a Volkswagen van. I could tell that much. You remember Old Zeke?'

Rolly nodded. 'I remember.'

'Old Zeke sounded just like that,' said Moogus.

'I wrote a song about Zeke.'

'We used to get the whole band in there and a couple of girl-friends sometimes too. What was the song?'

Rolly leaned his head back against the crocodile. He rubbed his temples, trying to access the memory. One verse. That was all he could remember. And the melody. His voice cracked as he sang it.

> *Old Zeke's got a number, stashed in his glove box*
> *A number he's waiting to play*
> *She gave him her number, the day that he met her*
> *A wahine from Hanalei Bay*

'Oh, man, that sucks,' said Moogus. 'A wahine from Hanalei Bay? Really?'

Rolly shrugged. 'I was going for a surf-rock kind of thing.'

'Zeke deserved better than that.'

'That's why I never played it for you.'

The fuzziness in Rolly's head began to clear. He stood up and dusted himself off.

'We sure got our asses kicked, didn't we?' said Moogus.

'Yeah.'

'I shouldn't have jumped that guy.'

'You should have stayed by the truck.'

Moogus laughed. 'I guess I'm not much of a bodyguard, am I, buddy?'

'I wouldn't give up your skin-beating job.'

'Let's get the hell out of here.'

'Yeah.'

They walked back down the path. The boulders looked smaller now, less foreboding.

'As I was saying,' Moogus continued as they wound their way down the trail, 'all those Volkswagen vans, they got the same sound. Once you own one, you'll never forget it. That's useful, right? Knowing what kind of car the guy drives.'

'What did you mean, it looked like a spaceship?'

'I only saw it for a couple of seconds. There was this gap in the rocks. It looked like a spaceship to me.'

'How so?'

'It had these little wings on the side, kinda like the space shuttle wings, and some more things jutting out of the top that looked like old TV antennas. There were these round cones, like rocket engines or something, stuck to the back. Just some shapes I could see.'

They reached the bottom of the hill and walked to the truck. Moogus pulled out his keys. They opened the doors and climbed into the truck.

'I'd know that sound anywhere,' said Moogus. 'A VW van. That helps, right? You just gotta find a VW van that looks like a spaceship. How hard can that be?'

'It helps,' said Rolly. 'A license plate would be better.'

'Yeah, well, I'm not sure I could have read it anyway, in this light.'

Moogus turned the key in the ignition. Nothing happened. He tried it again. There was a small click but no engine sound.

'What the hell?' Moogus said.

'Did you leave the lights on?' said Rolly.

'No, I turned 'em off,' Moogus replied, looking over the dashboard instruments. He tried the key one more time and got the same result. He reached into the glove box and pulled out a flashlight. He climbed out of the car, popped the hood and inspected the engine.

'Shit dammit,' he said.

Rolly got out of the truck, went to look at the engine with Moogus. 'What is it?' he said.

'Somebody pulled my relay fuse.'

'Can you fix it?'

'Not unless you happen to have one in your pocket.'

As they stood staring at the truck's engine, an old blue Toyota pulled out onto the road a hundred feet down from them.

'Hey,' Moogus called, waving his arms. 'Over here.'

The Toyota turned and drove away.

'Asshole,' said Moogus.

Rolly pulled his phone from his pocket. 'I don't get any signal here,' he said.

Moogus walked to the truck cab, pulled out his phone and tossed it back in the cab.

'Me neither.'

'So what do we do now?'

'Walk back to the freeway, I guess. See if I can get a signal there, find a call box.'

'How far is that?'

'Mile. Mile and a half.'

Moogus turned and pointed back towards the Desert View Tower. 'You think somebody lives in this place?'

'It says they don't open until eight-thirty,' Rolly said, pointing at the gate. 'You want to wait that long?'

'What time is it now?'

Rolly checked his phone. 'A little after five,' he said.

'Sign says it's only a quarter-mile. Let's go wake 'em up.'

They locked the doors of the truck, walked around the gate and headed towards the tower.

'I wish you'd stayed with the truck like I asked you to,' Rolly said.

'Yeah, I do too,' Moogus said. 'This detective stuff is really starting to suck.'

NINE

The Cop

They got home around eight the same morning. Rolly unloaded his gear from the truck. He didn't bother to wave as Moogus pulled out of the driveway. They'd spent longer and more exhausting nights together, but not since their youth.

Rolly's mother opened her back door and stepped onto the stoop. She looked concerned.

'Is everything OK?' Rolly said, walking over to greet her.

'I'm not sure,' she replied. 'Aren't you home rather late?'

'Car troubles. Moogus' truck wouldn't start.'

His mother sighed.

'What's wrong?' he asked. 'Is everything OK at the hospital?'

'Oh, everything's fine there. We talked to the doctors.'

'What'd they say?'

'They expect him to recover, but they'll want to keep him a few more days.'

'He won't be too happy about that. How's Alicia?'

'The police were here. That friend of yours, the blonde woman.'

'Bonnie?'

'Yes. I don't know why I can never remember her name.'

'What'd she want?'

'She wants you to call her.'

'Did she say why?'

'I told her about your father. Just so she'd be aware, if you were acting peculiar.'

Rolly sighed. Those who knew him, like his mother or Bonnie, were always on watch for suspicious behavior, looking for clues that he'd slipped off the wagon. He hadn't been sober long enough to slacken their vigilance. He didn't know how long it would take.

'I just want to say,' his mother continued, 'it's quite disconcerting to come home and find a police car in the driveway. Especially when you've returned from the hospital at seven in the morning and your son is missing.'

'I wasn't missing. I was working.'

Rolly's phone rang. He pulled it out of his pocket and looked at the screen. It was Bonnie. He answered. 'I just got home,' he said. 'What's up?'

'I talked to your mom,' said Bonnie.

'Yeah. She said you'd come by.'

'How's your dad doing?'

'It looks like he's gonna pull through.'

'Glad to hear it. Listen, you got any idea why tribal police might be looking for you?'

'You mean, like Indians?'

'That's usually what tribal means.'

'Um, no. I don't think so.'

'Did you play any of the casinos recently?'

'We were at the Jincona reservation last night.'

'Any problems?'

'No. Not that I'm aware of.'

'You usually get home this late?'

'We had some car trouble. Moogus' truck wouldn't start.'

'You were up there with Moogus?'

'He's our drummer, you know. We sound better when we have a drummer.'

'Don't get smart with me.'

'I'm sorry. I'm tired.'

'I'm gonna stop by.'

'I need to sleep.'

'It'll only be ten minutes. I'm still in the area.'

'OK. Fine,' said Rolly. He hung up. Bonnie didn't like Moogus. She had her reasons, besides his ex-con status. Moogus had talked Joan into going to bed with him once. Joan was Bonnie's girl-friend. All these years later, Bonnie still didn't like him.

'Is everything OK?' asked Rolly's mother.

'Hmm, oh, everything's fine. That was Bonnie. She's coming over.'

'Well, at least I'll expect her this time.' His mother crossed her arms and pursed her lips. 'Are you feeling all right?' she said.

'Me? Oh sure. Just thinking about some things.'

'Do we need to talk about your father?'

'I don't think so.'

'I thought perhaps you might want to discuss things. When something happens like this . . .'

'The doctors said he's going to be OK, right?'

'They said he'll be fine. He'll need to make some life changes, I expect.'

'I expect so.'

'I thought maybe you could advise him on that.'

'Me?'

'You've had your own experiences – you could talk to him.'

'What? About his drinking?'

'Well, yes, that, and your brush with . . . mortality.'

'You want me to talk to Dad about dying?'

'I'm just saying it's something you can share now: getting a second chance. You were able to make positive changes in your life.'

'I'm not talking to dad about his drinking unless he apologizes to me first.'

'Apologizes for what?'

'Something, anything.'

'This kind of life event might change him.'

'I think you're too hopeful. We'll see.'

'You don't drink anymore.'

'I kind of wish I had a drink now,' said Rolly, under his breath.

'What's that?'

'Nothing,' said Rolly. 'I'll think about it, but let's wait until he gets settled at home.'

'Don't let this get you upset. You can talk to me if you need to.'

'Thank you. I will. I'm not upset.'

'All right, dear.' His mother gave him a peck on the cheek and turned back into her house. Rolly grabbed his guitar and amplifier from the driveway, opened the door to his house and walked in. He stashed his equipment, plugged in his phone to recharge it then dumped the contents of his pockets on the kitchen table: wallet, guitar picks, keys and a postcard of Desert View Tower.

As Moogus had surmised, the proprietors of the tower lived on the premises. A young married couple, they had been awake by the time Rolly knocked on their door, more than happy to help out and share a cup of their morning coffee with marooned strangers. The woman had been awakened earlier by the sound of something being dropped through the mail slot on the front door. It was a gift for Moogus, a brown paper bag containing his truck's relay fuse. Both she and her husband seemed relieved to have the mysterious incursion explained.

As it turned out, they'd seen a VW van decorated like a spaceship. Many times. It was a regular visitor, at least once a week, in the parking lot and along the service roads. They knew little about the owner. Someone had told them the man lived in Slab City, an unincorporated enclave of hippies and retirees camped out in an old army base near the Salton Sea. The woman gave Rolly a brief history of Slab City, describing its genesis as a

training ground for troops during World War II. The army demol-
ished the camp soon after the war, leaving only the concrete
foundations of buildings behind. Years later, a vagabond traveler
happened on the abandoned slabs and decided they made a perfect
place to park a mobile home for the winter. There were no fees
or rents to pay, no rules to obey. Word soon got out and others
followed. Before long, an offbeat, off-the-grid community of
like-minded nomads had bloomed in the desert.

Rolly heard a car pulling into the driveway. A car door opened
and shut. Footsteps scrunched across the gravel. Rolly's front
door swung open. Bonnie Hammond walked in.

'Aren't you supposed to knock?' Rolly said.

'Door was open,' said Bonnie. 'And you invited me here.'

'Not exactly invited.'

'Is there anything you need to tell me about? Before you get
in trouble? You need help with one of your cases?'

'I don't need any help. I just need some sleep.'

Bonnie picked up the postcard from the table. 'Desert View Tower,
huh?' she said, reading the back. 'Teotwayki. What's that mean?'

'I don't know.'

'You got any clients you want to tell me about?'

'Not really.'

'No lights going on yet? About why the tribal police want to
talk to you?'

'No.'

'Aside from your casino gig last night, have you been in the
back country lately, on the reservation?'

'Moogus and I stopped at Desert View Tower this morning
after the gig. That's the only other place we've been.'

Bonnie looked at her watch. 'Sounds kind of early for you.'

'Moogus and I wanted to see the sunrise.'

'Uh huh.'

'We're sentimental that way.'

Bonnie put the postcard back on the table. She picked up
Macy's flyer. 'DJ Crazy Macy,' she said, reading the flyer.
'Doesn't sound like your style.'

'I like to keep an open mind.'

Bonnie pulled her phone out of her pocket and tapped on the
screen. 'Take down this number,' she said.

'Who is it?'

'Her name's Kinnie Harper. She's chief of police for the Jincona Tribe.'

'You're working with her?'

'No. Luckily for you, this is just a personal call. Kinnie wants to talk to you.'

'Why?'

'Originally she just wanted to find out if I'd ever heard of you. She had your name, for some reason.'

'How'd she get it?'

'She's trying find a woman named Macy,' said Bonnie, waving the flyer. 'Ring any bells?'

'Why didn't this Kinnie woman just call me directly?'

'I said I'd talk to you first, make sure you called back, which you will now.'

'Is this Macy in some kind of trouble?'

'I don't know. Not my business. Not yet, anyway. Kinnie's dad has gone missing. He used to be chief of police up there. Kinnie grew up in the business.'

'Daddy Joe?'

'I see you've heard of him. Kinnie said it's not the first time he's gone missing. He's gone a bit non compos mentis, now that he's retired.'

'She was adopted. Macy, I mean. She told me she grew up on the reservation. Why is Kinnie looking for her?'

'I don't know. Kinnie just mentioned her name. Like I said, she wants to talk to you.'

'How did Kinnie get my name?'

'You'll have to ask her that when you call. Listen, this is not official business on my part. I got no skin in the game. I'm just doing a personal favor for Kinnie. She's part of a professional group I'm in. I thought it'd be easier for both of you if I talked to you first. So you wouldn't start freaking out.'

'Appreciated. Thanks.'

'You ready?' Bonnie said, indicating her phone.

Rolly nodded. Bonnie spelled out Kinnie's name and read him the number. Rolly entered the information into his phone.

'Anything else?' he said.

'That's it,' Bonnie said. She turned to leave, then stopped to look back at him. 'How are you doing?' she said. 'With your dad and all?'

'My mom wants me to talk to him. About his lifestyle. She thinks I could influence him, I guess – get him to stop drinking.'

'I talked to my dad once, when he was in the hospital with cirrhosis. About cutting back, eating better and stuff.'

'How'd that go?'

'He said he wasn't taking nutrition advice from a girl who ate pussy.'

'Your dad was an even bigger asshole than mine.'

'He looked scared to death in that hospital, before he died. I really saw him for who he was then, just a lonely, fucked-up bastard with nothing left in life but getting plastered and calling people names, pushing everyone away so he could crawl into that bottle.'

'I guess we both turned out OK, under the circumstances.'

'Yeah, well, you know what they say: you can't pick your parents. Make sure you call Kinnie. I told her you would. I don't want her telling me you're acting like a jerk.'

'I won't be a jerk,' Rolly said.

Bonnie left. Rolly locked the door. He reached into the back of his amplifier and pulled out the roll of paper he'd stashed there. The woman from the Desert View Tower had found it rolled up in a slot in the shop's map case. She'd been looking for a map to show Rolly the location of Slab City. The shop had all sorts of maps for sale – road maps of California and the Southwest, elevations and trail maps for local parks and wilderness areas. But this map wasn't like any of the others. The proprietors had never seen it before.

It looked like a schematic diagram for some kind of electronic device. There was a nine-digit number printed in the bottom right-hand corner. He couldn't remember the exact number embossed on the gold tube that hung from Macy's necklace, but he had a feeling this one was the same. There was a word printed above the number. *TEOTWAYKI*. There were two more words printed above that. *Astral Vibrator*.

Rolly had realized that the man in the rocks had left it for him, the birdman from Slab City with the VW van that looked like a rocket ship. He'd offered the woman ten dollars for the rolled-up tube of paper. She said he could have it for free. He'd left a ten-spot in the tower's donation box on his way out. The roll of paper was worth at least that much to him.

He walked to the sofa, sat down and took off his shoes. He rolled out the diagram and stared at it for a minute. He had a marginal familiarity with the symbols used in electronic diagrams but this one was too complicated for him to assess, especially in his present condition. He rolled the diagram up, dropped it onto the floor and leaned back on the sofa. Two minutes later, he fell asleep.

Three hours later, his phone rang, waking him. He rolled off the sofa, crawled to the table and checked the number. It was Macy. He answered. 'Hey,' he said. 'We need to talk.'

'Fuck you, Waters,' said Macy. 'Fuck you and that cop you put on my ass.'

TEN
The Plans

'Astral Vibrator, huh?' said Marley Scratch, glancing over the diagram Rolly had handed him. He laughed. 'How come every time you ask me to look at something, it always ends up involving female anatomy?'

'I don't think it's that kind of vibrator,' said Rolly.

'You try Googling it yet? I bet that's what you'll end up with.'

'I imagine I would. I think this is for a guitar, though, like a stomp box or something.'

'Is this a musical or sleuthing endeavor?' said Marley.

'Detective work,' said Rolly.

'Where'd you get a hold of this?'

'Long story,' said Rolly. 'I wouldn't believe it myself if I hadn't been there.'

The two men stood in the kitchen of Marley's loft on Broadway and Seventh, the second floor of the old Apex Music store, which had been replaced many years ago by a Super Discount grocery outlet, an early casualty in the decline of independent music stores brought on by the rise of chain stores and the Internet. It was a dingy old building, spared from its inevitable demolition by the recent economic downturn. The developers would return someday, but Marley could enjoy his twelve-foot ceilings and cheap rent another few years.

Rolly often called Marley when he needed assistance in deciphering computer data that needed to be recovered, analyzed or decrypted. When Marley wasn't working for Rolly, he made a hodgepodge career out of repairing computers and writing for game magazines. He also traded in antique toys and black Americana.

'I need more light to read this,' said Marley. Rolly followed him back to the work area. Marley clipped the schematic to the top of a drafting table, turned on the table lamp and picked up a pair of reading glasses. He studied the document, tracing the signal path with his finger.

'You might be right about the guitar thing,' he said. 'The input impedance is the right level. There's no output, though, just a switch at the end of the signal path. Doesn't make sense for a stomp box. You'd want to feed the signal back out somewhere.'

'Does that number mean anything to you, below the name?'

'It could be a patent ID. Maybe the SKU.'

'There was a guy here in town, a guitar tech, named Buddy Meeks.'

'You think he designed this?'

'I've got this guitar he built. Well, not really a guitar. It's called a diddley bow. There's only one string.'

'Yeah, I know what a diddley bow is,' said Marley. 'Hey, I gotta show you the Molo that I picked up on my trip to the motherland.'

Marley stepped away from the table and returned with a primitive-looking stringed instrument. It had two strings stretched over a hollowed-out gourd and a broomstick for the neck. There was some sort of skin stretched across the gourd opening, like a drum.

'When were you in Africa?' said Rolly. He plucked at the strings. The instrument had a buzzy, lutish sound.

'Took a trip last year.'

'I didn't know that.'

'You've been out of touch, my friend.'

'Yeah. I guess so. How was it?'

'Some beautiful musical expressions. Alternate tunings and stuff. Some beautiful ladies, too.'

Marley hung the Molo back on the wall, next to a movie poster of Amos 'n' Andy.

'Hey, have you ever heard of the term Solfeggio?' said Rolly.

'Don't think so? Why?'

'This guy told me I needed to practice it. I think he's the same guy who left me the diagram.'

'You can Google it on the laptop, if you want.'

'Thanks.'

Marley returned to inspecting the diagram. Rolly moved to the sofa and opened the laptop sitting on the coffee table next to a red Tonka truck. You could count on there being at least a dozen computers scattered about Marley's loft at any given time, in variable states of functionality. There was usually one nearby. Rolly typed 'solfeggio' in the search field. He read through the entry at the top of the results page.

'Do, Re, Mi,' he said. 'That's what it is.'

'Hmm?'

'Solfeggio. It's vocalizing a scale with different sounds, like Do, Re, Mi.'

'Well, there you go.'

Rolly looked down to the list of search results. There was a video link for something called the Solfeggio frequencies. He clicked the link and played the video. A low tone played through the computer's speaker.

'What's that?' said Marley.

'It's one of the Solfeggio frequencies,' said Rolly.

'Doesn't sound like no Do, Re, Mi.'

'This is something different.'

'That's all it plays?'

'It says there are nine different frequencies. This one is a hundred and seventy-four hertz.'

'Kind of lacking on the funkiness level.'

'They claim it's for meditating. And entrainment, whatever that is.'

'I know what entrainment is,' said Marley. 'You know it too. Everytime you play with your band.'

'So what is it?'

'It's when people get synced up to music, how we all get hooked into the beat. Rhythmic patterns. People dancing as a group, trancing out together. It's like an evolutionary skill human beings developed.'

'Huh,' said Rolly. He flipped back to the listings on the search page, read through more of the list. There were all sorts of entries for Solfeggio frequencies.

'Each of the frequencies represents a different consciousness level,' he said, reading one of the entries. 'Consciousness Expansion. Awakening Intuition. Transcendence.'

'Sounds kinda woo woo to me.'

'My mom would love this stuff.'

Rolly continued reading. He thought about Dotty, the woman he'd met at the Alien Artifacts store. Universal Vibration Technologies. The paintings of flowing energy fields. The UVTs. She'd talked about frequencies, how they were used to release the alien within. The claims made on the Solfeggio websites were similar. Some even claimed that listening to the tones could realign your DNA.

Marley muttered something under his breath.

'What's that?' said Rolly.

'What was that number you said earlier, that Solfeggio thing?'

'Umm, let me look: one hundred and seventy-four hertz.'

'Interesting,' said Marley.

'What?'

'That number's written on here. It's on one of the resistors. You say there's nine of them?'

'Yeah.'

'Read me the rest.'

Rolly read the frequency numbers listed on the website.

'They're all here,' said Marley. 'That's gotta mean something.'

'Really?'

'Take a look if you want to.'

Rolly rose from the sofa and joined Marley at the drafting table.

'You see, here,' said Marley, running his finger down the paper, 'above each of these squiggles.'

'Maybe this Astral Vibrator plays those frequencies or something?'

Marley shrugged. 'Maybe. Sure looks like it's got something to do with it.'

Rolly pulled his phone from his pocket and checked the time.
'I have to meet with a client,' he said. 'Can I leave this with
you?'

'Sure,' said Marley. 'I'll do some more research. Maybe I can
find that number on the bottom somewhere in a patent search.
If I can find an abstract, it would help me figure it out faster.'

'I'll be over at the cantina. Give me a call if you find out
anything.'

'Will do, Sir Roland.'

ELEVEN
The Cantina

R olly sat in a back booth at the Villa Cantina, nursing a
mug of Mexican cocoa and coffee. He'd finished his lunch
– red enchiladas with an egg over easy. A satisfying meal
was all the meditation he needed. It had provided both sustenance
and gratification, greasing the wheels of his corroded feelings
towards Macy. She had texted him a half hour ago to let him
know she'd be late, which he hoped was a sign of appeasement.
Neither of them had expressed themselves well on the phone.
They were tired and angry, but they'd agreed on a truce and a
face-to-face meeting to be held at the cantina. He opened his
composition book and jotted down a few lines to keep his mind
occupied while he waited.

I'm sitting and eating huevos rancheros.
Drinking black coffee and falling behind.
I'm feeling tired, bewildered and beaten.
Chasing old shadows and losing my mind.

His phone rang. He didn't recognize the number. He answered
anyway. A sequence of tones played on the other end of the line,
like a fax machine or computer calling. He hung up. The phone
rang again, the same number. He muted it, then looked up to see
Vera ushering Macy to his table.

'There he is,' said Vera. 'The great detective. You want something to drink?'

'Dos Equis Amber,' said Macy, plopping down on the booth cushion across from Rolly.

Vera wagged a finger at Rolly. 'You be nice to her, Mr Rolly,' she said. 'Macy's my home girl.'

'This is business, Vera,' said Rolly. 'Just business.'

'Yeah, well, I haven't forgotten the nasty business you brought into my place with that little chica a while ago.'

'That was an unexpected situation,' said Rolly.

'What happened?' said Macy.

'No big deal,' said Vera. 'Just some *tunante* who tried to kill me. I shot a hole in the wall upstairs and Hector ended up with some kind of skin condition on his face.'

Macy looked over at Rolly. 'Don't tell me,' she said. 'Your middle name is Trouble?'

'You be careful with this one, girl,' said Vera. 'Don't let those eyes fool you. He can talk you into anything. You gotta be cool.'

'I'm gonna be one chilly bitch,' said Macy.

'Like ice?' said Vera.

'Freezing.'

Vera laughed. Rolly smiled. It was all he had sometimes.

'Could I have a glass of bubbles, Vera?' he asked. 'With a lime? Please?'

'There he goes, Macy,' said Vera, 'With those eyes. You watch yourself.'

Vera walked away.

Macy drummed her fingers on the table. 'Bubbles, huh?' she said. 'Club soda.'

'Yeah, I know what it is. You don't drink alcohol, do you?'

'Not anymore.'

'Why'd you stop?'

'Health reasons. My car tried to kill me.'

'You OK if I drink?'

'No problem.'

'I need a beer. Your lady cop friend really got me riled up.'

'Bonnie can be very . . . focused.'

'I'll say. I thought you weren't allowed to tell people about me? Because I'm your client, right? I'm supposed to have some sort of immunity?'

'Yes. You have client privilege. I didn't give her your name.'

'She told me she'd talked to you.'

'It was that flyer you gave me,' said Rolly. 'It was sitting out on my table when she came by.'

'Damn,' Macy said.

'Sorry. She had your first name already and put two and two together.'

'She asked me where I was two nights ago.'

'Did she say why?'

'Daddy Joe's disappeared. Weird, huh? Same night he was here.'

'You told Bonnie about that?'

'Sure. Why wouldn't I? Daddy Joe gets kind of distracted sometimes. I'm betting he got lost driving home, ran out of gas or something and drove into a ditch.'

Rolly flipped through the names on his phone and found the one Bonnie had given him.

'You know Kinnie Harper, right?'

'Yeah. I told you about her. Kinnie's a bitch.'

'You know she's with the police up there? The tribal police?'

Macy laughed. 'No shit,' she said. 'Kinnie's a cop now?'

'Bonnie told me she's chief of police.'

'Just like her daddy.'

'Bonnie wants me to call her.'

'What about?'

'I assume it's to ask about you.'

'How'd Kinnie get your name?'

'No idea. Did you tell anyone you'd hired me?'

'No. Vera's the only one knows I talked to you. Unless someone else saw us the other night.'

'Someone like who?'

'How would I know? I'm just speculating. Don't get on my case.'

They were silent a moment. Rolly waited, letting Macy cool down.

'Kinnie's like my big sister,' she said after a moment. 'She took care of me after Mama Joe died. Kinnie hated me, but I guess I understand where she was coming from.'

'What do you mean?'

'Daddy Joe put a lot of weight on her shoulders, taking care of the house, watching me. She was eleven or twelve, something like that, when her momma died. Daddy Joe didn't give her much of a break. He's kind of a hard case, real strict about men and women and what he expects. You know what I mean?'

'You think he abused Kinnie?'

'Oh, no, I never saw nothing like that. He just worked her to death.'

'When was the last time you talked to her or Daddy Joe?'

'I don't talk to them. Haven't since I left. I still can't figure how Daddy Joe found me. Your friend, that cop, was asking if I was up there recently, on the rez.'

'Were you?'

'I don't go to the rez. Period. Not since I left. I got too much history there – bad mojo.'

'You want to tell me about it?' said Rolly.

'Just some stupid teenager stuff. DNA.'

'OK. I'll assume it's not relevant.'

'Waters?'

'Yeah?'

'Are you setting me up?'

'What do you mean?'

'I don't know. It feels like I'm in a movie or something. Are you working with the cops to put me in jail?'

'I'm not working with the cops, but if you've done something illegal you need to tell me about it.'

'Hmm, let's see. I smoke weed sometimes. There, I confess. I smoked some weed Friday night. I used to do E when I first started clubbing. I've done a lot of things once. And I totally roll through stop signs.'

'You stole that necklace.'

'Yeah, I did. And I told you about it. That was over five years ago.'

'Here's my scenario. Daddy Joe goes missing. Kinnie Harper, his daughter, looks around the house and notices the diddley bow is missing. Kinnie knows you stole the necklace. Maybe she thinks you came back and stole the diddley bow, too. Took it from Daddy Joe's house.'

'I get what you're saying, Waters, but I didn't steal it. It's just like I told you. Vera gave me that thing Friday night after the guy brought it in.'

'I guess we can ask Vera.'

'Ask me what?' said Vera, arriving with their drinks.

'About the guy that was here the other night,' said Rolly. 'The one that gave you the package for Macy?'

'Oh, yeah. I remember. Big guy. Looked kind of Indian.'

'What'd he say to you?'

'Nothing. He just pointed at Macy's picture and handed me the package. I must've nodded at him or something. Then he left.'

Macy chuckled. 'He's a man of few words, that Daddy Joe.'

'You want anything to eat, Macy?' said Vera.

'I'm not that hungry,' said Macy. 'Maybe bring me some guac.'

Vera left them alone again.

'You satisfied now, Waters?' said Macy. 'I didn't steal the diddley bow.'

Rolly nodded. He felt satisfied, in both stomach and mind. He felt ready to share what he'd found out so far.

'I found someone who will give you a thousand dollars for it,' he said.

'Really?' said Macy. 'That thing is worth money?'

'I was surprised too.'

Rolly told Macy about his visit with Norwood and his confrontation with the man at the Alien Artifacts store.

'What's this guy's name again?' Macy asked when he'd finished.

'Randy Parker.'

'I went out with a guy named Randy once,' she said. 'Randy No Pants.'

'Nopanz?'

'No Pants,' said Macy, separating the words. 'That was his nickname.'

'What'd he look like?'

'Couple years older than me, I think. Even whiter than you. Good hair. Nice ass.'

'Any tattoos?'

'No.'

'The guy I met was a lot older,' said Rolly. 'He had some prison tattoos and a really bad wig.'

'Definitely not the same Randy.'

'Doesn't sound like it,' said Rolly.

Macy took a sip of her beer. Rolly stirred his club soda, watching the slice of lime spin around in his glass.

'What was the name of that weirdo group again?' said Macy. 'The one the lady at the store told you about?'

'She called them Yoovits. U-V-Ts. Universal Vibration Technologies.'

'She said the diddley thing belonged to them?'

'Yes.'

'Damn. That's kinda creepy.'

'What?'

'I think it was them that lived up near the rez. Daddy Joe was there when they found the bodies.'

'What are you talking about?'

'Well, not *there* there. It was after they killed themselves.'

'Wait. Back up. When was this?'

'I don't know. Before I was born. Look it up on Wikipedia or something. They all died. It was one of those suicide cult things, I think. That's how Daddy Joe got involved. He saw the people after they were dead. He arrested one of the guys.'

'How many people were there?'

'That died? It wasn't that many; I mean, compared to Jonestown or something like that. Kinda creepy though, huh?'

Rolly nodded his head and made a mental note to get more information on the UVTs. It was time to creep Macy out even more. He pulled the postcard from his pocket and passed it to her.

'Take a look at that,' he said. 'Tell me what you think.'

'Desert View Tower,' said Macy, looking at the card. 'I remember that place. Daddy Joe used to take Kinnie and me. We'd run around in the rocks.'

'Read the back,' said Rolly. Macy read the back of the card out loud. She stopped after the first line.

'Where'd you get this?' she asked.

Rolly described the ill-fated trip to Desert View Tower and its aftermath.

'Seriously,' Macy said. 'You got tasered?'

Rolly nodded.

'Teotwayki,' said Macy. 'Daddy Joe had that on the dry erase board in his room.'

'Is it an Indian word?'

'Kinnie could tell you what it means. Are you going to call her?'

64
Corey Lynn Fayman

'Bonnie will kill me if I don't.'

'You got some kind of thing going on with her?'

'Who? Bonnie?'

'Yeah. Are you two swapping fluids?'

'No. We're just friends.'

'I didn't think she'd be your type.'

'You could say that.'

'Yeah, I thought so. I was kinda digging on her, actually. She looks kinda hot in that uniform.'

'Uh huh,' said Rolly. He couldn't figure out Macy at all.

'A woman in uniform gets me hot and bothered. I think it's a sex and authority thing, you know, like a fetish.'

'Thanks for sharing,' said Rolly. 'But can we get back to what's on the card?'

'"Golden eyes key,"' said Macy, reading the card again. 'You think that's got something to do with me?'

'It's the first thought that came to me.'

'OK. I get it, now, Waters. I get why you're giving me a hard time.'

'Do you know anything about a key?'

'No. Do you?'

'Yeah. Maybe.' Rolly pulled out his phone again and tapped into his notes app. 'Read me the number,' he said. 'The one on your necklace.'

Macy read the number to him. It matched the number he had entered in his notes, digit for digit.

'So?' said Macy.

'You know that electronics schematic I told you about, the one I got from the maps display at the tower? It's got that word and that number written on it.'

'What's it mean?'

'I don't know. Could be a serial number or something.'

'Why is it on my necklace?'

'I don't know.'

'This is kind of freaking me out,' said Macy. 'They must be connected, right?'

'It's something simple. We'll figure it out.'

'I got something else freaky for you,' said Macy. 'That guy with the rocket-ship van?'

'Yeah?'

'I know him.'

'You do?'

'Slab City. Me and No Pants were there for a couple of days. After Coachella.'

'You and Randy No Pants were in Slab City together?'

'Yeah. I met that guy with the van. His name's Bob.'

'Does Bob have a last name?'

'I don't know. Everybody calls him Cool Bob.'

'Do you know anyone with a normal name?'

'That's weird about the van. I should go talk to Bob.'

'Maybe I should go with you.'

Macy took another sip of beer. 'Bob might let me stay with him. Don't think he'd go for you being around.'

'We'll just drive out and come back the same day.'

'Folks are kind of tight-lipped out there. I'm not even sure Bob will want to talk to me. We might have to camp out a couple of nights. We'd need a trailer or an RV. You don't want to sleep on the ground. Too many spiders and scorpions and other weird stuff.'

Rolly rubbed his head and sucked the last of his club soda up through the straw. It made a squelching sound. He knew he was going to say something stupid, something he shouldn't. But his tongue and his lips conspired against him. They said the words before he could stop them.

'I know where we can get an RV,' he said.

TWELVE
The Rez

Rolly drove the Tioga along Interstate 8, heading up the grade into the mountains of East County on the way to Slab City. Macy rode shotgun, her bare feet propped up on the dash. They would pass the Jincona Reservation soon, then Desert View Tower, and begin their descent into the desert. The Cuyamacas weren't the loftiest mountains to cross, but it was still slow going in the Tioga. It would take them at least three hours to arrive at their destination.

He'd felt embarrassed asking his stepmom, Alicia, if he could
borrow the motorhome, but she been more than happy to lend
it to him. She'd seemed relieved to get it out of the driveway,
the two-ton elephant that had caused her so much distress.
Rolly's father was still in the hospital. His condition had been
upgraded to stable, but he wouldn't be taking
any trips for a while. The great adventure would have to be
rescheduled, put on the back burner for a few months, while
he recuperated.

Alicia had primped her makeup and made herself presentable by the time Rolly and Macy arrived at the house. The
larder of the Tioga was stocked and the gas tank was full. A
great weight seemed to lift from Alicia's shoulders as Rolly
backed out of the driveway. He pointed the Tioga in the right
direction and set the cruise control. As mobile homes went,
the Tioga wasn't that large, but it still felt like he was driving
a house.

'You wanna see where I grew up? On the rez?' said Macy.

'I thought you never wanted to see the place again.'

'Now that we're out here, I guess I'm kind of curious. I could
show you the place where those people died. The UVTs.'

'It's on the reservation?'

'It's next door,' Macy said. 'You can see the house from Daddy
Joe's place.'

'You sure about this?'

'C'mon, Waters. I said I wanted to go. DNA.'

Rolly took the casino exit and crossed the bridge back over
the freeway. They drove down a narrow country road that twisted
through rocks, manzanita and sagebrush.

'Beautiful, isn't it?' Macy said. 'Not.'

'I didn't really get to see the terrain the other night. It seems
kind of nice.'

'Not to me.'

'A bit austere, I guess.'

'Desolate is more like it.'

'We can still turn around if you want.'

Macy stared out the window. She'd lost interest in talking to
him. Rolly checked his speedometer. The Tioga felt huge on the
backcountry road, with the driver's side hanging over the center-
line or the passenger side hugging the gravel shoulder. Two cars

passed in the opposite direction. Small herds of sheep, horses and cows dotted the landscape.

'That's it, over there, the UVTs place,' said Macy, pointing at a wood sign set close to the ground on the opposite side of the road. Rolly slowed. A dirt road led away from the sign, blocked by a gate.

'Beatrice House for Girls,' he said, reading the sign.

'Yeah, that's the place. Kinnie used to say Daddy Joe was going to send me there. Like all the other bad girls.'

'I don't see any house,' said Rolly.

'It's over that rise, looks out on the mesa. You can see it from Daddy Joe's place.'

Rolly continued down the road. A large, open vista came into view, a mountain peak in the distance. Macy pulled her feet from the dash.

'Holy crap!' she said, pointing at the building that loomed in the foreground. 'Is that the casino?'

'That's it,' said Rolly. 'That's where we played the other night.'

'Sure is ugly.'

A small green sign on the right side of the road informed them they were entering the Jincona reservation. They passed the sign, then the casino.

'Hard to believe they could make this place even worse,' said Macy. 'I guess they're all gonna get rich.'

'Some of those casinos don't do that well,' said Rolly. 'We played this place near Julian. There were only three people in the room.'

'Maybe that was because of your band.'

'Nice. Thanks.'

'You want to see Daddy Joe's place?'

'I'm not sure that's a good idea.'

'I grew up there, you know. I got a right to visit my old house.'

'I haven't been able to get in touch with Kinnie yet.'

'So what? You called her, right?'

Rolly nodded. He'd left two messages for Kinnie. She'd left one for him.

'She might not like us snooping around.'

'If Kinnie shows up we'll just say we were coming to see her. We've both got alibis for the other night.'

'Yeah.'

'Daddy Joe might've shown up by now, anyway.'

Rolly bit his lip. He hadn't told Macy what the man with the taser had said to him, that Daddy Joe was a dead man. He didn't want to tell her. He didn't want to tell anyone, not without some kind of proof.

'C'mon, Waters,' said Macy. 'A trip down memory lane might help me remember something important. Take a left at the intersection.'

Rolly turned at the stop sign. The road got rougher. He did what he could to avoid the larger potholes, but the bumps and ruts weren't friendly to the Tioga's suspension. They crested a small hill. Below them the road ran straight down to the edge of a triangular mesa. A small ranch-style house stood on the edge of the mesa, overlooking the intersection of two canyons.

'That's Daddy Joe's place,' said Macy.

Rolly lifted his foot off the gas. The Tioga inched down the road like a tiptoeing elephant. The house was surrounded by a yard, if your definition of yard included an open space filled with gravel and cactus and tumbleweeds. A low chain-link fence helped keep the tumbleweeds from entering or leaving the yard. He pulled to a stop in front of the gate.

'This is where you grew up?' he said.

'Yep. I lived here with Daddy Joe and Kinnie. Aunt Betty too, I guess, although I don't really remember her, just from photos.'

'How old were you then?'

'Two or three,' said Macy.

Macy opened her door and stepped down from the cab. She was all the way to the front door of the house before Rolly could protest. Macy seemed oblivious to caution, unconcerned with self-control, that imprint of age and experience. Rolly knew he'd acted that way himself once. His compulsions weren't as strong anymore, but he often found himself in conflict with his natural tendencies. Macy's impulsiveness felt exciting, almost sexy. She opened the door to the house and walked in.

He jumped out of the Tioga and looked around to make sure no one was watching. Across the canyon he could see a large house, the Beatrice House for Girls, if he'd understood Macy correctly. It looked much nicer and newer than Daddy Joe's rundown hovel. He walked to the front door. Macy had left it ajar.

'Macy?' he whispered. No one answered. He pushed the door open then raised his voice. 'Macy!'

'I'm in back,' she said. 'There's nobody home.'

'We shouldn't be in here,' said Rolly. 'What if somebody shows up?'

'Chill out, Waters. It's cool. It's my house as much as anybody's.'

'Macy . . .'

'There's something in here you need to see.'

Rolly took a deep breath and entered the house. The kitchen was piled with dishes and the living room was dusty. It had dank green carpeting and a dirty brown sofa. Heavy curtains prevented any sunlight disinfectant.

'Where are you?' he said.

'In here,' said Macy, from a doorway off to his right. He walked to the doorway and peeked in. Macy sat at a small desk in the corner. The desk was piled high with papers. All sorts of papers, drawings, photos and maps covered the walls.

'What is it?' he asked. Macy turned from the desk.

'My flyer,' she said. 'Daddy Joe's got my flyer.'

She handed Rolly a flyer, just like the one she'd handed him the night they met.

'It was here on the desk?' Rolly said.

'There's a letter, too. It's not finished . . .'

'What?'

'It's addressed to me,' she said, handing him the letter.

Rolly inspected the paper in his hand. It felt coarse, like an autumnal leaf. The handwriting was rough too. You could almost see the quiver of the hand that had written it. But the words were legible.

'"My Little Alien,"' he said, reading the salutation.

'Daddy Joe called me that sometimes,' said Macy.

Rolly continued reading the note. '"I have seen a photograph of this woman. The one called DJ Crazy Macy. I know it is you. You are old enough now. I must tell you some things. About the gold charm which I see you still wear. The one stolen from me. It is yours now. I have something else for you. It is an instrument of great power."'

Rolly looked over at Macy. She nodded. Rolly turned back to the letter.

"'I had intended to make it a gift to you on your eighteenth birthday, when you would have your freedom, but you left us before that time came. There is more I still hope to give you. So that you may be free. But you must speak with me first, before I can—"

'He didn't finish,' said Rolly.

'Flip it over,' said Macy. Rolly flipped the paper over. Three words were scrawled on the back.

TEOTWAYKI? TEOTWAYKI? TEOTWAYKI?

Rolly looked over at Macy. 'What's this stuff on the walls?'

'Kinda creepy, huh?' she said. 'He's still obsessed with the UVTs. It's up there still.'

Macy pointed at the dry erase board on the wall, at the capital letters in red lettering. TEOTWAYKI.

'We shouldn't be here,' Rolly said.

'Yeah,' said Macy. 'This is totally spooky.'

'I don't want anyone finding us here,' Rolly said. 'Especially if Daddy Joe's still missing. It would look suspicious.'

He handed the letter back to Macy, who placed it back on the desk. Their fingerprints were all over it now. They trooped back out to the Tioga and climbed in.

'That was stupid,' said Rolly, as he buckled himself in. 'Let's get the hell out of here.'

'Yeah, I'm sufficiently creeped,' said Macy. 'But at least we know how Daddy Joe found me.'

Rolly turned the Tioga around and headed out the same way they'd come in. It was the only way to go.

'Why didn't he send me the letter?' said Macy as they jounced along the road that was more like a ditch.

'He couldn't wait, I guess. Maybe he thought you wouldn't talk to him if he only sent you a letter.'

'Shit,' said Macy. 'Everything's different now. I thought I didn't care. Coming back here, suddenly I'm worried about Daddy Joe. Maybe he's in trouble or something. Maybe he's dead.'

'Don't worry,' said Rolly, trying to manage his own sense of uneasiness. 'They'll find him soon.'

They crested the hill and started back down into the middle of the reservation. Rolly resisted the urge to drive faster. The Tioga didn't belong here. It was too large, too obvious. He felt like an alien in a crippled spacecraft. As they approached the intersection to the main road he spotted a truck, parked on the other side of the road, shaded under a tree.

'You see it?' said Macy.

'I see,' Rolly replied.

'That's tribal police.'

'I know. Be cool.'

'Too late,' said Macy. 'I'm hyperventilating. I gotta lie down, in the back.'

Macy took off her seat belt, lowered her head, snuck back to the dining room and laid down in the booth. Rolly pulled up to the stop sign facing the patrol truck across the intersection. He made a full stop, checked for traffic and turned left onto the main road.

'Was it her?' Macy whispered. 'Was it Kinnie?'

'I don't know. I couldn't see anyone.'

Macy crawled along the floor and into the bedroom. She climbed on the bed and looked out the rear window.

'Shit,' she said. 'It's her. I know it. She's pulling out.'

Rolly checked his rearview mirror. The tribal police truck came into sight, following them at a well-measured distance. He checked his speedometer, looked in the mirror again and took a deep breath. No one knew him here. He hadn't broken any rules. No one could prove he'd been in Daddy Joe's house.

'I can't see if it's her,' said Macy. 'She's staying too far back.'

'Sit down and stop staring. Don't act so suspicious.'

The police truck continued to follow them. Macy crawled back up to the front. She got up on her knees and pointed out the front window.

'That's the reservation border up ahead – that sign,' she said. 'If she's going to stop us, she'll have to do it soon.'

Rolly checked his mirror again. He relaxed his hands on the wheel. They passed the boundary sign.

'She stopped, didn't she?' said Macy.

Rolly checked his mirror. The police truck had pulled off to the side of the road. 'Yeah. How'd you know?'

'She had to. That's the rules.'

Rolly watched in the rearview mirror as the police truck turned around and headed back in the opposite direction.

'Sovereign nations,' said Macy. 'Tribal police can't arrest you once you're outside the rez. The county sheriff can't arrest you once you're inside.'

'Sound pretty complicated,' said Rolly.

'Oh, yeah,' said Macy. 'I took advantage of it a couple of times.'

THIRTEEN
The Mountain

'Oh, God, I remember that smell,' Macy said as they drove through the town of Calipatria, just south of the Salton Sea. It wasn't much of a town, more like a gathering of buildings not quite as far apart as others they'd recently passed. There was farmland for miles around, long rows of tilled earth on either side of the road – desert farms irrigated by water diverted from the Colorado River. There was a notable scent of fertilizer in the air.

'You see that weird castle thing over there?' said Macy, pointing at a long purple wall adorned with yellow turrets. 'We took some pictures there when I came out with No Pants. You ever been to Coachella?'

'Big festivals aren't my kind of thing. Not usually my kind of music, either.'

'Yeah. I hear what you're saying. It was hot as fuck during the day. I'd love to play for a big crowd like that, though, get some serious entrainment going.'

'Entrainment?'

'Yeah. You know what that means?'

'I just learned it yesterday.'

'That's what being a DJ's all about. Everybody moving to the music. Mass-altered states. In a good way.'

'Have you ever heard of something called the Solfeggio frequencies?'

'No,' said Macy. 'What's that?'

Rolly explained what he'd read on the website the day before.

'Sounds like it might be good for my downtempo stuff,' said

Macy. 'Chillout or Lounge. Those are kinda like the New Age of dance beats.'

Rolly considered all the things he didn't know in the world. There were a lot of them.

'How long were you out here with Randy No Pants?' he asked.

'Less than a week. I dumped him. It was not a healthy relationship.'

'You want to tell me about it?'

Macy stared at Rolly for a moment. 'Sure, Doctor Phil,' she said. 'Let me tell you all about my dysfunctional relationships. How guys ask me to dress up in little girls' clothes, call them daddy and suck on a lollipop.'

'Really?' said Rolly.

Macy rolled her eyes. 'I'm being sarcastic, Waters. Don't be my shrink. Just be you. You're cool the way you are, almost like an adult.'

'To tell you the truth,' Rolly said, 'I thought you liked girls.'

'Because I got all hot and bothered about that butch girlfriend of yours? Bonnie the Copper?'

'Well, I did consider it a possibility.'

'She's gay, right?'

Rolly nodded. Bonnie didn't advertise, but she didn't hide either.

'Yeah, Waters, you've been trying to figure me out since we met. I saw the way you checked me out at the cantina. You been calculating the odds, trying to figure out if I'm doable, wondering if an old guy like you could get lucky.'

'I don't sleep with my clients.'

'Doesn't stop you from thinking about it though, does it?'

'Well,' said Rolly, 'some things are hard not to think about.'

'Your friend Bonnie is kinda hot. I'd let her strip-search me anytime.'

'So . . .'

'DNA, Waters. Don't try to label me. If I get a vibe, I go with it. You got a problem with that?'

'No. No problem,' said Rolly. He smiled.

'There you go,' Macy said. 'With that look. Just like Vera warned me. It makes you seem so . . . decent.'

'Sorry.'

'You ever seen the place that crazy Christian guy built? Salvation Mountain?'

'I don't think so.'

'We should stop there. You should see it.'

'I'm not exactly religious.'

'Neither am I. Not really. Not any organized shit, anyway. I just think it's cool when someone goes crazy like that, dedicates their whole life to something non-remunerative.'

'Uh huh.'

'There it is,' said Macy. 'Pull off at the sign.'

Rolly pulled off the road in front of a large sky-blue sign: *God Never Fails – Salvation Mountain*. He parked the Tioga. Salvation Mountain was an exuberant monument made of paint and plaster. A modest hill rising above the desert floor, it was covered in bright washes of green, blue, purple and yellow, adorned with the words 'Love' and 'Repent' spelled out in large letters. Biblical quotations had been lettered into the mountain's nooks and crannies. Primitive illustrations of flowers, trees and rivers flowed down the sides. A camper truck had been parked out in front with similar embellishments.

Macy opened the door and jumped out. Rolly followed her. The hot desert air hit his face like the belch of an underworld demon. He regretted letting Macy talk him into this adventure. He hoped the Tioga's air conditioning would hold up.

'Let's walk to the top,' said Macy, pointing at the cross on top of the mountain.

'It's OK to do that?'

'Oh, yeah,' Macy said. 'I've been up there before.' She pointed to a large yellow step at the base of the mountain. 'Follow the yellow brick road,' she said.

Rolly cleared his throat, wondering how long it would take heat stroke to set in. Macy could afford to be enthusiastic in this heat. She was young and skinny.

'C'mon, you infidel,' Macy said. 'Let's go find God, see if he wants to talk to us.'

Rolly followed Macy up the bright yellow stairway that curved around the mountain. They reached the peak, stood at the base of the cross and looked out at the desert panorama. You could see for miles in every direction.

'You OK?' said Macy.

'I'm fine.'

'You look a little flushed.'

'It's hot out here.'

'Hotter than fuck,' said Macy. She put her hand over her mouth. 'I really need to watch my language.'

'Don't be sacrilegious.'

'At least I wasn't taking the Lord's name in vain. I should watch my mouth, though. Out of respect for Leonard.'

'Who's Leonard?'

'The guy who built this place. The crazy guy.'

They walked around the cross, taking in the scenery and bright decorations on the sides of the mountain below them. Streams of blue and white flowed down the mountain, painted to look like waterfalls. Pink and orange paint blossoms bloomed against fields of green. A benevolent deity ruled over Salvation Mountain.

'So, Waters,' said Macy, 'you ready to repent? You have anything you need to confess?'

'Do you?'

'I asked first.'

Rolly thought for a moment. 'Yeah. Sure. OK,' he said. 'The guy in your photo – the one with Aunt Betty, the baseball player. I talked to him.'

'You found the guy?'

'Yeah. Well, this is the confession part. I knew who it was when you showed it to me. I thought I did, anyway. I was right.'

'So who is he?'

'Eric Ozzie. The Sneaker.'

'Wait. Is that the guy on TV? With those ads?'

Rolly nodded.

'What'd he say?'

'He said the photo's from his minor league days. In Hawaii. He doesn't remember your Aunt Betty.'

'That's all you found out?'

'Afraid so.'

'You think he was telling the truth?'

'He said he'd be willing to talk to you, that he'd take responsibility.'

'In case he's my daddy?'

'Yeah. I think that's what he was saying.'

'Yeah, well, like I said earlier, if he and Aunt Betty hooked up and I'm the result, there were a lot of recessive genes getting together. It'd be a million to one, ten million to one that I'd look like I do.'

'You really understand all that heredity stuff?'

'I've done some reading on it. DNA.'

'Why can't I ask?'

'No, sorry. I meant the genetic thing. That DNA.'

'I have another confession,' said Rolly. 'Something the man said to me, the guy at Desert View Tower, the one with the taser.'

'What'd he say?'

'He said Daddy Joe was a dead man.'

Macy wrinkled her nose. She sniffled. 'This dry air makes me crazy,' she said.

'Why did you take me to Daddy Joe's house?' said Rolly.

'You ever feel like you're going crazy?' said Macy.

'I used to. Not so much now.'

'The Gold Drinkers. That's what Daddy Joe called the UVTs. He said they drank gold, like the medicine man made him do once, when Daddy Joe was sick. He told me the UVTs drank gold every day.'

'That doesn't sound very healthy.'

'Actually, gold's inert. It won't hurt you. You ever seen that five-thousand-dollar chocolate sundae the guy makes in Vegas? They put gold flakes all over the thing. People eat it right down. It wasn't drinking the gold that killed them. They'd just be trace amounts anyway. The UVTs would boil this big nugget in water, then everyone drank the water. Gold soup. That's how they died.'

'You just told me it was safe,' Rolly said.

'They got something else in their soup one day. This other chemical. Some kind of cyanide. Daddy Joe told me that miners use it to separate the gold from the rocks. He arrested the guy.'

'I thought they committed suicide,' said Rolly.

'Sodium cyanide. That's what it's called. That's how they died. Fucks up your system so you can't breathe. I snuck into Daddy Joe's desk once, looked through some papers he had. There were some photographs, too. Of the dead people. And some other stuff. I wanted to check.'

'Check what?'

'One of those diddley bow things. I remember seeing it in one of the photographs.' Macy walked away from him. She pointed into the distance. 'That's Slab City, over there,' she said.

Rolly turned to look in the direction she pointed. He didn't see much: a collection of trailers and broken-down buildings.

'Something's going to happen,' said Macy. 'Something that changes things.'

'What makes you say that?'

'You'd tell me, wouldn't you, if you thought I was crazy?'

'You're not crazy.'

'I got my own confession to make, Waters, about that word. I know what it means.'

'Teotwayki?'

'It's not an Indian word. It's an acronym.'

'What does it mean?'

'The end of the world as you know it.'

A chill ran up Rolly's spine. His sweat evaporated in the dry desert heat. He rubbed the stubble on his chin, stared at the ground. *TEOTWAYKI.* Daddy Joe was obsessed with the word. The man in the rocks at Desert View Tower had chirped the word like a bird call. The end of the world.

Two years ago a preacher had purchased billboard space along the San Diego freeways, advertising his predicted apocalypse date to disgruntled commuters, providing them with a number to call for more information. You could make a good living on Doomsday predictions. Apocalypse preparers even had their own TV shows now. Geeks freaked out over the Y2K bug and that collider thing the scientists had built in Switzerland. The end was coming. It always had been. It always would be.

He wondered if the UVTs knew they were going to die when they drank the poisoned soup. Had they believed that the aliens would really take them away? There was nothing anyone could do for them now. There were only the living, people with problems, with troubles and crazy thoughts, people who hadn't left Earth yet. His father and Daddy Joe. Macy Starr. He hoped he could help Macy find what she wanted without any apocalypse.

'Onward,' he said.

They walked back down the mountain and climbed up into the Tioga. Rolly started the engine and cranked up the air conditioner.

He'd never done well in hot weather. Getting older and fatter hadn't made it any easier. He hoped the desert air would cool down tonight.

They left Salvation Mountain in the rearview mirror and continued down the road. Macy pointed to an abandoned concrete guardhouse on their right. Someone had painted the guardhouse like the sky, a blue background with dusty white stencils of bird and tree shapes. Words had been stenciled along the upper molding as well. *Welcome to Slab City.*

FOURTEEN
The Garden

Rolly and Macy stood under a rusty rebar archway. Old propane tanks were encased inside the rebar, and a spinning bicycle wheel was stuck to the top of the arch. Car doors reinforced the base, one on each side. It was the entryway to a well-tended garden of sculptural junk. A perimeter line of old tires encircled the garden, embedded halfway into the ground.

'East Jesus,' said Macy. 'The discarded afterbirth of the Industrial Age, repurposed for aesthetic enhancement.'

'What's that?'

'That's how Bob described it to me. He gets kinda philosophical. All the art in here is built out of trash and junk people collected. It's their ethos. Making art from our modern refuse.'

'Is it OK for us to go in?' asked Rolly.

'Sure. In the daytime. You need to make a reservation if you want to come by at night.'

'How do you get a reservation?'

'I don't really know. Cool Bob just told me to get here before dark. He said people start shooting at night.'

Rolly swallowed. They walked through the arch, into East Jesus.

'Hey, this is new,' said Macy, inspecting a spiral installation of jagged metal triangles.

'Uh huh,' said Rolly, keeping an eye out for any gunmen who

might be setting up for the evening. He pulled out his cell phone and checked the time.

'It's ten after six now. You sure Bob said to meet him here?'

'Relax, Waters,' said Macy, walking towards a tall pile of black rubber. 'Cool Bob will show up. Time is fluid around here. Check this out.'

Rolly put his phone back in his pocket and walked over to Macy.

'Looks like some kind of elephant,' he said.

'A mammoth,' said Macy. 'It's called Definition of a Grievance.'

'What's that mean?'

'I don't know, but it's pretty cool, huh?'

'Yeah. Pretty cool.'

The Mammoth, or Grievance, loomed over them, raised up on its hind legs. It had been built out of reclaimed strips of automobile tires fastened together with wire and string. The Grievance had two headlights for eyes, car fenders for tusks and a corrugated rubber tube for a trunk.

'Looks like he's wearing a gas mask,' said Rolly, but Macy had already moved on. He followed her. They stopped at a low wall of reclaimed television sets, various models and sizes stacked on top of each other. Each of the TV screens had been painted white, and words were painted in red letters on the white screens. *Bad News. Some Things Never Change. Dear God No.* Some of the screens had only one word on them.

'Blah,' Macy said, reading the screens. 'Blah, blah, blah.'

'Everyone's a critic,' said Rolly.

'I don't see the dolls,' Macy said. 'There used to be these gold dolls.'

Moving on, they saw the top half of a house, set askew, sunk halfway into the ground as if caught in a flood. They passed a group of beer keg animals that had bottles for legs and a short piece of watering hose for tails. The heads on the beer kegs were bleached animal skulls.

Macy stopped beside a circle of rusted tin cans, different sizes of cans set in the ground at varying heights.

'They're supposed to be drums,' she said.

Rolly squatted down by the cans and tapped on a couple of them.

'Bob says they sound really cool when it rains,' said Macy.

'I bet they do,' said Rolly. 'Doesn't seem like you'd get to hear them much in the desert, though.'

Macy squatted down beside him and spoke in a whisper. 'Don't freak out, but somebody's spying on us.'

'Where?'

'Over my right shoulder, behind that stand of creosote bushes.'

Rolly swiveled his head, surveying the scene. 'Yeah, I see him,' he said. There was someone standing outside the garden perimeter, hiding behind a bush. The bush covered the man's face but you could see his body. 'You think it's Cool Bob?' said Rolly.

'Bob's a lot taller.'

Rolly stood up and turned to face the man. 'Hello,' he called. The man yelped and ran away. They watched him run out of sight.

'There was this guy, when I came here with No Pants,' said Macy. 'He started following me around.'

'What'd he want?'

'I don't know. He'd stand about ten feet in front of me and just stare. That chicken-ass Randy wouldn't confront the guy. I started screaming, finally scared him off.'

'You think that was the same guy just now?'

'Maybe. The other guy made this weird sound, like a bird.'

'Teotwayki?' said Rolly. He chirped the word a couple of times, imitating the sound of the birdman at Desert View Tower.

'Holy shit, Waters!' said Macy. 'That was it. Teotwayki! Holy shit!'

'My goodness,' said a voice from behind them. 'Such fervent ejaculating.'

Rolly and Macy turned towards the voice. A tall man with a scraggly beard and long hair stood behind them. He wore shorts and sandals, and nothing else.

'Bob!' said Macy. She ran to the man and gave him an ardent hug. Rolly glanced down at the dirt.

'Hey, Bob,' said Macy, breaking the clinch, 'this is Rolly Waters.'

'Hi,' said Rolly, offering his hand. Bob shook it.

'He's older,' said Bob. 'Older than the last guy.'

'Yeah. Waters here is an adult.'

Rolly let Bob and Macy exchange niceties a bit longer, then got down to business. 'I'm trying to find a VW van,' he said.

'Macy told me you had one. A customized one that looks like a spaceship?'

Bob's face clouded over. 'Whoa,' he said. 'That's supernormal.'

'It was unusual,' said Rolly. 'I've never seen one like it.'

'No, man,' said Bob. 'I mean, this is paranormal. Fatalistic. I traded with a guy three days ago.'

'You got rid of the jam van?' said Macy.

'Temporarius only, Mace, not a mooch. The guy left some collateral. He'll bring it back.'

'When's he supposed to return it?' said Rolly.

'Could be tomorrow. Could be next week. Could be a year from now.'

'Does he live around here? Could we talk to him?'

'Not for me to say,' said Bob. 'The guy's prodigious. Totally singular.'

Bobspeak – that's what Macy had called it earlier, describing Bob's unusual speaking style. Bob's vocal inflections imparted the intended meaning but the words themselves made less sense the more you thought about them.

'What's his name?' Rolly asked.

'Can't say.'

'You don't know his name?'

'Not allowed. No designating.'

Rolly wasn't sure if Bob was refusing to give him the name or if the man in question didn't actually have one. It sounded like both. Macy tried to help.

'It's OK, Bob. This guy's cool,' said Macy. 'Not like the guy who was with me the last time.'

'No Pants was heinous,' said Bob. 'Left me in shambles.'

'Yeah, I know. He was an asshole.'

'What happened?' said Rolly.

'Randy broke into Bob's trailer,' said Macy. 'We figured he was looking for Scooby Snacks.'

'He was looking for dog food?'

Macy laughed. 'You see, Bob? This guy's one hundred percent. He doesn't even drink.'

'Way orthodox,' said Bob. 'Theological.'

Macy nodded. 'What did this guy give you for the van? For collateral?'

'A metal box.'

'That's it? A metal box?'

Bob nodded his head. 'I got it in the trailer,' he said. 'You wanta' see?'

Macy turned back to Rolly. Rolly nodded. Bob turned on his heels and walked away. Macy and Rolly scrambled to catch up with him. They tramped to the far end of East Jesus, stepped across the tire perimeter and headed further into the desert. Bob took long strides. It was hard for his shorter companions to keep up.

'Where are we going?' said Rolly as he and Macy dropped into a steady trot ten feet behind Bob.

'Bob's trailer is out on the range,' said Macy.

'Home, home on the range . . .' Rolly said, singing the cowboy tune.

'Not exactly. It's a shooting range.'

'That doesn't sound peaceful, or safe.'

'Depends on who's around. Bob likes guns, anyway.'

Rolly's stomach grumbled. He wished he'd eaten before they set out, but daylight had been waning. They'd wanted to find Bob before sundown.

'We're almost there,' Macy said.

Cool Bob turned in behind an embankment of dirt. Rolly and Macy followed him. There was an old Coachmen trailer parked on the other side of the embankment. An awning had been stretched from the top of the trailer, providing a rectangle of shade. A white plastic table sat under the shade, a mismatched assortment of chairs gathered around it.

'Wait there,' Bob said, indicating the table. He opened the door to his trailer and went in, then closed it behind him. Rolly and Macy sat at the table, across from each other. The sun was lower now but it still felt good to be in the shade.

'What are Scooby Snacks?' said Rolly.

'Ecstasy. MDMA. You know what that is, right?'

Rolly nodded. 'Is Bob a dealer or something?'

'No Pants thought so, I guess. I asked Bob to show me around the Slabs. Randy was going through his trailer when we got back.'

'Did Bob think you set him up?'

'At first. I found a way to make up with him.'

'Oh.'

'Bob's hung like a horse.'

'Didn't need that information.'

'Sorry. Oversharing again.'

The door of the trailer opened. Cool Bob stepped down, carrying an assault rifle. Rolly glanced at Macy, wondering if he should be nervous. She looked nonchalant. Bob handed Macy the gun.

'This is beautiful, Bob,' said Macy. 'Is it new?'

'Yeah,' replied Bob. 'You wanna go shoot some stuff?'

'Maybe later,' said Macy. 'We wanta' see that metal box thing.'

'Okey-doke,' said Bob. He trudged back to the trailer.

'Whattya think, Waters?' said Macy. 'You like crazy chicks with guns?'

Macy looked perfectly relaxed holding the rifle. She'd clearly handled one like it before, unperturbed by the firepower held at her fingertips. Rolly wondered if he'd have to go to the gun range with them later and peel off a few rounds to be sociable. Both Macy and Bob would outshoot him – he felt sure of that. He just hoped he wouldn't embarrass himself.

Bob returned with a black metal box and placed it on the table. He remained standing between them. The box was rectangular, about two feet wide, eight inches tall and perhaps a foot deep. It looked like a wall safe, solid black steel with a panel in the front, thickly bolted. There was no slot for a key; no keypad or combination to spin. There was only a single extruded hole in the front panel, held in place by a six-sided nut.

'You traded the van for this?' said Macy. Bob nodded.

'What is it?' she said.

'Don't know. He said it was valuable.'

'You must really trust this guy,' said Macy.

'Impeccable,' said Bob.

'That looks like a quarter-inch jack there in the front,' said Rolly. 'Like you could plug a guitar into it.'

Bob giggled and put his hand over his mouth. 'What is it?' said Macy.

'He calls it a vibrator.'

Macy laughed. 'What's it a vibrator for – Robbie the Robot?'

Rolly pursed his lips and leaned forward, put his hand on the box, inspecting it.

'Does this mean something to you?' said Macy.

'Maybe. I'm not sure.'

Rolly turned to Bob. 'The guy who gave you this – does he play guitar?' he asked.

'Not a player,' Bob said. 'He builds guitars, though, these one-stringed things, like for kids. He builds all kinds of stuff. Totally Edison.'

Rolly felt a glimmer in the back of his brain. He needed to talk to the man and show him the diddley bow to confirm it. The man could be Buddy Meeks.

'You play guitar, huh?' said Bob.

'Yeah,' said Rolly. 'I play.'

'You any good?'

'Are you kidding, Bob?' said Macy. 'This guy's the hottest guitar slinger in San Diego. He's a killer. Hall of fame.'

Bob folded his arms and squinted at Rolly. 'How many frets on a guitar?' he asked.

'What?'

'Macy says you're the shit. So answer the question.'

'I didn't know I'd be taking a test.'

'C'mon, Bob,' said Macy.

Bob didn't say anything. He stared at Rolly. 'How many?' he said.

'Well,' Rolly said, 'first I'd want to know what kind of guitar you were asking about. Classical or Electric?'

'Why?'

'Well, classical guitars usually have nineteen frets. The electrics I've played usually have twenty-two, though there can be more.'

'Outstanding,' said Bob. 'What's the tuning frequency?'

'Concert A, you mean?' said Rolly.

Bob nodded.

'Four hundred and forty hertz is the modern tuning,' said Rolly.

'Exemplary,' said Bob. 'Now, what's a Solfeggio?'

'That's not a guitar question, is it?'

Bob had a glint in his eye, like he'd just won the shootout. Rolly smiled. He still had a bullet left in the chamber. He sang the notes of the major scale.

'Do, Re, Mi, Fa, So, La, Ti, Do.'

Bob laughed. 'I like this one Macy. Smiling Jack.'

'Smiling Rolly Waters,' said Macy. 'The last decent man in the West.'

'How 'bout it, Bob?' said Rolly. 'Can you help us meet with this guy?'

Bob put his hands on top of his head and closed his eyes.

'There must be something you can do, Bob,' said Macy. She placed her hand on Bob's thigh.

Bob's eyes popped open. 'I got it,' he said. 'You can sit in with the band. If you're any good he'll want to talk to you afterwards. He always talks to the guitar players, if they're virtuoso. You up for it?'

Rolly nodded. 'Count me in,' he said.

'I'm looking forward to this,' said Macy. She leaned back in her chair.

'What?'

'Tonight only. At The Range. Rolly Waters and the Slab City Rockers.'

FIFTEEN
The Camper

The jam session went on past midnight, well into the morning. Cool Bob and the Slab City Rockers were better musicians than Rolly had expected. Their style leaned towards psychedelic jams with a looser groove than Rolly preferred, but still agreeable. It was fun to play without the usual worries about the schedule, the P.A., the audience or the club owner. He loosened up, had a good time just letting things rip. He even pulled out the diddley bow for a couple of songs. The crowd loved it. They cheered. They went wild.

After the concert, he and Macy returned to their camping spot. They sat in the Tioga's dining booth munching on Yo-Hos and tortilla chips they'd found in the larder. Macy drank a couple of beers. And they talked. A lot. Macy asked questions about his glory days, back when The Creatures were the hottest band in town. She asked him about everything: the gigs, the girls, the chemicals and the craziness. She even managed to get him to talk about the accident, about Matt's death, how everything had imploded. He told her about his recovery, how far he'd come, how far he still needed to go. He told her more than he'd ever told anyone.

And when he'd finished talking, when he'd told Macy all the things he'd never said to anyone but himself, she got quiet. She stopped asking questions. She leaned in to him and kissed him on the lips.

'How about we go in the back,' she said, 'and have a good fuck.'

He was more than willing to let Macy take charge at that point. She led him to the bedroom and took off his clothes. She pushed him onto the bed, then took off her own and climbed on top of him, shoving herself onto his mouth, then down on his hips, then back to his mouth, spending time in each position until they'd both had as much as they wanted, as much as they could take. Macy slid off him and turned on to her back. They stared up at the ceiling.

'You remember when we were at Salvation Mountain,' Rolly said. 'You said I should let you know if I thought you were crazy.'

'Yeah?' said Macy. 'What?'

'Well,' Rolly said, 'that was crazy.'

'Shut up, Waters,' said Macy. 'I'm still digging on the afterglow.'

'You did sound a little crazy, you gotta admit.'

'Shut up,' she whispered, putting a finger on Rolly's lips, 'Or I'll climb on your face and make you do me again.'

Rolly massaged his jaw. 'I may have to drink through a straw for a day or two.'

'You got yours. Ungrateful bastard.'

Rolly chuckled. He stroked Macy's hair. 'Oh, I'm grateful,' he said.

'Been a while?'

'Yeah.'

'Well, you passed inspection,' said Macy.

'Glad I could . . . measure up.'

'Waters, you are pathetic.'

'What?'

'I didn't fuck Cool Bob.'

'I thought you said . . .'

'I know what you thought. You thought Macy Starr was a size queen. I've seen Bob's equipment at the hot springs. That's how I know. People get naked a lot around here.'

'Where are the hot springs?'

'Near the water tower, other side of the shooting range. You wanna go later?'

'Maybe. We'll see.'

'Everyone gets naked there. There's no hiding your junk.'

'I doubt Bob would want to.'

'Yeah. He probably picks up a few dates at the springs.'

'So how did you make up with him?'

'I posed for some pictures.'

'What kind of pictures?'

'Bob's got a thing for naked chicks shooting guns.'

'Oh.'

Rolly dropped his head back on the pillow. Macy tucked her head into his shoulder. It had been quite an evening.

'Who was that guy you were talking to?' Rolly said.

'When?'

'At The Range. Looked like you were having an argument.'

'You saw him, huh?' Macy sighed. 'That was No Pants.'

'Your old boyfriend?'

'An old mistake, coming back to haunt me.'

'What'd he want?'

'He wanted to know what I was doing, like I got no right to be here. He's a douchebag.'

'I guess you got rid of him.'

'I told him I was with you. He got really quiet, then, when he saw you on stage.'

'Rock gods have that effect on people.'

'Yeah. Just like the old days, right, Waters?'

'What's that?'

'The crowd goes wild. You nail another groupie, add a notch to your guitar.'

'Shut up, Macy.'

Rolly drifted to sleep, the half sleep that comes with a new bed and a new place. His body was past tired but his mind stood on alert. There was a lot to process. Something clattered against the window. He jolted out of his post-coital haze.

'Ow,' said Macy, rubbing her nose.

'Sorry,' said Rolly. 'What was that?'

'I don't know,' she said. 'Sounds like the wind's kicking up.' The window clattered again.

'Someone's out there,' said Rolly. 'It's him.'

Macy turned over, crawled to the window and peered through the shades.

'Do you see anyone?' Rolly asked.

'No. Not yet.'

Pebbles scattered against the window again. Macy jerked her head away.

'Teotwayki!' The bird cry came from outside. 'Teotwayki!'

Rolly climbed out of the bed and put his pants on.

Macy sat up. 'It's that guy, isn't it? The one who followed me? It's him.'

Rolly flipped on the light, found his shirt, slipped it over his head and turned back to Macy.

'I guess Bob's plan worked,' he said.

The window clattered again. Macy climbed out of bed and started putting on her clothes.

'I'm going with you,' she said.

'No,' said Rolly. 'You need to stay here.'

'Don't pull that macho protection thing on me, Waters.'

'Just let me talk to him first,' Rolly said. 'Find out what he wants.'

'I'm your client. I got as much stake in this as you do.'

Rolly knew he couldn't stop her. 'OK,' he said. 'Just let me go out first and look around.'

'Yeah, yeah, whatever,' said Macy. 'Let's go.'

They walked to the front of the trailer. Rolly stepped down, unlatched the bolt and cracked open the door. He looked outside. There wasn't much to see except the night sky.

'Hello,' he called. 'Who's out there?'

No one responded. He pushed the door open wider and stepped down onto the dirt. The light from inside the Tioga spilled out onto the desert floor. He walked out past the circle of light and saw the gray shapes of other trailers and mobile homes. In this part of Slab City, at least, everyone was asleep.

'Who's out there?' he called again. Someone spoke, out of sight.

'You're the guitar player. The Waters.'

'Yes.'

'I remember you.'

'I remember you, too.'

'The Waters doesn't play it right. The Waters must practice.'

Macy stepped down from the trailer and took Rolly's arm. 'I think he plays great,' she said.

They heard scuttling noises, like a large beetle hurrying through the brush.

'You think I scared him away?' said Macy.

As if in answer, a stuttered sequence of vocalizations began to emanate from the other side of the Tioga. They sounded like moans of sexual pleasure. They sounded like Macy.

'Freakin' pervert,' she said.

'Ooo, aaa . . . yes, yes, yes,' the voice continued.

'OK,' said Rolly. 'We get it. You heard us. What do you want?'

The moaning stopped. There was silence. They waited.

'Who is the golden eyes?' the voice asked.

'My name's Macy. Who the hell are you?'

'The Macy makes funny noises.'

'Uh huh.'

The man spoke again but his voice had changed, as if he were conversing with someone behind the trailer.

'The Macy has golden eyes. The Macy has the key. The Macy is the Sachem.'

Macy looked at Rolly. She shrugged her shoulders. Rolly thought about the woman at the Alien Artifacts store – Dotty. He remembered the gold doll at the store. Dotty had called it by the same name – *the Sachem.*

'The Waters must practice now,' said the man. 'The Sachem has the key.'

'The key to what?'

'The Astral Vibrator,' said the voice, returning to its previous tone.

'What does the Astral Vibrator do?'

'The Sachem is here. The Conjoinment is near. The Waters must practice.'

'Who are you?' said Macy.

'I'm the cool Dionysian. That's my religion.'

'I've heard that line before,' Macy whispered to Rolly. 'It's from one of Bob's songs.'

'You think it's Bob back there?'

'No. Do you?'

'No. Not really. He's probably heard Bob singing it.'

The voice chirped. 'Teotwayki!'

Rolly chirped back, imitating the call. 'Teotwayki!'

They traded calls again. A light went on in one of the trailers nearby. Their bird calls had woken the neighbors.

'Open the Astral Vibrator,' said the voice. 'The Sachem has the key.'

'Who's out there?' It was a new voice, from one of the trailers.

'Teotwayki! Teotwayki!' the voice behind the RV called, sounding alarmed.

'Shut up!' said the voice from the trailer.

The bird calls continued. They became muted and drifted into the distance. Rolly walked to the other side of the Tioga. No one was there. He listened as the last of the bird calls faded away. Macy walked up beside him. They stared into the darkness. Macy spoke first.

'I gotta say, Waters, this is definitely the most batshit crazy date I've ever been on.'

'Me too.'

'What's he talking about? About me having the key? What's this Sachem thing?'

'I don't know exactly. Some kind of alien the UVTs believed in. That lady at the Alien Artifacts shop showed me a doll, a baby doll painted gold. She called it the Sachem.'

'This guy thinks I'm an alien?'

'It would appear so.'

'Man, this is weird. It would explain a lot, though.'

'What?'

'Like maybe I don't have any parents. I mean, earthling ones. Maybe I came from that Oort place. You saw what Daddy Joe wrote in the letter. *My little alien.* He used to call me that. I used to think about it sometimes, being so different from the rest of the kids on the rez.'

Rolly faced Macy, put his hands on her shoulders. 'You are not an alien.'

'How do you know?'

'I don't sleep with aliens.'

'Too late, Waters. You told me the stories. You'll sleep with anyone.'

Rolly pulled Macy close. She buried her face in his chest.

'Do you think Daddy Joe's dead?' she said. It was the first chink he'd felt in Macy's armor, the first hint she was vulnerable.

'I don't know,' Rolly said, holding her tighter. He kept one arm around her shoulders as they walked to the end of the trailer. 'I still think he'll show up.'

'Little Alien DJ, that'll be my new name,' she said. 'I'll make some Space Disco mixes, or maybe Bleep Techno.'

'I have no idea what that means,' said Rolly.

They turned the corner of the trailer. Rolly stopped and pulled Macy back. 'Someone's coming,' he said.

They watched a dark figure approach the Tioga. The light from the window of a nearby trailer caught the man's face as he passed.

'It's Cool Bob,' Macy said.

They waited in the shadows, watching. Bob entered the dark space between the two vehicles, then into the light again as he got close to the Tioga. He was carrying a box. He set the box down and knocked on their door.

Rolly stepped out from the end of the trailer, keeping Macy behind him.

'Hey, Bob,' he said.

Bob peered over at him. 'Hey man,' he said. 'That was some righteous riffage you laid on the Slabbers last night.'

'Thanks. I had fun. What can I do for you?'

Bob indicated the box. 'He liked how you played. He asked me to give this to you. The vibrator thing. He said I should give it to you.'

'What about your van?'

'It's been returned to my domicile. Accountability justified.'

Macy stepped out from behind Rolly.

'Hey Macy,' said Bob. 'Your new boyfriend's a killer.'

'Much cooler than No Pants, huh?' Macy said.

'Way cooler.'

Rolly and Macy walked over to Bob.

'You wanta' come in?' Rolly asked.

'No worries,' said Bob. 'Just wanted to make the delivery.'

Rolly looked down at the black box. 'Is this the Astral Vibrator?'

'He wants you to practice. He said you were worthy.'

'What's his name, Bob? Can I talk to him?'

Cool Bob smiled. 'See you later,' he said. They watched him walk away until he disappeared from view.

'Oww!' said Rolly. A stinging pain shot through his ankle, like a sharp needle.

'What's wrong?' said Macy.

'I don't know,' Rolly said, stumbling towards the door of the Tioga. 'I think something just bit me.'

SIXTEEN
The ER

A *spider loomed in the darkness. It was huge. It had long fangs that gleamed like glittering gold sabers. Rolly turned to run, but his legs wouldn't work. It was like running in deep sand. The spider captured him in its web. It bit into his leg with its giant gold fangs.*

He jolted awake and looked around. The light in the emergency ward of Brawley General Hospital seeped under the edges of curtains surrounding his bed. It was a strange shade of green, like something you'd see on the bridge of a movie spaceship. He felt better now, stronger and clearer. There were no giant spiders.

The monitoring equipment had been unhooked from his arm. He checked his left leg, lightly wrapped in white gauze. His leg felt better, too. His stomach felt settled, with only an occasional flutter to remind him of the dry heaves and retching he'd endured a few hours ago. He was going to live.

A nurse entered the room, pushing a wheelchair. She looked young enough to be a high-school cheerleader.

'Looks like we're awake,' she said.

'We are,' Rolly said.

'How're you feeling?'

'OK, I guess. What time is it?'

'Almost eight. We're ready to check you out. Your mom's here.'

Rolly raised up off the pillow, rested on his elbows.

'My mother?'

'Yeah. She's a real sweetheart.'

'How'd she get here?'

'Well, most people drive their cars.'

'No, I mean, how'd she know I was here?'

'Your friends called her, I guess. They had to leave. Let's have you try standing up now.'

Rolly lifted himself to a sitting position, then swiveled his legs so they hung off the bed.

'Be careful,' said the nurse, taking his arm. 'Your left ankle and lower leg might hurt a bit when you put weight on them.'

Rolly slid down from the bed. A hot pain shot through his left ankle as his feet touched the floor. He leaned against the nurse for support. Her hair smelled like freshly cut grass.

'Just take your time,' she said.

Rolly waited for his head to clear. He nodded at the nurse and took his arm from her shoulders.

'Have you ever used crutches before?' she said.

Rolly nodded. After the car accident, he'd been on crutches for two months.

'OK, hang on to the gurney here if you need to,' the nurse said. 'We're going to put you in the wheelchair first to get you out of the hospital. We'll give you the crutches to take home.'

She grabbed a pair of crutches and handed them to Rolly. He took them, placed them under his arms.

'OK on the height?' the nurse asked, stepping back and assessing the adjustment.

Rolly nodded. 'They're fine.'

'Let's go see your mom and get you checked out.'

The nurse took the crutches while Rolly lowered himself into the wheelchair. She handed them back to him and pushed him out to the waiting room. He spotted his mother in the corner, engaged in conversation with a young Latino woman and her two children.

'Mrs Waters?' said the nurse. 'He's ready to go.'

Rolly's mother said goodbye to her new friends and walked over to Rolly. 'How do you feel, dear?' she said.

'I've felt better,' said Rolly.

'You've got all the instructions?' said the nurse.

'Right here,' said Rolly's mother. 'I took care of the insurance.'

'He's all yours then, I guess,' said the nurse.

'Thank you,' said Rolly's mother.

'Yes,' Rolly said. 'Thanks.'

The nurse returned to the emergency ward.

Rolly looked up at his mother. 'Does Dad know about this?' he said.

'Alicia can worry about your father,' she said. 'It's you I think we should worry about.'

'Sorry you had to drive all the way out here.'

'That's all right, dear.'

'The Waters men sure cause you a lot of trouble, don't we?'

'That's my cross to bear.'

'How did you get here?'

'I drove my Mini, of course.'

'No, I mean how did you find out I was here?'

'A woman called. She told me what happened.'

'Macy?'

'I don't remember her name. I don't think she told me. She said they'd brought you here but she had to leave. There was something important she needed to do.'

'Did she say what it was?'

'No. I don't think so. She gave me the address and the phone number for the hospital here, and asked if I'd be able to come over and get you. She said you'd been bitten by a black widow spider and that you wouldn't be able to drive.'

'What about the Tioga?'

Rolly's mother looked perplexed. 'I don't understand, dear.'

'We drove out here in Dad's RV,' Rolly said. 'Alicia let me borrow it.'

'Was it some sort of romantic liaison you had with this Macy woman?'

Rolly shook his head. 'It's business,' he said. 'She's looking for someone.'

Rolly's mother stared down at him, parsing his statements, assessing their truthfulness.

'We have to stop somewhere,' said Rolly. 'To check on the Tioga. I'll explain on the way.'

'All right, dear,' said his mother. It was what she always said when her vigilance meter had peaked, the needle pegged to red. She had stored up a lot of questions.

His mother wheeled him out of the hospital. He waited while she went to pick up her car. His leg still hurt, but the nervous weight in his stomach worried him more. It might be the last vestiges of spider poison, but an uncertain certainty roiled his belly; the feeling that Macy had a secret she hadn't shared with him. He worried that she'd gone rogue, extemporizing on the events of last night. Macy had the diddley bow and the Astral Vibrator. She knew they were valuable. She might even know why.

It took thirty minutes for them to drive to Slab City from Brawley General. He spent most of that time explaining what had happened to him over the last several days. His mother had always been embarrassed by his day job, almost to the point of denying it existed. When asked, she told people her son was a musician. Macy Starr's case seemed to intrigue her, though. Looking for a young girl's missing parents was more reputable than his usual assignments, even noble. At least he wasn't digging up dirt for divorce lawyers and ambulance chasers.

At any rate, by the time they reached Niland, his mother had finished her interrogation and returned to her usual state of enthusiasm. New adventures were afoot, after all. They pulled off the main road and passed Salvation Mountain. She reminisced about her year on an ashram in New Mexico, reflecting on the aesthetic and spiritual appeal of stark desert landscapes.

When they arrived at Slab City, Rolly directed his mother to the Tioga's old camping spot. The Tioga wasn't there. They drove around looking for it, to no avail. Macy had taken it. He didn't know where or why she had gone.

His mother pulled the Mini to a stop across from The Range.

'What shall we do?' she said.

'Let me think,' Rolly said.

'Perhaps she's gone home.'

Rolly checked his phone again. He'd called Macy from Brawley but she hadn't called him back. She hadn't left any message. His phone indicated there wasn't much signal in this part of the world. The battery had run down. His charger was in the Tioga. He looked out the window. A man dressed in shorts and a carpenter's belt stepped out on the stage at The Range.

'It's Bob,' he said.

'Who?'

'Cool Bob. Honk your horn.'

His mother tapped on the horn. Bob turned to look at them. Rolly rolled down his window.

'Hey, Bob, it's me, Rolly Waters, the guitar player from last night.'

Bob walked over to them. 'Hey,' he said. 'You doin' OK?'

'Yeah, I'm OK.'

'You were looking kinda gruesome the last time I saw you.'

'You were there, weren't you? You helped me get to the hospital?'

'Yeah. I tied on a tourniquet and took you down there in the rocket ship.'

'I remember. Thanks for taking care of me.'

'Macy was freaking.'

'Yeah, I expect so. Speaking of which . . .'

'I've seen folks bit by spiders before, but I never seen it that bad. You were seriously messed up. Explosive. I just got the rocket ship clean.'

'Sorry about that. Have you seen her?'

'It was really trippin' me out. Scandalous.'

'Have you seen Macy? Do you know where she went?'

'I think she went home.'

'To San Diego?'

'There was some odious spirits blowing through here last night.'

'I'm feeling better now. I'll be OK.'

'It was Macy that found him, you know. That's why the police are on location. At the hot springs.'

'Wait. What are you talking about?'

'Macy's old boyfriend. No Pants. He's dead. Extinguished.'

A cold shiver ran down Rolly's bad leg. It was at least eighty degrees outside.

'What happened?' he said.

'They sink before they float. That's what the cops told me. Never knew that before. Didn't see the guy down there 'cause the water's so cloudy.'

'You found him?'

'Macy did. We went to the hot springs after we got back from the hospital. We were both stressing, you know. She suggested we take a soak, get some relief on the musculature. I'd already gone back to my place when she comes running and shouting, all naked. I went back to the springs and saw the guy floating around. That's when I called the cops.'

Bob stroked his beard, looked down at the ground. 'People are kind of hating on me,' he said. 'They don't like having cops around.'

'What can you tell me about Macy's boyfriend?' said Rolly.

'No Pants? He was mucho inquisitive,' said Bob. 'Really bugged people. Pestilential.'

'Macy said he broke into your trailer; that he was looking for something?'

'Yeah, assuredly. With massive intent.'

'You think he was looking for drugs?'

'That's what Macy conjectured. I didn't really peg him for a tweaker, though.'

Rolly stared out the front window, wondered if he should talk to the police. He decided against it and turned back to Bob. 'I saw Macy talking to him last night,' he said, 'when we were playing at The Range.'

'Yeah, I discerned that encounter too. They looked kinda quarrelsome.'

'He didn't like her being here, I guess. Said this was his territory, for some reason. That's what she told me, anyway.'

'He asked a lot of questions. Like you.'

'What kind of questions?'

'He was looking for someone, asking about gold. He brought another lady the last time he was here. Couple of weeks ago.' Bob lowered his head and peered into the car to see who was driving.

'This is my mother,' said Rolly.

'Hello,' said his mother.

'Hello,' said Bob. 'You got white hair. I thought maybe you were the same lady.'

'Oh, no,' said Mrs Waters. 'I don't think we've met before.'

'Yeah. She was different than you.'

'What was the other lady like?' said Rolly.

'She had some interesting postulations about stuff.'

'What kind of stuff?'

'Therapeutical frequencies and gold. She talked about aliens. Like they were real.'

SEVENTEEN
The House

Rolly sat in the passenger seat of Tribal Police Chief Kinnie Harper's Ford Bronco, staring into the sideview mirror as the truck churned up a trail of dust in their wake. Kinnie was driving down the hardscrabble dirt road to Daddy Joe's house. Rolly's mother was tucked away in the reservation's general store, a slatted wooden structure that looked like a set piece from an old Western. There were plenty of trinkets there to keep his mother occupied, and a coffee stand where she could get a cup of tea. She might drive the elderly proprietor crazy with chitchat, but at least she'd be out of Rolly's hair for a while.

Just after driving into the reservation they'd spotted a tribal police truck parked at the casino. It turned out to be Kinnie Harper's. After administering a short but intense interrogation Kinnie agreed to drive Rolly out to her father's house. Daddy Joe was still missing.

'Officer Harper?' said Rolly.

'I guess you can call me Kinnie,' she said. 'Since you're friends with Bonnie.'

'How'd you meet Bonnie?' he asked.

'I know Bonnie from WILES.'

'What's that?'

'Women in Law Enforcement and Security. It's a professional support group. Bonnie was president there for a while.'

Rolly smiled and nodded. Even Bonnie needed encouragement sometimes.

'Kinnie, do you remember anything about Aunt Betty?'

'Who?'

'Aunt Betty. Macy told me she lived with you. That's why she hired me. She wants me to find Aunt Betty.'

'I don't know any Aunt Betty.'

'Macy showed me a photo. It's a young black woman standing with a baseball player.'

'There was a black lady who worked for us a little while. I don't remember her name. She wasn't here long – just while my mother was in the hospital during her last days. The lady was helping us out.'

'Daddy Joe hired her?'

'I guess. I don't remember.'

Rolly felt mystified. The photo of Aunt Betty had become real to him, the story Macy had told him, her memories of Aunt Betty. Kinnie's disavowal of Betty threw him off. It was unexpected.

'Do you know anything about Macy's parents?' he said.

'Her parents? No. Daddy Joe's the only one who would know something about that. We never talked about it in our house. We didn't talk about a lot of things.'

'Macy just appeared one day?'

'Yeah. That's about it. I was ten, I think. You don't really ask questions about stuff like that when you're ten. Daddy says you got a baby sister now and you just accept it.'

'How about later?'

'Macy and I used to talk sometimes. I told her she was an alien. Daddy Joe never said anything. Who's the baseball player?'

'Hmm?'

'The guy in the photo. The baseball player. Is he somebody famous?'

'He's a minor leaguer. The Hawaii Coconuts. They're not even around anymore.'

'Is it that guy on TV? Eric Ozzie?'

Rolly rubbed his chin. He felt like an imbecile. 'Why'd you say that?'

'This guy called Daddy Joe a couple days ago. Left a message. Said he was The Sneaker. He had your name too, said you were snooping around, asking questions. That's why I called Bonnie, asking about you.'

'Well, that explains a lot. I showed him the photo a couple of days ago. He said he didn't recognize the woman in the photo. Said he didn't know anything about her.'

'He must've called Daddy Joe straight afterwards,' said Kinnie.

'They don't call him The Sneaker for nothing, I guess.'

'You think maybe he's Macy's father?'

'I'm not checking him off my list yet, that's for sure.'

Rolly fell silent, ruminating on Macy's motivations. Had she known the man in the photo was Ozzie? Had she hired Rolly to help shake him loose? Did she know Ozzie would call Daddy Joe?

'Kinnie, have you ever heard of a guy named Randy Parker?'

'Yeah. I know him. He used to visit Daddy Joe sometimes.'

'Any time recently?'

'Not that I know,' Kinnie shrugged.

'You ever been to his shop?'

'Nah. I hate that stuff. Aliens. Stupid.'

'What did Randy talk to Daddy Joe about? Was it about the UVTs?'

Kinnie gave Rolly a prickly look. He was trying to pick fruit from a cactus.

'Did Macy tell you about the UVTs?' she said.

'She told me a few things,' he said. 'That they killed themselves. That Daddy Joe was obsessed with the case. I guess he arrested someone.'

'Did she tell you about the gold mine?'

'She told me the UVTs liked to drink gold,' said Rolly.

'The story goes they were hoarding it,' said Kinnie. 'Gold. For this big event when the aliens were going to arrive.'

'The Conjoinment,' said Rolly.

'Some of the people, they sold their houses and stuff. They handed the money over to the people in charge. Their leaders, that's who converted the money to gold – this one guy, anyway. The one Daddy Joe arrested. Caught him on his way to Mexico with a bag full of gold chips.'

'You remember his name?' Rolly said. 'The guy they arrested?'

'Parnell Gibbons. They couldn't prove it was murder, not first degree anyway, so they got him on manslaughter and put him away for a while. There's stuff on the Internet about what happened. Randy Parker's got a website, one of those blog things.'

'I'll look it up,' Rolly said.

'Anyway, it became kind of a legend,' Kinnie continued. 'The gold that went missing, I mean. Daddy Joe had to shoo people away. He got bat gates installed to keep people out of the mine. They'd come around looking, thinking the gold had been buried somewhere around here. The story kind of built up over the years. That Randy Parker guy had kin there that died. His parents, I think. Their names are on the marker.'

'Where's that?'

'Out on the mesa, near that home for girls.'

'That's where the UVTs lived, isn't it?'

Kinnie sighed. A dark sigh. Deep. 'It's old history, you know,' she said. 'Bad history.' She turned her head and looked out the side window. They crested the hill that led down to Daddy Joe's house.

Kinnie said, 'Is that your RV in front of the house?'

'Looks like it,' said Rolly.

'You sleep with her yet?' said Kinnie. The truck bounced through a deep pothole. Rolly winced and rubbed his hand along his lower back to make sure his spine hadn't cracked. He didn't reply. Kinnie laughed.

'Bonnie warned me, you know. She said you got some hound dog in you. All droopy-eyed and rumpled, look like you always need a nuzzling. I bet Macy had you on a leash in five minutes.'

Rolly smiled. Kinnie might be right but he wasn't going to admit it.

'Is it true she doesn't get any proceeds from the casino?' he said.

Kinnie looked over at Rolly with what he hoped was grudging respect for the way he'd slipped in the question. The grudge part was definitely there. He wasn't sure about the respect.

'She had her chance,' said Kinnie. 'Daddy Joe was going to make her official.'

'What's that?'

'He never officially adopted her. He was thinking about it, doing it before she came of age, so she'd be part of the tribe. This was before the whole casino thing. But she ran away. She can't be part of the tribe now. Not retroactively. She had her chance.'

Kinnie parked her truck in front of the Tioga, blocking its escape.

'I'm starting to regret this,' she said. 'I talk too much.'

'I appreciate it. You haven't done anything wrong.'

'That's not what I'm talking about. Me and Macy, we got some history. I don't like to feel like this. Not on the job. Not around some smart-ass private investigator from the big city who I know is going to turn out to be some big-shot lawyer's ass wipe.'

'Look, Kinnie,' said Rolly, making his plea, 'I'm not anybody's asswipe – not any lawyers, anyway. I like Macy. I don't really know why, except that she's younger than me and keeps pushing my buttons, some buttons I didn't even know I had anymore. I doubt she'll be able to pay me for all the time I put into this case, but I don't like to lose people like her, even if they tell me to get lost. I want to give her a chance.'

Kinnie laughed. 'Man, you're a mess.'

'Yeah, I know. I do this a lot.'

'Well,' Kinnie said, 'I like her too. I want to apologize.'

'For what?'

'For something that happened a long time ago. Between her and me.'

'What was it?'

Kinnie looked at the house. 'Let's take a look, find out what she's up to.' Kinnie opened the door of her truck and climbed out. 'You coming?' she said.

Rolly nodded, climbed down from the truck and grabbed his crutches. They walked to the front of the house. Kinnie turned the handle and opened the door. They walked in. The dim light that filtered through the drawn curtains revealed a layer of dust on the thrift store furniture. A thump, like a shutting drawer, came from the back room. Kinnie and Rolly exchanged glances. Kinnie unholstered her pistol. Macy walked into the room.

'Waters?' said Macy when she saw them. 'How's your leg?'

'Macy?' said Kinnie.

'Kinnie?' said Macy. 'What's with the gun?'

Kinnie Harper slipped her gun back into the holster. 'What the hell did you do to your arms?' she said.

'They're called tattoos,' said Macy. 'When'd you get so fat?'

'I'm sorry, Macy,' said Kinnie. 'I'm sorry what I did to you.'

'It's OK, Kinnie. Water under the bridge. I'm sorry, too.'

'Not as sorry as me. You're under arrest.'

'What?' Rolly said.

Kinnie waved her hand at Rolly and put her other hand on the butt of her gun. 'Sit down, Mr Waters. I'm taking you in as well.'

'What for?'

'Trespassing. Breaking and Entering.'

Rolly protested. 'But you brought me here.'

'You were both here the other day. I saw an RV, just like that one outside. You were driving back from here.'

'We didn't take anything,' said Rolly.

'Where'd you get that?' Kinnie asked, pointing at the gold charm on Macy's neck.

'It's mine,' Macy said. 'Daddy Joe gave it to me.'

'That's not true.'

'He gave it to me five years ago, before I left.'

'You stole it.'

'Cut it out, Kinnie. Stop being so mad at me.'

'Why'd you come here?' said Kinnie. 'Why'd you come back?'

'I'd like to know that, too,' said Rolly. 'Why are you here?'

Macy looked from Rolly to Kinnie and back to Rolly again. 'I think someone killed Daddy Joe,' she said. 'And now they want to kill me.'

EIGHTEEN
The Jail

On the whole, Rolly found the accommodation at the tribal jail an improvement on his recent overnight arrangements. It was quieter than the emergency room at Brawley General and less cramped than the Tioga. He would have preferred sleeping in his own bed, but the cell cot wasn't uncomfortable. The throbbing in his leg had settled down, thanks to a couple of Tylenol Kinnie Harper had been kind enough to provide him with. He'd told his mother to go home and call Max when she got there. Max would get him out of jail. Max had done it before. Rolly lay back on the cot and closed his eyes. Fatigue settled in.

'Hey, Waters,' said Macy, who occupied the cell next to him. 'What're you thinking about?'

'I was trying to sleep.'

'You ever been arrested before?'

'I'm not talking to you.'

'I didn't do nothing.'

'You stole my Tioga.'

'It's not yours. It's your dad's.'

'You still stole it.'

'I only borrowed it.'

'Like you borrowed that necklace?'

'That necklace belongs to me. Besides, I didn't know you were gonna get out of the hospital so soon.'

Rolly heard Macy padding around in her cell. They were small cells – one cot and a toilet. There were three cells in the jail – metal cages set side by side – with open bars between them. Macy and Rolly could hold hands if they wanted to. There was another man, asleep, in the third cell. He snored like a boozehound.

'Kinnie's upset about Daddy Joe,' said Macy. 'I guess she thinks I killed him or something. That'd be a twist, wouldn't it, Waters? Me killing Daddy Joe?'

'Did you?'

'C'mon, Waters, what do you think?'

'I don't know. Did you kill No Pants?'

'You heard about that?'

'Cool Bob told me what happened. He said you were there.'

'Did you tell Kinnie?'

'Sure, I told her.'

'I guess she'll call the sheriff then, won't she? Out in Imperial, tell 'em she's got their suspect in custody?'

'I imagine she will. What happened to No Pants?'

'I don't know. That's why I'm freaked out. He said he'd met somebody who knew my parents.'

'Wait, what?'

'OK. I lied to you a little bit. About that argument you saw, with me and No Pants. He said he'd met this guy. He said it was important, that this guy knew stuff about my parents. I told him about you, how you were working for me and that you had to be there too. He got kind of quiet then, said he was going to meet with the guy anyway, that I had to come by myself if I wanted to do it. He said he'd be at the hot springs in the morning, at sunrise, to meet the guy. I wasn't going to do it, but after you ended up in the hospital I couldn't stop thinking about it. I asked Bob to go with me, just to be safe. We stayed for a while but no one showed up. Bob said he had to get back. I sat there a little longer, thinking Randy might still show up. He did, just not like I expected.' Macy shivered. 'Ugh,' she said. 'Ugh, ugh.'

'You should have waited to talk to the police.'

'Yeah. I know.'

They were silent for a few minutes. Rolly closed his eyes.

'Hey, Waters,' whispered Macy. He didn't answer.

'Are you asleep?' she said.

'I'd like to be,' he replied.

'Don't be mad at me.'

'You got us thrown in jail, Macy.'

'Let's have some fun.'

'What kind of fun?'

'I could give you a blow job.'

'Stop it, Macy,' he said. As attractive as the offer might be, he felt resolute.

'C'mon, Waters,' said Macy. 'I know what you got. I bet we could do it.'

'Just stop it.'

'OK, OK. It's just that I got this heavy submissive tingle going on right now. It must be the bars and the handcuffs and everything. Makes me want to get down on my knees. I feel kind of bad too, about taking the Tioga. I want to make up.'

Rolly turned on his side and faced the other cell. What did he know about women? About anyone? Ten years ago he'd walked into his apartment at three in the morning to find Matt and Leslie together because they both knew he'd be out all night with a Gauloise-smoking groupie wearing tiger-striped stretch pants – a girl he'd picked up at the bar. The only thing he really knew about women was when they were available and willing. That was all he'd learned in his forty-odd years on the planet. It didn't feel like much of an achievement.

'Kinnie's probably got cameras in here anyway,' Macy continued. 'Spying on us. I'm not into sharing that kind of way, especially with Kinnie.'

'What's the story with you and her anyway?' said Rolly.

'What do you mean?'

'That apology thing. When she saw you, and even before we went in, she said she wanted to apologize to you.'

'I don't know.'

'Yes, you do.'

'Sure was a surprise seeing Kinnie again. She's put on some weight since the last time I saw her.'

'She's put on a gun, too.'

Macy laughed. 'Yeah. That was a surprise as well. She looked like she knew what she was doing with that pistol, don't you think?'

Rolly sighed. 'Are you gonna tell me the truth?' he said.

'What about?'

'I don't know. Anything. How about your Aunt Betty, for one?'

'What about her?'

'Kinnie says she doesn't remember anyone named Aunt Betty.'

'Really? Kinnie's such a bitch. Why would she say that?'

'That's what I'm asking you.'

'Kinnie had to take care of me. That's why she hates me.'

'Can we get back to Aunt Betty?'

'It wasn't my fault. I was just a little kid. I couldn't help that Daddy Joe liked me better. It wasn't my fault her mom died.'

'Why doesn't Kinnie remember Aunt Betty?'

Macy walked around her cell – a pacing shadow. The snoring man rolled over on his cot. Macy grabbed the cell bars, facing Rolly. 'Sure you don't want a hummer?' she said.

'Macy . . .'

'OK, OK. It's just that I can't really remember Aunt Betty either, when I try to picture her for real. It's mostly from Daddy Joe showing me that photo over the years, telling me about her. That's what I remember. She's like a shadow or something. Maybe she's not real. Maybe Daddy Joe just made her seem real, with those stories.'

'It would explain why Kinnie doesn't remember her.'

'Kinnie hates me because I was Daddy Joe's little pet. His little alien with the curly gold locks. Kinnie had it tough after her mama died. She was only ten or eleven when it happened. Daddy Joe expected her to take care of the house, cooking and doing the chores. And she had to look after me, of course, when Daddy Joe was out working. When he got home, he'd sit with me on his knee after dinner, in his office, while Kinnie was in the kitchen washing dishes and stuff.'

'Uh huh,' said Rolly.

'Not much in the way of child care on the rez back then. Probably still isn't. We went to school sometimes, but it was kinda sporadic, our education.'

'So you think Daddy Joe only talked about Aunt Betty with you? He didn't show Kinnie the picture?'

'Not like he did me. That's what I'm saying. Maybe she saw it a couple of times, but mostly it was me. Daddy Joe treated Kinnie like she was the maid or something. That's why she hates me.'

'That's why you left?'

'Kinnie left before me. She was older, though. After she left Daddy Joe had me doing the chores. I couldn't take it anymore. That's why I skedaddled. Daddy Joe's a mean bastard.'

'How old were you when you left?'

'Sixteen.'

'Kinnie told me Daddy Joe was going to adopt you, so you could be part of the tribe, but you ran away before he could do it.'

'I never heard anything about that. Wouldn't have made a difference.'

'She says you would've been able to get some of the casino money if you hadn't left.'

'I don't care about that. I had to get out.'

Rolly considered what Macy had told him. It sounded truthful, lacking the usual embellishments. Daddy Joe had told stories, planted memories of Aunt Betty. But why? Daddy Joe was the only person who could tell them, for sure. Daddy Joe was still missing. He might be dead.

'Why'd you come back here?' said Rolly. 'I mean, today? Why'd you come back to the house?'

'I told you.'

'Macy, c'mon . . .'

'It was something No Pants told me. Kinda freaked me out. Especially after I saw him there, floating up dead. When I was with him before, when we went to Coachella that time, he would get these weird phone calls. It was just these tones, played over and over.'

'Like a modem or fax machine, that kind of thing?'

'That's what I thought too, like it was one of those robo-dial things. But when Bob and I took you to the hospital and we were sitting in the waiting room, I got a call too. Beep, beep, beep, over and over again. I disconnected the guy but he called back. Again and again. I stopped answering, but then I remembered about Randy No Pants, how he kept getting those calls. I had to talk to him, find out what he wanted to tell me. That's why I left.'

'OK, but why did you come here, to the reservation?'

'I was freaking out after seeing him dead. And then I thought about Daddy Joe, how he went missing, like maybe he was dead too. Two people I know in one week. It freaked me out. I started thinking maybe there's a psycho killer out there who's calling people with this beeper thing as a warning. Like you're next on the list.'

'You're sure it's a person who's calling, not a computer?'

'You can hear stuff in the background, like those sales calls you get where they don't pick up right away and you hear the people talking in the room. Except I think it's outside somewhere.'

'Do they say anything?'

'No. Nobody says anything. You just kind of get this sense that there's somebody there and then these beeps start going off. I got some on my voicemail. I can play 'em for you if Kinnie ever gives me my phone back.'

'Did you tell Kinnie about this?'

'Sure, I told her. Except for the part about Randy. But I guess you told her about that. I told her she needed to go back and listen to what was on Daddy Joe's phone machine.'

'That's why you went to the house?'

'I couldn't stop thinking about it. Daddy Joe's phone machine. When you and I went there the first time, it was blinking like crazy. What if Daddy Joe got those calls too?'

'Did he?'

Macy nodded. 'They were on there. The same beeps.'

Rolly stood up and walked over to her. He reached through the grate, put his hand on her shoulder. She reached up and held it there.

'I'm scared, Waters,' she said. 'I'm freakin' terrified.'

NINETEEN
The Memorial

Kinnie Harper strode into the holding area. She stopped in front of Rolly's cell.

'They found Daddy Joe's car,' she said.

'Where was it?' said Rolly.

'Over near In-Ko-Pah,' said Kinnie.

Kinnie pulled a key from her belt and opened the door to Rolly's cell. 'Your lawyer called,' she said. 'I told him I'd let you go if you helped me out with something.'

'What is it?' he asked.

'We need to go someplace. You tell me what you know when you see it. It'll save your lawyer having to come out here and post bail.'

'Max said it was OK for me to do this?'

'It's up to you. Your choice. That's what he said.'

'Can I call him?'

'Sure. If you want.'

Rolly stood up and walked out of his cell.

'What about me?' said Macy as they walked past her cell. Kinnie stopped and gave Macy the evil eye.

'You got a lawyer?' she said.

'Did you listen to those messages on Daddy Joe's phone machine – those beeps?'

'Yeah. I heard 'em. You think that means somebody wants to kill you?'

'Yes. It's just like I told you. Somebody's after me.'

'In that case, the safest place for you is right here.'

'You're such a bitch, Kinnie. Did you talk to Vera at the restaurant yet?'

'Yeah. I talked to her.'

'So you know Daddy Joe was there. You know I got an alibi.'

'I still got you on breaking and entering.'

'Come on, Kinnie. It's my house as much as it's anybody's.'

'You had no right to be in there, not without me or Daddy Joe letting you in.'

'Waters, can't you do something? You know I'm right.'

Rolly looked at Macy. He didn't say anything. He followed Kinnie into the office. She motioned to a chair across from her desk. Rolly sat down.

'If you're wondering, I'm just keeping her until the Imperial County Sheriff shows up.'

'They don't really think she killed that guy, do they?'

'I don't care what they think. They want me to keep her here.'

Kinnie picked up a photograph from on top of her desk and passed it to Rolly.

'What's this?' he asked.

'I found it in Daddy Joe's files,' she said. 'From the UVTs crime scene.'

Rolly looked at the photo. It was a room in a house. There were bodies on the floor of the room, so close to each other they looked like they'd been stacked.

'You notice anything?' said Kinnie.

Rolly looked at the photo again. He looked past the bodies at the walls of the room, into the corners. He found it.

'There's a whole row of them,' he said. 'Diddley bows.'

'Here's something else,' said Kinnie, pushing a yellow sheet across the desk. It was a receipt from the San Diego Sheriff's office. Rolly had one like it in his files back home, from the confiscated property auction the sheriff ran twice a year. He'd bought a black Paul Reed Smith guitar there once for two hundred bucks. Daddy Joe had also purchased something at the auction, almost fifteen years ago. The receipt listed it as a homemade one-string guitar.

Kinnie took the documents from Rolly and put them back in the folder. She stood up. 'There's something else I want you to see,' she said. 'We gotta take the truck.'

'What about Macy?'

'What about her?'

'You aren't just going to leave her here, are you?'

'She'll be OK. She's got Bert.'

'Who's Bert?'

'The guy in cell one. Bert's pretty friendly once he's slept things off. She'll remember him from high school.'

'You're not concerned about what she said?'

'You really buy that stuff? That somebody wants to kill her?'

'Daddy Joe's missing. And this No Pants guy is dead. You don't think those phone calls are connected?'

Kinnie looked at Rolly a moment, as if to make sure he was serious. She turned her head, put two fingers to her mouth and whistled. A door in back corner of the office opened. A man stuck his head out.

'Yeah, boss?' he said.

'Manny, I'm gonna be out a little while. You see anybody suspicious hanging around, you go on lockdown and radio me right away.'

'Suspicious, like how?'

'Oh, you know, trained assassins, death squads, anything like that.'

'Really?'

'Mr Waters here thinks we got a high-security risk in back.'

'Wow. OK.'

'You remember Macy, right?'

'Your little sister, with the eyes?'

'Yeah. That's her in the tank. Opposite Bert.'

'You got your sister in the tank?'

'Just keeping her safe from herself. Keep an eye on things, will you?'

'Sure, boss.'

Kinnie turned back to Rolly and raised her eyebrows to confirm his approval. He nodded, raised himself up on his crutches and followed her out of the office. They climbed into Kinnie's truck.

'Where are we going?' said Rolly.

'Over to Beatrice House,' said Kinnie. She pulled out onto the main road.

'Macy said you don't have jurisdiction off the reservation,' said Rolly.

'I don't,' said Kinnie. 'Doesn't mean I can't take you there and show you something.' She adjusted the air conditioning and picked up speed. Rolly tugged on his ear and stared out the window. Dry blades of grass passed in battered clumps by the side of the road, quivering in the wind like frayed nerve ends of the cracked earth.

'That place where they found Daddy Joe's car,' said Rolly, 'that's the same exit you take for the Desert View Tower, right?'

'Yep.'

'I was out there the other night,' he said. 'After our gig at the casino.'

'I had a feeling that might've been you,' Kinnie said. 'I talked to the owners.'

'What did they tell you?'

'Said a couple of crazy musicians showed up yesterday morning, with this story about some guy in a rocket ship who gave them the runaround, took some fuses out of their truck. They would have thought you were high, except somebody dropped the fuses through their mail slot that same morning.'

Rolly nodded. 'What kind of car does Daddy Joe drive?' he asked.

'It's just an old Toyota.'

'Blue?'

'Yeah.'

'We saw a blue car that morning. I think it was a Toyota. It pulled out on to the road, when we were standing around, trying to figure out what to do. We tried to flag the guy down, but he drove away.'

'You get a look at the driver?'

'Not enough to tell anything. He was too far away.'

'That's the back road,' said Kinnie. 'To get down to the gold mine.'

They rounded a curve in the road. The casino came into view. Rolly opened the window and rested his arm on the frame. The truck interior felt oppressive. He needed to feel the outside air on his skin, in his eyes. They passed the casino and left the reservation. Kinnie turned in at the sign for Beatrice House. She stopped at the gate and entered some numbers in a keypad attached to a post by the side of the road. The gate opened. Kinnie drove through it and over the hill.

A white wood fence ran along the road as they descended to the mesa. A pretty white house sat behind the fence. Another gate blocked the driveway to the house.

'That's Beatrice House,' said Kinnie. 'The people that bought the place, they tore down the old one, the one where the UVTs died. They built this place, brand new for the girls. It's for unwed teens, ones that got pregnant and don't have family, on their own.'

They passed the house and continued down the mesa.

'You see across the canyon there? That's Daddy Joe's house.'

Rolly looked across the canyon and spotted the house. The Tioga was still parked there. Kinnie continued down the road to the narrow end of the mesa. She pulled up next to a circle of concrete. Two black iron benches had been set inside the circle, facing a granite tablet about four feet high. They climbed out of the truck.

'I remember the UVTs being out here on the mesa,' said Kinnie. 'I could see 'em from our house. Every morning and every night. I'm not sure what kind of music you'd call it, but you could hear it over to our place. They'd line up in pairs and start banging away on those diddley bopper things.'

'Diddley bows,' said Rolly. 'Why am I here?'

'I thought you might want to read the names,' said Kinnie, indicating the marble slab.

'Why?'

'Just read the names.'

Rolly crouched down by the monument, read through the names. He found one of interest.

'Wanda Ozzie,' he said. 'Is she related?'

'Eric Ozzie's mother,' said Kinnie. 'I looked it up in Daddy Joe's files, after Ozzie called him.'

Rolly looked up at Kinnie. She nodded and put her hands on her hips.

'I got this weird flashback,' she said. 'When I heard Ozzie's voice on the answering machine, I remembered this time at the house, when I was a kid. It was night. Some guy came over, sat with Daddy Joe in the living room. He was a black guy. I was pretty young, you know. You don't see many black people out here, living on the rez. Only on TV.'

'You think it was Ozzie?'

'I don't know. I hadn't thought about it until a coupla days ago, after I heard the message. Daddy Joe had people showing up all the time, all hours of night. Part of being a cop.'

'Is that what you wanted to show me?'

'There's some other names, too,' Kinnie said. 'The ones after Ozzie.'

Rolly read the names. *Tom Parker. Gladys Parker*. He looked up at Kinnie.

'Randy Parker's parents,' she said. 'They died here too. He was only a little kid. I think that's why he visits with Daddy Joe sometimes. Because of his parents. They're both kinda obsessed.'

'What do they talk about?'

'Where the gold went, I think. People were always asking Daddy Joe about that, thinking he had something to do with it – the gold that was missing. Some people straight out thought he stole it.'

'Why would they think that?'

'The amount they found didn't add up, you know. That was pulled from the bank accounts. It came out in the trial. That

Gibbons guy was taking money out, converting the cash into gold. He said it was for the aliens or something. They took that lady to court. Some of the relatives sued her. She ended up having to sell the place to settle with them.'

'What was her name?'

'Dorothy Coasters. She owned the place – all this land. She got some kind of immunity for testifying against Gibbons. Didn't protect her in the civil court, though. She took people's money. They gave it to her when they joined the UVTs. That's why they sued her. She said she didn't know where the money was, that Gibbons or somebody took it.'

Rolly closed his eyes. He felt exhausted, overwhelmed with the information. There was too much to take in, about Ozzie and Randy Parker, the whole UVT disaster. It was like a huge tangle of tumbleweeds had piled up in one corner of his brain. And Macy was caught in the tumbleweeds. Daddy Joe, too. Maybe Kinnie. And the bird-call man. They all needed to find a way out.

'One more thing,' said Kinnie.

'What's that?' Rolly asked.

'Check out the other side of the slab. The sheriff called me about it this morning.'

Rolly lifted himself up on his crutches. He walked around to the back. A word had been spray-painted on the reverse side of the granite slab, sprayed across the date etched in the stone.

TEOTWAYKI.

The damn word was everywhere.

TWENTY
The Return

An Imperial County Sheriff's car was parked outside the tribal police station when Kinnie and Rolly returned. They found the detective sitting inside, nursing a cup of coffee and shooting the breeze with Officer Manny. Kinnie let Macy out of her cell and listened in while the detective interviewed both Macy and Rolly. There'd been no further identification of the man who died in the hot springs other than the colorful moniker he'd gone by in Slab City. Everyone knew No Pants was dead. No one knew who he was.

The interview took twenty minutes. Afterwards, Kinnie followed the detective out to his car and re-entered the office five minutes later. Rolly and Macy signed some release papers, then she drove them out to Daddy Joe's house. She made sure they both got in the Tioga and followed them down the road until they'd left the reservation. Rolly's gimpy leg made it difficult for him to drive, so Macy took the wheel. Her mood seemed to lift as they headed back to the city, back where she could be DJ Macy again, no longer the insubordinate, outcast little sister. Back in the city, she wasn't the only alien. There were plenty of them, with weird haircuts and tattoos.

'So Waters, whatta' ya think now?' she said.

'About what?'

'About Macy Starr. You planning to dump me? Get rid of this crazy, scheming bitch?'

'I'm not going to dump you.'

'Professionally or personally?'

'Neither.'

'You think we'll have sex again?'

'I have no idea.'

'Do you want to?'

'I'm not sure.'

'Yeah. Me neither. We might never be able to live up to last night. Situational sex. That's my thing, I think. You think you'll ever settle down with somebody?'

'I thought you hated talking about "Doctor Phil" stuff?'

'Yeah, whatever,' said Macy. 'It depends.' She looked in the rearview mirror and switched lanes to pass a slow-moving truck. They dropped down through the rocky hills of Alpine and headed into the flatlands of El Cajon.

Macy laughed. 'One thing I can't figure out,' she said. 'It's really stupid.'

'What's that?' said Rolly.

'Why I want you to like me. I don't usually care.'

Rolly smiled. He looked out the window. An aqueous sliver of blue appeared in the distance – one of the local reservoirs cradled between mountains of rock.

'I haven't had this much fun since Vera almost shot me,' he said.

'What was that all about, anyway?'

'That's between me and Vera.'

'Rolly Waters doesn't kiss and tell, huh?'

'There was no kissing involved.'

'I'm gonna get Vera drunk sometime and find out what happened.'

Macy's phone rang. She looked over at Rolly. 'You want to see who it is?' she said, indicating the phone in the cup holder between them. Rolly lifted the phone and checked the screen.

'Justin Beeper?' he said, reading the caller's name.

'That's the guy,' said Macy. 'The one who punches in tones all the time. I entered a name so I'd know it was him. Go ahead and answer if you want.'

Rolly tapped the answer button and put the phone to his ear.

'Hello,' he said. There was no answering voice, but he could hear something in the background. It sounded like a car passing. A tone beeped. Then another. A whole set of tones, nine or ten, then a pause.

'Who is this?' said Rolly.

The sequence of tones repeated, paused and repeated. He hung up and checked the number on the display. The area code was 760, which covered a lot of territory. Most of that area lay behind them in the great desert empire. It didn't mean the caller was in the desert, though, if it was a cell phone.

'Was it that tone thing?' Macy said.

Rolly nodded.

'Freaky, huh?' Macy said.

'When did this start?'

'In the hospital, in Brawley, while I was waiting for you.'

'It's the same pattern of beeps on Daddy Joe's answering machine?'

'Yeah. I saved one of the calls on my voicemail so I could compare 'em. Same little tune. You think it's a code or something?'

'Maybe. Did you hear anything else on Daddy Joe's machine?'

'Like what?'

'Kinnie said Eric Ozzie left him a message.'

'The Sneakers guy?'

'Yeah. Kinnie said Ozzie called Daddy Joe about me. He wanted to know how I got the photograph. Look out for that camper up there.'

Macy tapped the brakes as a truck and camper combo swerved in front of them. Its left blinker popped on halfway through the lane change.

'Asshole,' said Macy, tapping the brakes again.

'Did you hear the message from Ozzie?' asked Rolly.

'C'mon, Waters,' said Macy. 'I woulda told you about that. All I heard were those beeps. Kinnie must've erased it.'

'Someone did, I guess.'

'The Sneakers guy lied to you, didn't he, about never seeing the photo?'

'Appears so.'

'We need to confront that guy.'

'We?'

'You're going to talk to him, aren't you?'

'Yeah. Sure.'

'I want to meet him. He told you he'd be willing to meet me, right?'

Rolly put the phone back in the cup holder and considered his choices.

'Yeah,' he said. 'You should go too. I'll call when I get home, try to set something up.'

'You think I'm all wrong? That he's my father?'

'Maybe he is.'

'Aunt Betty can't be my mother then.'

'Ozzie's mother died. She was one of them. The UVTs.'

'No shit? That's crazy.'

They descended into a bank of dust and smog that hung like cement over the city of El Cajon. Macy's phone rang again. Rolly checked the name on the screen. He looked at Macy, then checked it again.

'What is it?' she asked.

'It says No Pants.'

'What? I don't . . . Randy's dead.'

'They probably found his phone. The cops. They're going through his recent calls list and contacts.'

'You gonna answer?'

'I don't know.'

'It'll go to voicemail after six rings.'

The phone had rung four times already. It rang again. Rolly tapped the screen and put the phone to his ear. 'Hello,' he said.

'Who's this?' It was a woman's voice.

'It's me,' Rolly said. 'Who are you?'

'I was looking for . . .' said the woman. 'Oh dear.' She hung up. Rolly tapped Randy's name on the screen to call back and got sent straight to voicemail, the default message. He tapped off the call.

'Who was it?' said Macy.

'Some woman,' said Rolly. 'Not the cops. She hung up.'

'How'd she get Randy's phone?'

'I don't know.'

He realized he did know as soon as he said it. Randy No Pants was Randy Parker. They were one and the same. The man he'd met in the Alien Artifacts shop was an impostor. Kinnie had said something, back at the monument, but he hadn't realized what it meant until now. *Randy was a little kid.* The man with the bad wig and the prison tats couldn't be Randy Parker. He was too old.

'Tell me about Randy,' said Rolly.

'It was just those four days I was with him, you know.'

'How did you meet him?'

'He came to the club one night, chatted me up on the break, said he dug what I was doing. He came back the next night, said he had two tickets to Coachella, the whole weekend and asked if I wanted to go. I said sure.'

'Uh huh.'

'I know. I'm a concert whore. Those tickets are like three hundred bucks.'

'What did you talk about?'

'Not much. We got high, listened to music, fucked around. I told him about rez life. He seemed pretty interested in that stuff, in my growing up. We kinda bonded because we were both orphans. I remember talking about that. His parents died when he was young. His grandparents raised him or something.'

'Did he say how they died?'

'No. Not that I remember. He was wearing this goofy T-shirt the night I met him. What was it? Oh, yeah. *My parents were abducted by aliens and all I got was this lousy T-shirt.*'

Rolly rubbed his forehead.

'What is it?' said Macy.

'No Pants – his name's Randy Parker. He owns that shop. Kinnie showed me some names on the memorial. His parents were UVTs too.'

'No shit? That's seriously demented.'

Rolly nodded. He thought about the woman in the Alien Artifacts store. He wondered if she could be Randy's grandmother.

'What else?' he said. 'When did you go to Slab City?'

'He told me about East Jesus and that stuff while we were at Coachella, said he wanted to check it out. I didn't need to be anywhere after the weekend. I guess he didn't either, so we spent a couple of days at the Slabs, like I told you. We walked around a lot. It was almost like he was showing off, wanting to make sure everybody saw us together. He was trying to find somebody, too.'

'Who?'

'He didn't have the guy's name. He kept asking about gold, asking people if they knew a guy with gold fingers. That's how we met Cool Bob.'

'Bob doesn't have gold fingers.'

'No, but people kept bringing up Bob's name when Randy asked about the guy, said Bob might know somebody. Maybe it had something to do with that guitar. Then there was that thing with Bob's trailer, when Randy broke in. That's when I dumped him.'

'What happened with Bob's trailer?'

'We met Bob and talked to him for a while at his trailer. He wasn't giving up anything, kinda like he acted when you and me went there. He said he knew a guy that made gold, extracted it from old computers or something. He said the guy was real private, though – didn't like talking to people. Bob said he could give the guy a message, but that's all he could do.'

'Did Randy leave any message?'

'Not that I remember. He got all weird after that.'

'How so?'

'It was like he was done with me. The morning after he said he had to go see somebody. In Calipatria, I think – his brother or someone. He just took off. I thought he'd dumped me. Sad

Macy, ditched in the desert. Anyway, I went to East Jesus to hang out some more and ran into Bob. I asked him if there was any other stuff I should see. He showed me the water tank. They got it all painted up. No water, though. He showed me the shooting range and the golf course. We went back to his trailer for a beer. That's when we caught Randy tearing up the place. Bob was pissed at me.'

'He thought you set him up.'

'That's what I felt like. After Bob threw him out, Randy waited for me out on the road, like I was his dog or something and I was going to follow him home. I told him to fuck off, to get out of my life. He finally gave up. That's the last time I saw him until the other night at The Range. I thought maybe he was looking for drugs.'

'Why'd you think that?'

'Nothing, really. Bob didn't make Randy for a tweaker.'

'Yeah, he told me. Did you know Randy Parker used to visit with Daddy Joe?'

'I never heard of Randy Parker until you mentioned his name at the cantina.'

Rolly looked out the window. They were entering Mission Valley, approaching the football stadium. He spotted an exit sign. 'Take Fairmount,' he said.

Macy put on the right blinker, moved over a lane. 'Where are we going?' she said.

'The Alien Artifacts store,' Rolly replied. 'You're going to call Randy.'

TWENTY-ONE
The Relics

Macy followed Fairmount Drive south into Mid-City, then turned onto El Cajon Boulevard. Rolly pointed out the Alien Artifacts store. They pulled into a grocery store parking lot two blocks away, climbed out of the Tioga and walked to the store. Rolly leaned on his crutches and tried the doorknob.

It turned. He couldn't see anyone inside but there were lights on in back, behind the partition. He looked at Macy.

'Got your phone?' he asked. Macy showed it to him. He'd outlined the plan in the parking lot before they came over. They opened the door and walked in.

'Hello?' said Rolly. 'Is anyone here?'

Something stirred in the back of the store. 'We're closed,' said a woman's voice.

'The door was open,' said Rolly. 'Is Randy here?'

'Randy's gone,' said the voice.

Rolly looked over at Macy. She inspected an elongated crystal skull displayed on the front table.

'Dotty?' said Rolly. 'Is that you?'

Dotty entered the room through the door in the back. 'Oh, hello,' she said, walking towards them.

'Hello,' said Rolly. 'Do you remember me?'

'Yes. You're that detective person, aren't you?'

'That's right. Rolly Waters. I was here a couple of days ago. I talked to you and Randy. That was Randy I met, wasn't it?'

'Yes,' said Dotty. She looked past Rolly, assessing his new companion.

'This is Macy,' said Rolly.

'Hello,' said Dotty.

'Hi,' said Macy.

'You have beautiful eyes,' said Dotty.

'Thank you.'

'Very unusual. I used to know someone with eyes like yours.'

'They're amber,' said Macy.

'They look like gold,' said Dotty. 'Have they always been that way?'

Macy shrugged. 'As long as I can remember,' she said.

'We'd like to talk to Randy,' said Rolly. 'It's important.'

'Randy's not here.'

'Is he still in the desert?'

Dotty pulled her fascinated gaze away from Macy and returned her attention to Rolly. 'Yes,' she said. 'In the desert. That's right.'

'When did you last hear from him?'

'Oh, goodness, that must've been when you were here the last time. When he came back to the shop to pick up his phone. Is there some way I can help you?'

'I don't think so. Unless you know why Randy called Macy.'

Dotty turned back to Macy. 'Do you know Randy?' she asked.

Macy shrugged again. 'I camped out with him once,' she said. 'At a concert.'

Dotty stroked her long white hair, fiddling with it. Her eyes stayed on Macy.

'You must be the young lady he was telling me about,' she said. 'I was so glad to hear that he'd found someone. He doesn't get out much, you know. This shop takes up all his time.'

'We were just out in the desert,' said Rolly. 'At a place called Slab City. We saw Randy there.'

Dotty tugged at the sleeves of her dress, re-arranging the diaphanous purple fabric until she found it acceptable. She went back to stroking her hair.

'There's been a disturbance,' she said. 'I feel the vibrations.'

'Have the police been here?' said Rolly. 'Have you talked to them?'

'Randy was supposed to come back yesterday,' Dotty said.

'Who was that man?' Rolly asked.

'What man?'

'The one with the tattoos. The man you told me was Randy. Who is he?'

'I wanted to warn you. I didn't know he'd come back.'

'Who came back? Who is he?'

Dotty turned and walked away from them.

'Randy's dead,' Rolly said.

Dotty stopped. She turned back to face them. 'I am blameless,' she said. 'I am blameless in all of this.'

Rolly and Macy exchanged glances. Dotty took a step towards the wall. She stared at the UVT paintings that hung there, of the planets and energy fields, the man playing the diddley bow.

'Randy's been preoccupied,' she said. 'Much more than usual.'

'How so?' said Rolly.

'He gets like that when he's collecting things, when he thinks he's found something exciting.'

'This lady's dotty all right,' said Macy, *sotto voce*. 'Want me to make the call?'

Rolly nodded his head. Macy tapped on her phone once then hid it behind her. A phone rang in the back of the store. Dotty looked confused.

'Would you like to answer that?' said Rolly. Dotty said nothing, so he continued, 'That's Randy's phone, isn't it? The man didn't take Randy's phone with him because he wasn't Randy.'

'I don't know what you're talking about.'

'You tried to call Macy, didn't you? From Randy's phone. Twenty minutes ago. When I answered you didn't know what to do so you hung up.'

Dotty played with her hair.

'Why did you call Macy?' said Rolly.

'I warned him,' said Dotty, talking to herself. 'I am blameless in all of this.'

'You went out to Slab City with Randy a couple of weeks ago. Who were you looking for?'

Dotty stopped playing with her hair. She looked at Rolly as if she might say something. Then she bolted past them and ran out the front door. Macy dashed after her.

'Macy!' said Rolly.

Macy paused in the doorway and looked back at him. 'I'll catch the old lady,' she said. 'Find Randy's phone and I'll call you.'

And then she was gone. Rolly stumbled to the front door. He stepped out on the sidewalk and looked up and down the street. He couldn't see either woman. There was no chance he'd catch up with them. He hobbled back into the store and made his way to the back. He opened the door leading into the back office and saw a small desk, stacks of metal shelves filled to the edges with alien bric-a-brac. There was a cell phone on the desk. He laid his crutches against the side of the desk and sat down in the chair. He turned on the magnifying lamp attached to the desk. There were maps on the desk and all sorts of papers. He looked at the top map – *Geology and Mineral Deposits of the Jincona District, San Diego, California.* He looked through the other papers. They were technical articles on gold mining and chemicals. There were road maps, trail maps, elevations. They all covered the same area. They always included the Jincona Indian reservation.

He picked up Randy's cell phone and searched through the call list. Dotty's call to Macy was the most recent one listed. A call to Joe Harper was next. It had been made two days ago. The next number on the list had no name next to it, but the prefix was 760, like the beeper's number. Rolly tapped the number and put the phone to his ear. He stayed on the line, hoping to get through to the caller's voicemail, thinking he might get a name or hear a recorded voice.

As he waited for voicemail to pick up, he heard a scraping sound, like metal against metal. He swiveled in the chair to see where it came from. A thin line of sunlight leaked out from underneath the back door. There was another door, next to the exit, a bathroom or closet. He hung up the phone, grabbed his crutches and stood up. The scraping sound came from behind the interior door.

'Hello?' he said. There was a different sound, like a grunting animal, a dog perhaps, trapped behind the door. He stepped towards it and took a deep breath, hoping he wouldn't have to defend himself from any protective canines, a Pit Bull or Doberman.

'Hello?' he said. 'Is someone in there?'

He tapped out 911 on the phone's keypad but stopped short of making the call. He reached for the handle and cracked the door ajar. Nothing growled or barked at him. He opened the door further.

A pair of cowboy boots was the first thing he saw. They were standing upright in the far corner, next to the toilet. Two stock-inged feet were splayed out next to them. There were two legs attached to the feet and a massive body attached to those legs. Rolly flipped on the light switch.

'Uhnnn!' said the man with the large body. He was handcuffed to base of the sink. There was a hood over the man's head and long black hair spilling out from beneath it.

'Daddy Joe?' said Rolly.

The man raised his head. He nodded. Rolly placed his crutches in the corner, hopped over to the toilet and took a seat. He placed Randy's phone on the edge of the sink.

'I'm a friend,' he said. 'I'm here with Macy.'

'Uhnnn,' the man said.

Rolly reached down and pulled the hood from the man's head. The man stared at Rolly, blinking his eyes as they burned with the light. His eyes were bloodshot and bleary, but in all other ways he was the man Macy had described, with long black hair and broad features. Rolly leaned down to peel off the duct tape that covered Daddy Joe's mouth. It was wet, covered in sweat and spittle and hard to grip. He gave up, leaned back on the toilet and picked his phone up from the sink.

'I'm calling the police,' he said, tapping the button. He looked out the door to the office. 'You'll be safe now.'

A shadow moved across the line of sunshine on the floor in the office near the back door. Someone fumbled at the lock. Rolly waited, expecting Dotty or Macy to open it. The latch clicked. Rolly stood up.

'Nine-one-one. What is your emergency?' said the operator, coming on line.

'Wait a minute,' said Rolly. He bolstered himself in the doorway. The shadow moved away from the door. He glanced at the door handle. There was a double-keyed bolt on the door.

'Do you wish to report an emergency?' the voice on his phone asked.

'Yes, an emergency,' Rolly said, putting the phone back up to his ear.

'Do you need police assistance?'

'I found a man here. I think he needs help.'

A bell tinkled on the other side of the wall. It was the bell inside the front door. Someone had entered the shop.

'Macy?' said Rolly. No one answered. 'Macy?'

'Someone's here,' Rolly said to the operator.

'Do you need an ambulance?'

'Yes, an ambulance and the police. He's going to kill us.'

'Can you describe your location, sir?'

'The Alien Artifacts store. El Cajon Boulevard off Fairmount. Please hurry.'

Rolly glanced down at Joe Harper, who stared back at him with unfocused eyes.

'Who's out there?' said Rolly. 'I called nine-one-one. The police will be here soon.'

There was a sound from the other side of the partition, muted electronic pings. Rolly jammed his crutches into the floor and hurried back towards the shop. He cut the corner too close and the left crutch jabbed into his ribs, knocking him into the display shelves. A collection of plastic *Doctor Who* figurines scattered across the floor. He stepped on one of the figurines, lost his footing and joined them on the floor. A steady beep emanated from the ceiling. He looked towards the front of the shop. Dotty stood by the door, watching him.

'I am blameless in this,' she said. She opened the door, stepped outside and keyed the lock.

Rolly stood up and steadied himself on the table. He heard the bolt set. Dotty walked past the front window and out of sight. He walked towards the door. The beeping continued. He reached for the latch but it had a double-keyed bolt, just like the back exit. The electronic countdown pitched higher. The alarm bell went off, a short ring, and the shop was silent. He was trapped. The police would arrive too late. Macy was gone.

TWENTY-TWO
The Interview

The San Diego Police Department's Mid-City station was attractive, for a police station. It looked new, both inside and out. In matters of government largess, the Mid-City neighborhood wasn't always treated as generously as other parts of Rolly's fair metropolis. He was glad to see his tax dollars had been spent on something regular folks could appreciate.

It was still a police station, though. On general rules of principle, Rolly preferred not to be in one. He greatly preferred not arriving at one in the back of a squad car with his arms handcuffed behind him. But that was how his day had gone. He'd have to put up with these inconveniences a while longer.

After finding himself locked inside the Alien Artifacts shop, he used Randy Parker's cell phone again to call emergency services again and update them on his situation. Unfortunately, the shop's alarm system had been equipped with infrared sensors. As soon as he pulled the phone from his pocket the alarm bell went off. It left him with the difficult task of explaining his situation to the emergency operator while the alarm bell rang in the background. Within five minutes, a squad car had arrived, followed shortly by firemen and paramedics.

The arresting officers were both polite and professional. One of them took notes as the other inspected the shop. The paramedics attended to Daddy Joe. The officers gave no indication they doubted Rolly's story, or suspected Rolly had anything to do with Daddy Joe's condition. They tried calling the owner of the business, but the owner's phone was, as Rolly explained to them, the same phone he'd used to call them. Now he sat in limbo at the attractive Mid-City Police station, waiting to find out if he would be spending another night in jail, hoping he would get to go home.

He shifted his weight in the hard plastic chair and closed his eyes to ward off the nervous jitter of the fluorescent lights. The police had taken his wallet and keys, as well as Randy's phone. No one seemed concerned he might be a flight risk. No one expected a paunchy forty-something on crutches to make a break for it. They were correct in their assumptions.

He heard a familiar voice, turned his head and spotted Bonnie speaking with the officer at the front desk. She glanced Rolly's way but didn't acknowledge him. A man in a coat and tie walked up to greet Bonnie. They spoke for a moment. The two of them walked over to Rolly. The man in the coat crossed his arms.

Bonnie looked down at him. 'Breaking and entering, huh?' she said.

'I entered. I didn't break,' Rolly said.

'I hear they had to break in to get you out. That some white-haired lady got the drop on you?'

'I'm not particularly agile right now,' Rolly said, indicating the crutches.

Bonnie picked up his crutches. 'Where'd you get these?' she asked.

'I got bit by a black widow spider. Wanna see?'

'I asked where you got them, not why.'

'Brawley General Hospital. It's in the desert, north of El Centro.'

'I know where Brawley is. What were you doing out there?'

'I was working. On a case.'

'For this Macy Starr woman? She's your client?'

Rolly nodded.

'You say Macy ran after the old lady,' said Bonnie.

'Dotty,' said the man in the suit.

'Dotty,' said Bonnie. 'Macy chased after this Dotty and left you holding the bag.'

'I don't think Macy had anything to do with my getting locked inside.'

'You sure about that?'

'There had to be someone else there.'

'Who?'

'The man who tied up Daddy Joe. The one I met two days ago. The ex-con who pretended to be Randy Parker.'

'What makes you think he wasn't Randy Parker?'

'I think Randy Parker is dead.'

The man in the tie and coat exchanged glances with Bonnie. 'We better record this,' he said.

Bonnie nodded. 'C'mon,' she said, handing Rolly his crutches.

'What's going on?' Rolly asked.

'I'll explain in a minute.'

Rolly climbed out of his chair and followed the man in the coat and tie down the hallway. Bonnie followed behind them. The man walked into a room with a small table and some chairs and closed the door behind them. He asked Rolly to take a seat on the opposite side of the table and seated himself. Bonnie pulled up another chair across from Rolly. The man in the suit pushed a red button on the table.

'Detective John Creach interviewing Roland Waters,' he said. 'Assisted by Sergeant Bonnie Hammond.'

'Are you arresting me?' Rolly asked.

'Please state your name, for the record,' said Detective Creach.

'Roland Waters,' said Rolly. 'What's this about?'

'Mr Waters,' said Detective Creach. 'Are you acquainted with Randy Parker, proprietor of the Alien Artifacts shop at 5424 El Cajon Boulevard?'

'I met someone who claimed to be him. At the store.'

'You don't believe this man was Mr Parker?'

'Not any more.'

'Can you describe the man?'

'He was an older guy – older than me anyway. Kind of tough looking, in good shape for his age. Muscular. Taller than me.'

'How tall would you say?'

'Six-two, six-three.'

'Hair color?'

'Black. I think it's a dye job, though. Or a wig.'

'Eyes?'

Rolly shrugged. 'He had sunglasses on.'

'Any other distinctive features?'

'He had tattoos on his arms and neck. One was a watch, without any hands.'

Someone knocked on the door. A young woman entered the room. She handed a large envelope to Creach.

'Thank you, Denise,' said Creach. The woman left. Creach opened the envelope and pulled out some photographs. He passed one over to Rolly.

'Is this the man you met at the store?' he asked. Rolly looked at the photo – a young man in his early twenties.

'No,' Rolly said.

'Do you recognize the man in this photo?'

'It looks like Randy No Pants,' said Rolly. 'I saw him talking to Macy in Slab City.'

'We heard they were arguing.'

'It was an animated discussion.'

'Do you know what they were discussing?'

'He told Macy he'd met someone who knew her parents. He wanted her to go with him.'

'Where?'

'To the hot springs.'

'In Slab City?'

'Look, I know all about this. I know Randy No Pants drowned. I know Macy found him. We went through all this with the detective from Imperial County. Kinnie Harper was there.'

'Yes, we know. Sergeant Hammond has talked to Chief Harper.'

'So why are you asking me about this stuff?'

Creach picked up the photo and inspected it. 'Would it surprise you if I told you this was a photo of Randy Parker?'

'Two days ago, yes. But not now.'

'This is not the man you talked to in the store?'

'No,' said Rolly. He was tired of hearing himself answer the same questions. 'I started to think that Randy Parker and Randy No Pants might be the same person, which meant the guy I talked to in the shop wasn't Randy Parker. That's why I went there with Macy. I wanted to talk to Dotty and find out for sure.'

'What did this Dotty woman say?'

'Not much.'

'You remember anything specific from your conversation?'

'She said she was blameless.'

'Blameless for what?'

Rolly shrugged. 'Blameless in all of this, that's what she said.'

'Do you have any idea what she meant by that?'

'No idea,' he said. 'She was into this alien stuff. The Randy guy was too. They were looking for a one-string guitar owned by the UVTs.'

Detective Creach looked over at Bonnie. She nodded.

Creach handed Rolly another photo – a mugshot. 'You recognize this man?' he said. Rolly nodded. 'That's him,' he said. 'The man in the store. Who is he?'

'His name's Parnell Gibbons.'

'Uh huh.'

'You've never heard of him?'

'I think Kinnie Harper mentioned his name to me earlier.'

Bonnie cleared her throat.

'What?' said Rolly.

'C'mon,' she said. 'You really don't know who this guy is?'

'No. Kinnie said something about Daddy Joe arresting him.'

'This lady at the store talked to you about the Universal Vibration Technologies, right? The UVTs?'

'Yeah. They were this UFO cult who thought they were aliens in human form – something like that. Macy told me they drank this gold soup. That it was poisoned and that's why they died. I guess this Gibbons guy had something to do with it. Randy Parker's parents were there. They died with the rest. Kinnie showed me the memorial. Near the reservation.'

'What's this guitar thing?' said Creach. 'The diddley whatsis?'

'Diddley bow.'

'You say they were looking for one?'

'A friend of mine runs a guitar shop. Rob Norwood. This guy was in there, gave him Randy Parker's business card, said he'd pay good money if Rob could find him a special kind of diddley bow. It has something to do with the UVTs, I guess. Kinnie showed me a crime-scene photo. There was a whole rack of them in the back. Kinnie said she remembered the UVTs playing these things out on the mesa when she was a kid.'

'Anything else?'

'Daddy Joe purchased a diddley bow from the sheriff's property auction. He was looking for one that was built by a guy Rob and I used to know. The guy worked up at Guitar Trader a long time ago. His initials are on the back. B-M, for Buddy Meeks.'

Detective Creach wrote the name down. 'Parnell Gibbons was released a few days ago. From Calipatria State Prison.'

Rolly remembered a road sign just north of Brawley. Calipatria State Prison. On the way to Slab City.

'Macy said Randy Parker went to see someone in Calipatria. He said it was his brother.'

'Mr Parker was a regular visitor at the prison,' said Creach. He shuffled through some papers. 'He talked to Gibbons many times over the last year.'

'What was Gibbons in for?' said Rolly.

'Manslaughter and embezzlement,' said Creach. 'Multiple counts.'

'He killed those people,' said Bonnie. 'Gibbons purchased the poison. The D.A. didn't think they could convince a jury the poisoning wasn't accidental so they charged him with manslaughter.'

Rolly rested his elbows on the table and put his hands over his face. 'You think Gibbons killed Randy?' he said.

'We'll wait to see what the coroner out in Imperial has to say,' said Creach. 'Intentional drowning is tough to prove, unless there's some kind of a struggle. There's some marks on the body that suggest he might have been shocked with a stungun. Joe Harper has similar marks on his body.'

'So do I,' said Rolly.

'Excuse me?' said Creach. Rolly turned around in his chair and lifted his shirt, exposing the two brown dots on his lower back. He turned back to the table.

'When did this happen?' said Bonnie.

'The other night, after we played the casino, at this place called Desert View Tower.'

Bonnie clenched her jaw and gave him her blue-eyed beam-of-death look. That was all she could do with Creach there and the recording machine going. He would get an earful later.

'Did you report this incident to anyone?' she said.

'I told Kinnie about it. Except for the stungun part.'

Creach looked through his papers for something. He found it.

'Joe Harper's car was found near there,' he said. 'Off the In-Ko-Pah exit.'

'Yes. I talked to Kinnie about that too. I saw his car that morning driving away from us.'

'You saw Joe Harper in it?'

'No. I couldn't see who was driving. It was an old blue Toyota. I saw it about a hundred feet from us, pulling out from this secondary road. We were parked near the gate.'

Creach made a note.

'Has anyone seen this Gibbons guy since he got out?' asked Rolly. 'Did anyone see him in Slab City?'

'No witnesses, so far,' said Creach. 'Did Macy Starr ever mention his name?'

'No.'

'But you believe Macy Starr was taken by force?'

'I don't know. She ran out after the woman, Dotty. That was the last time I saw her.'

'You think it's possible she ran out on you?' said Bonnie.

Rolly slumped back in his chair. Anything was possible at this point. 'What about Dotty?' he said. 'What's she got to do with this guy? Why did she keep saying she was blameless?'

'We're working on something,' said Bonnie.

'What?'

'Too soon,' said Bonnie. 'First we need you to tell us more about your case.'

'Like what?'

'How about everything?'

Rolly closed his eyes and rubbed his temples. It came out in a rush. He told them everything he could remember about Macy, the photo of Aunt Betty and Eric Ozzie on the back of the diddley bow, Cool Bob and the bird-calling gravel thrower, and the schematic he'd found in the maps display at Desert View Tower.

Bonnie and Creach let him run. He told them about TEOTWAYKI and the Astral Vibrator, about Daddy Joe and his files and the mysterious beeping phone calls. He purged his memory, vomited up everything in his brain. It kept him from vomiting up whatever was left in his stomach. He felt better when it was done. He leaned back and opened his eyes. Bonnie and Creach both stared at him. It was a lot of information to take in. He hoped they could make more sense out of it than he could.

TWENTY-THREE
The Patents

Rolly parked the Tioga at the Rite Aid in Hillcrest and walked to his house. Negotiating his own driveway in the motorhome seemed like too fine a task to attempt in his present condition. Backing it out would be even more problematic. No spaces of sufficient size were available on his street, but there was plenty of room in the drugstore's parking lot. Security services wouldn't call for a tow unless the Tioga had been there for more than twelve hours.

He opened the door to his house. Everything looked clean and neat, more so than when he left. His mother had been there, doing her bit in his time of duress. He sat down on the sofa. His phone rang. 'Hey,' he said, answering.

'Where you been, Brother Waters?' said Marley.

'Talking to cops,' said Rolly.

'Having an enlightened conversation with our local constabulary?'

'Something like that.'

'Everything copacetic?'

'We worked some things out. I'm at home now. What's up?'

'I found a patent abstract for the Astral Vibrator thing. There's a couple of names listed; thought you might want to hear them.'

'This would be the guys who invented it?'

'There're two names on the filing. I think the first one's the real inventor. I searched on his name after I found it. He's got three other patents.'

'What's his name?'

'Buddy Meeks. Ever heard of him?'

'Yeah. He was a guitar tech at a shop here in town. He made the diddley bow I told you about.'

'Well, other than the Astral Vibrator, the guy has patents on something called an Astrotuner and something called a Melodylocker.'

'Sounds like they might be guitar effects.'

'Irie, my friend. It's in the patent abstract, that's like the general description you have to fill out when you're filing a patent. You have to provide an abstract. All of this guy's patents are for processing audio signals. Let me read you the one for the Astral Vibrator.'

'Wait a sec,' said Rolly. He moved to the table and grabbed his notepad and pen. 'OK.'

'Here goes,' said Marley. 'The Astral Vibrator is a physical locking device for security systems. It utilizes a pitch-based system for encoding and decoding physical locking mechanisms via vibration-tuned tumblers.'

'What the hell does that mean?'

'My best guess is it uses special frequencies to unlock things. Could be a padlock or a deadbolt. So maybe you'd use this system instead of a physical key. Like instead of a keypad, you maybe have a beeper or something, and it opens the lock for you.'

Rolly made some notes. *Locks. Frequencies.*

'What's the other name on the patent?'

'I think the other guy's his business partner or something. Not a techie.'

'What makes you say that?'

'Well, on the Astrotuner, which is the patent previous to the Astral Vibrator, this guy only shows up on the revised patent. He shows up on all the revised patents, actually.'

'Revised patents . . . that's like a new version?'

'Could be. Or it could be you're just re-assigning the patent, if you sold it or something. Like if you sold half your company to somebody, you might give them fifty percent on all previous patents.'

'Is that what the other guy gets, fifty percent?'

'Ninety percent.'

'Ninety?'

'Guess he drove a hard bargain.'

'Did you find this guy's name anywhere else?'

'No. That's it. This guy never shows up on anything else. That's what I mean about this Buddy Meeks being the real inventor. This other guy's money, or management.'

'What's the guy's name?'

'Parnell Gibbons.'

'Say that again?' Rolly said, making sure he'd heard Marley correctly.

'Par-nell Gib-bons,' said Marley, accenting each syllable. 'You heard of him?'

'Yeah. I've heard of him,' Rolly said. 'He just got out of jail. The police showed me a photograph.'

'What was he in for?' said Marley. 'Embezzlement? Larceny?'

'He was part of an alien cult,' Rolly said.

'Loopy-Doopy and Crooky, huh?'

'Worse than that,' Rolly said. He rubbed his temples. 'They got him on manslaughter. Seventeen people died.'

'This wasn't that Rancho Bernardo thing, was it?'

'No, this was out in East County. In the mountains. Twenty years ago.'

'Before I arrived in this fair land.'

'I don't remember anything about it.'

'You could probably Google it.'

'Yeah. That's what everybody keeps telling me. I haven't had time.'

'I downloaded a .pdf of the Astral Vibrator patent. The schematic looks just like the one you gave me. You want me to email it to you?'

'Yeah, I guess.'

'You sound kinda beat.'

'I've felt better.'

'Stay strong, bredren.'

'Thanks.'

Rolly hung up his phone. He looked out the kitchen window to his mother's house and decided he should check in with her – let her know he was home. The last time they'd spoken he was about to be locked up in jail on the Jincona reservation. He needed to check in with Alicia, too – perhaps visit his father in the hospital. It was hard to keep up with family obligations when you were getting arrested all the time.

His phone rang again. There was no name displayed but the number looked familiar. His stomach tightened. He tapped the answer button and held the phone to his ear. The beeping tones played, followed by silence. The tones played again.

'Who is this?' he said. The tones continued to play, over and over, in the same order. He counted them: nine notes in the pattern. He hung up and checked the phone number again. He called Bonnie and left a message, telling her what had happened. He gave her the phone number for the beeper. If she hadn't looked it up already, it might prompt her to move it up on her priority list. Randy and Macy and Daddy Joe had all received calls from that number before they went missing. He didn't like being next one on the list.

Someone knocked on the door. Rolly jumped. He looked for something he could use as a weapon. He picked up his phone, ready to dial 911. There was another knock. The door opened.

'It's me,' said his mother, peeking around the door. 'Are you here?'

'Come in, Mom,' said Rolly, dropping his shoulders. 'I made it back.'

His mother closed the door and stood looking at him. She gave a weak smile. 'I talked to Max earlier,' she said. 'He said you got out this morning.'

'They let us both go.'

'I thought you'd be home sooner.'

'Sorry I didn't call. Still had some work to do.'

'How's your leg?'

'Better. I don't think I'll need the crutches tomorrow.'

His mother looked at the room for a moment, then back at him. 'How old is that Macy woman?' she said. 'She seems rather young for you.'

Rolly rubbed his forehead. 'She's in trouble, Mom. And it's my fault.'

'Is she pregnant?'

'No, no. I think she's been abducted. And I led her right into it.'

'Oh my goodness? Did you call the police?'

'I've just had a long talk with them. Bonnie was there.'

'I'm sure Bonnie will take care of it,' said his mother, as if finding a kidnapper was like paying off an overdue bill. 'It's been a quite a week.'

'Yes, it has.'

'Do you plan on getting arrested again?'

'I don't really plan on it. That's just the way it works out sometimes, depending on the case. I wasn't really arrested.'

'What do you call it, then?'

'Just having a conversation with our local constabulary,' he said, repeating Marley's line. 'Being held for questioning, maybe. Not arrested.'

'Do you remember how you used to say you were "just having a drink"?'

'This is different.'

'I hope so,' she said. She sat down at the table. His mother was at least four inches shorter than Rolly but she always seemed taller when she put on her concerned face.

'I'd hate to think you were developing a weakness for jail-houses,' she said. 'Or anything else.'

'I haven't been drinking. Or "just having a drink".'

'This job of yours seems rather stressful, and, well . . . dangerous.'

'It's not usually like this.'

'You had that man in your house a few years ago, remember? The police had to come. And there was that little Mexican girl who showed up last year. I had to stay with the neighbors that night. I worry about you.'

'How's dad doing?' said Rolly, trying to change the subject.

His mother furrowed her eyebrows and smoothed her dress. 'Your father is about as I expected,' she said. 'Back to his old unpleasantness.'

'He's feeling better then?'

'Alicia's beside herself. You really should talk to him.'

'I will,' said Rolly, hoping to end the conversation. 'After I get through this.'

'I like her, you know,' said his mother.

'Alicia's OK.'

'I meant your girlfriend. What's her name?'

'Macy. She's not . . .'

'Those tattoos, I don't know about that. All the young people seem to have them these days. But that Macy's got spirit. There's a sparkle about her. I read her flyer there, for the nightclub. I hope it's OK. I came in and cleaned up for you.'

'You didn't have to do that.'

'Things have changed so much from when I was a girl. I married your father so young. I never blamed him. We were both young. I thought it would be romantic, being a Navy wife.'

Rolly slumped into his chair. He'd heard the litany before. It was the Navy. It was the times. His mother stopped herself. Macy's flyer was still on the table. She picked it up and read it over.

'Is that her real name?' she asked. 'Macy Starr?'

'As far as I know,' he said. 'She was adopted. That's why she hired me to find her parents. She grew up on that reservation.'

'Yes, you told me.'

'The woman who arrested us, Kinnie Harper, was like her older sister. They grew up together. Kinnie's parents adopted Macy, but the mother died. Kinnie took over the household.'

'That must have been rather difficult, for both of them.'

'Macy hated it out there. She says she never fit in.'

'You really think she was kidnapped? Who was it?'

'There's this ex-con involved. His name's Parnell Gibbons. The police showed me a photo. He just got out of jail.'

'Why was he in jail?'

'It's got something to do with this cult that lived up there near the reservation. Some people were poisoned. This was about twenty years ago. They think he did it.'

'Oh, dear,' said his mother. 'I was afraid of that. I had an intuition, driving through the reservation, when I had to leave you in jail. It felt like I'd been there before.'

'What's that?'

'It was the Universal Vibration people, wasn't it?'

Rolly sat up in his chair. 'You know about the UVTs?' he said. His mother inspected the fingernails on her left hand.

'Of course, dear,' said his mother. 'I went and visited them. I thought you and I might live there for a while.'

'When was this?'

'After your father and I separated, of course – after we moved out of the house. I needed something. I had no one to turn to.'

'But Mom, I mean . . . aliens?'

'It's not that far-fetched, you know, dear. I was just reading today about these new planets the scientists have discovered with that Hubble telescope. There are thousands of them out there that could support life. And it's science people, real scientists, you know, saying this now.'

'Instead of crackpots.'

'They were nice people, the ones that I met. I thought you might enjoy the musical aspects of their teachings.'

'They were a cult. Everyone died.'

'Yes, I'm aware of that, dear. I'm alive. I didn't join them. I just stopped by to find out what it was all about. I didn't stay.'

'Did you ever want to?'

'I only went up to their camp that one time. Something wasn't right. I could feel it.'

'What do you mean?'

'I don't know exactly – something unhappy I felt there. I had you to take care of. I wanted to make sure you got to live your own life. It didn't feel right.'

They fell silent. Rolly's phone rang. He checked the screen. It wasn't Bonnie. It wasn't the beeper. The phone number had a local area code but there was no name. His mother gave him a wan smile, indicating it was OK for him to take the call. She looked tired. He answered the phone. 'Hello,' he said.

'Mr Waters?' said a man's voice.

'Yes, who is this?'

'This is Eric Ozzie, Mr Waters.'

'I talked to Kinnie Harper,' said Rolly.

'Who?'

'Daddy Joe's daughter.'

'I want to explain.'

'OK. I'm listening.'

'In person. Can we meet?'

'Now?'

Ozzie didn't respond. Rolly waited.

'Max Gemeinhardt is here,' said Ozzie. 'He tells me you live close by.'

'Why is Max at your house?'

'Max is my lawyer too.'

'Oh.'

'She's my sister, Mr Waters. The girl in the photograph is my sister.'

TWENTY-FOUR
The Sneaker

Eric Ozzie lived at the end of a cul-de-sac overlooking the wide end of Mission Valley, where the San Diego River widened into saltwater marshes and surrendered its meager waters to the Pacific Ocean. The house was an early twentieth-century mansion set in the hills behind the Spanish Presidio, as large as you might expect for a retired professional baseball player, but no larger. Max Gemeinhardt sat at the head of the table when Ozzie escorted Rolly into the dining room.

'Hey,' said Max.

'Hey,' said Rolly. 'What's going on?'

'All in good time,' said Max.

'Have a seat, Mr Waters,' said Ozzie. 'Can I get you a drink? I've got a Macallan 18.'

'Club soda if you have it,' said Rolly, not exactly sure what a Macallan 18 was. It sounded expensive. People with money never served bourbon, Scotch or vodka. It was always a brand or a label, sometimes a year.

'Pellegrino OK?' said Ozzie. Rolly nodded. Rich people used proper names for their carbonated water, as well.

Ozzie retreated to the kitchen to retrieve Rolly's drink. A large photo album sat on the dining-room table in front of Max. Rolly took a seat to the right of Max and resisted the urge to open the cover of the album and leaf through it. The album was there for a reason. It would be part of the show.

Ozzie returned with Rolly's Pellegrino and some sort of brown liquor on ice for himself. Max already had a beer. Ozzie sat down on Max's left, across the table from Rolly. He took a sip of his drink and placed the glass back on the table. He looked at Rolly, then stared down at the table as he spoke. 'Thank you for coming,' he said. 'Max is here as my lawyer, but also as a witness to what I'm about to tell you.'

Rolly turned to Max. 'You knew about this when I called you?'

'Yes and no,' said Max. 'I was afraid it might come to this.'

'You could have saved me a lot of trouble.'

'I couldn't say anything,' said Max. 'Not without Eric's permission.'

Rolly knew Max had done the right thing. He turned back to Ozzie. 'Why didn't you tell me she was your sister?'

'It was a shock, Mr Waters, to see that photograph. I couldn't understand how you were able to get it. Why it was on the back of that instrument. Joe Harper and I had an arrangement, you see.'

'Daddy Joe's in the hospital. The police are involved. Another man died.'

'What was his name, the man who died?'

'His name's Randy Parker. He runs a shop called Alien Artifacts.'

'That is disturbing,' said Ozzie. He took another sip of whisky and set his other hand on top of the photo album.

'Mr Parker was here,' he said. 'About a month ago. He claimed he was writing a book. It's been so long now, I wasn't sure I could tell him much. I never knew all that much, really. He insisted.'

'He wanted to talk to you about the UVTs?'

Ozzie nodded. 'My mother and sister were there,' he said. 'My mother died with the rest of them.'

'I saw her name on the memorial. I'm sorry.'

'It was my first year in the majors. My first real money. I was so focused on making the team. It was overwhelming. I couldn't save either of them – my mother or sister.'

'What was your sister's name?'

'Can I show you something?' said Ozzie as he opened the photo album. Rolly glanced over at Max. Max closed his eyes, scratched his beard. He didn't object.

'OK,' said Rolly.

Ozzie found the page he wanted. He slid the album back across the table to Rolly. The page he'd selected had a photograph of a group of teenage girls. They were standing on the porch of a house. It was the house Kinnie had driven him by only yesterday.

'This is Beatrice House, isn't it?' said Rolly.

'That's right,' said Ozzie. 'Beatrice. Betty, we called her.'

'It's named for your sister?'

Ozzie nodded. Rolly studied the faces of the girls, searching for Betty's face. Or Macy's.

'Is Betty in this picture?' he said.

'No, but she's the reason it could be taken.'

Rolly rubbed his forehead, just above his right eyebrow, massaging his head to keep his brains from falling out. Betty had appeared again, and vanished as quickly.

'What happened?' he said.

'I grew up around here, you know,' said Ozzie. 'In San Diego, but not in this part of town. I grew up in a hard part of the city. My parents were pretty messed up. We never had a home for long. My father couldn't keep a job because of his drinking. Both of my parents were alcoholics. We lived on the streets for a while.'

Rolly nodded.

'My father was killed one night, by some junky. He'd taken our spot under the overpass. I was twelve when it happened.'

'I'm sorry.'

'In a weird way, it saved me. My mom cleaned herself up after that. For a while. She took us into social services, got us lodging at St Vincent's. They found her a job, got me enrolled in school again. That's when I started to play baseball. I was always good at sports, you know, but I only played pick-up games before that. Someone at the shelter gave me a new glove, that Christmas, when they gave all the kids toys.'

Ozzie took another sip from his whisky glass and wiped his mouth. 'I guess you could say the rest is history. I got on the JV team at high school the next year and moved up to varsity halfway through my first year. Baseball became my whole life. Coach Sullivan kept me going. I got drafted out of high school, which was good, 'cause I woulda had a hard time in college. Double-A first, then to Hawaii for a year and a half before I got called up to the majors.'

'That's where the picture was taken?' said Rolly. 'Betty came to Hawaii?'

'They both did,' said Ozzie. 'I paid for their tickets. My mom and Betty. That's when I first heard about the UVTs. I thought it was weird stuff, but at least my mother was sober. She said she owed it to these UVT people, how'd they helped her see the power inside her, this golden alien thing. Betty seemed happy too. I figured it was better for them to believe in aliens and have a place to stay than it was being out on the street. I gave them some money. I wasn't seeing much yet, but I did what I could. It was later that I found out all the money I sent home went straight into the UVTs bank account. And then into gold.'

Ozzie paused and took another drink. The ice clinked in his glass. He tapped his fingers on the table. Rolly rubbed his sternum.

'So Betty was there too?' he said. 'With your mother and the UVTs?'

'Yes.'

'Why isn't her name on the memorial?'

'My sister was as much a victim as the others, just not at the same time.'

'Who else knows?'

Ozzie stood up. 'I think I'll freshen my drink,' he said. 'You want anything?'

Rolly shook his head. Ozzie went into the kitchen, got a new cube of ice and poured another shot of the Macallan 18. He returned to the table.

'I didn't even know what had happened until two days after they died,' he said. 'We were on a road trip, in Houston, my first year in the majors. I was batting one-ninety-seven, stinking it up. I heard a couple of the coaches talking about something they saw in the paper. Gave me this sick feeling inside. They showed me the article. I took some days off and flew back to San Diego. Identified my mother's body. That made the papers, too. The sportswriters knew me because of my prep days. I stayed at Coach Sullivan's house. That's where he called me.'

'Who?'

'Chief Harper. He'd figured it out. That she was my sister.'

'Betty was alive, then?'

Ozzie nodded. 'He asked if I'd like to see her, that we could avoid the press and the police. I wanted to make sure it was really her. He gave me directions to his place, this little house on a canyon, out there near that tower thing that looks over the desert.'

'Desert View Tower,' said Rolly.

'You know the place?'

'I had a meeting with someone there just the other night.'

Ozzie gave Rolly a funny look, as if Rolly were joking.

'So you know there's pretty much nothing out there,' he said. 'Chief Harper had my sister with him in the house. He said we could keep her out of the limelight, away from the police and the papers. He was married. He seemed like a good man. We came to an agreement.'

'Daddy Joe adopted your sister?'

'Betty, you see, she had challenges. She was kind of simple-minded. She couldn't really take care of herself. I thought I might have to put her in an institution or something. It seemed worth it just to give Chief Harper some money to keep her out of the way until the season was over and I had more time to figure out what I wanted to do.'

'How long did this last?'

'He called me a month later. He told me she was gone, that she had run away from their house one day. He promised to find her. I took him at his word. Chief Harper behaved like an honorable, decent man. He called me, once a week, then once a month. Later, we only spoke once a year.'

'Did you ever find out what happened to your sister?'

'Chief Harper had lots of theories, I guess, but none of them seemed to lead anywhere. I'd pretty much given up finding her, dead or alive. Then you showed me that photograph. All sorts of thoughts ran through my mind. I thought it might be some kind of extortion scheme you were running.'

'I understand.'

'My sister's disappearance haunts me, Mr Waters, even more so than my mother's death. I was young. I was under a great deal of pressure. I made an expedient choice instead of a wise one.'

Rolly rubbed his chin and looked over at Max. 'Did you know about this?'

'I didn't know the whole story until yesterday,' said Max. 'I helped Eric set up the trust for Beatrice House, so his name wasn't attached. I knew he named it after his sister, but I didn't know what had happened to her. Wasn't my business, really. We were able to get some money to the UVTs' relatives by buying the place.'

'When was this?'

'Maybe two years after the UVTs event. After the criminal trial there was a civil case against the lady who started the whole thing.

One guy had gone to jail, but she was the one who owned the house. She had to sell the house to pay for the judgement. Eric came to me, asked if there was some way he could buy the house without the newspapers finding out. I set up a charitable trust. He put in the money and we bought the property. We set up a non-profit and folded the home into it.'

Ozzie took the photo album back and leafed through it. 'These are my girls, you know. I'm taking care of them, helping them get through a tough time. I didn't do right by my sister, but I can help these girls, give them a chance.'

Rolly nodded. It was nice to know all this, but he wasn't sure it was going to help him find Macy. He pulled Macy's flyer out of his pocket and placed it in front of Ozzie. 'Have you ever seen this woman?' he asked.

'Not in person,' said Ozzie. 'I've seen her picture before, though.'

'Where?'

Max cleared his throat. Ozzie looked over at him. Max twisted his lips to one side and nodded. Ozzie left the table. He returned in a moment. 'Randy Parker gave this to me,' he said, placing another copy of Macy's flyer on the table. 'He asked if I knew this woman, just like you did.'

'What else did he say?'

'He seemed very interested in that charm around her neck.'

Rolly took the flyer from Ozzie.

'There's something on the back,' said Ozzie.

Rolly flipped the flyer over. TEOTWAYKI. 'Do you know what this means?' he said.

'I didn't before Mr Parker told me. How did he die?'

'He drowned, at these hot springs out in the desert. The police are investigating. They haven't ruled anything out. Macy was there.'

'They think she killed him?'

'I have to tell you this, Mr Ozzie: Macy thinks she may be Betty's daughter. Do you have any reason to believe that's possible?'

'I never heard anything about Betty having a baby. But . . . well, I noticed those eyes. I got a little of that gold in my eyes. My sister Betty had even more.'

'What else did Randy ask you?' said Rolly. 'Why did he come to talk to you?'

'He told me about his business, how he collected and sold UVT stuff. He said it was urgent he find some things of theirs soon.'

'Did he say why it was urgent?'

'He just said our time was getting short. There was some event happening.'

'The Conjoinment? Is that what he meant?'

Ozzie's phone rang. He reached in his pocket, pulled it out and answered it. A puzzled look came over his face. He hung up. 'I hate that,' he said.

'What?' said Rolly.

'You know, when there's just a bunch of beeping sounds, like a computer.'

TWENTY-FIVE
The Blog

There was a dim light on in his mother's house when Rolly got home. He changed his clothes, grabbed his composition book, slipped into a pair of hard-soled slippers he kept by the door and scrunched across the gravel driveway to his mother's back door. He needed to return her car keys and borrow her computer. He tapped on the door – two short taps, repeated three times. It was the same way he always knocked – a coded knock so she'd know it was him. He tried the door. It was locked. He found her house key on the ring with the car key, opened the door and stepped into the kitchen.

'Mom?' he said. 'It's me. I'm returning your keys.'

He continued on through the kitchen and into the dining room, where he found his mother sitting at the table, the ghostly glow of her laptop computer illuminating her face.

'Mom?' Rolly said, keeping his voice low.

'Hello, dear,' she said, without turning to look at him. 'Are you all right?'

'Sure,' he said. 'I'm fine. I wanted to use the computer.'

'I was looking up some things,' said his mother.

'It won't take long.'

'I should take a break, anyway,' she said, rising from the table. 'Can I get you some tea? I think I'll make chamomile.'

'Sure,' Rolly said.

'Chamomile's very soothing. For the nerves. I know I could use some.'

'That would be nice.'

His mother stood looking at him, as if she had something on her mind. 'I was reading about them,' she said. 'That's why it's on the screen.'

'Who?'

'The Universal Vibration Technologists. The UVTs.'

'Oh.'

'I couldn't sleep. I felt very agitated after we talked. It was a terrible thing that happened to them. That man you told me about, I remembered him. The one they arrested.'

'Parnell Gibbons?'

'He was quite imposing.'

'You met him?'

'Oh, yes. I think that's what gave me such unease when I visited. There was a kind of animal magnetism to him. Something dark under the surface. Very controlling. Of course, I'd just left your father, so I was hyper-aware of alpha male controlling behaviors.'

'Dad didn't start any cults,' said Rolly. If there was one thing his mother was hyper-aware of, it was pop psychology catchphrases.

'His cult was the U.S. Navy, dear,' said his mother. 'Giving orders. You've seen how he behaves when he gets around his buddies. Always making sure he's captain of the ship.'

'Dad likes to be in charge, I'll give you that.'

'Well, anyway, I left the article up there on the screen. Since you're involved with these people, you might want to read it.'

His mother went into the kitchen. It was a surprise to Rolly that there had been an event in his mother's life that she hadn't told him about. She'd dragged him to so many things when he was a teenager, from yoga sessions to music appreciation classes to lectures by mumbling dolts who thought that sending postcards would lead to world peace. It was his mother's revenge, of a sort, on his father, after the divorce. Rolly's father never wanted to go anywhere. He only cared about three things: his country, his Navy and his bourbon. The order of those allegiances changed daily, but his father remained consistent on general principles. He expected others to honor them. Dean Waters didn't want his wife attending yoga classes or his son playing the electric guitar.

Rolly sat down in front of the laptop and looked at the article his mother had been reading. He scrolled to the top of the page. It was Randy Parker's blog, also called Alien Artifacts. He read the article on screen about the trial and subsequent incarceration of Parnell Gibbons. It didn't answer all his questions but it filled in a few gaps.

The UVTs had all died from drinking their morning soup – the gold soup, as Macy had described it. Except on that particular morning, the soup had somehow been laced with sodium cyanide. There were two known survivors: Parnell Gibbons and a woman named Dorothy Coasters. Gibbons went to jail. He'd worked as a professional exterminator, killing rats and vermin. A purchase receipt he'd signed for sodium cyanide was the key evidence against him, as well as Dorothy's testimony that Gibbons had embezzled money from the organization.

The circumstances of Gibbons' arrest went against him, as well, though anyone who had just found seventeen people dead might be expected to panic. Gibbons had been pulled over in his car, heading for the Mexican border at Tecate. Found in the car with him was a tote bag filled with one-ounce gold bars worth about thirty thousand dollars at the time. Gibbons offered the gold to the arresting officer, under the impression that tribal policemen were underpaid dupes. The arresting officer was Sergeant Joe Harper. The bribe didn't work. Rolly made a note in his composition book.

In his initial deposition, Gibbons claimed that two other members of the UVT group had been responsible for the poisonings. Neither of those people had ever been found, dead or alive. The first was a young black woman Gibbons claimed had been with him when he was arrested. Officer Joe Harper denied Gibbons' claim on the witness stand. The jury found Daddy Joe to be a more creditable witness than Gibbons. Daddy Joe had turned down the bribe, after all.

Gibbons also claimed that he'd purchased the cyanide at the request of another member, a man named Buddy Meeks.

According to Gibbons, Meeks had asked him to purchase the sodium cyanide solution in order to process gold ore from other rocks and minerals they found in an old gold mine near the property. The use of sodium cyanide for this purpose was well known and accepted among gold miners. Gibbons testified that he and Meeks had explored the old mine together, looking for ways the UVTs might use it. Rolly made another note in his composition book.

At the end of the page there was a link to the next article – *Alien Gold?* Rolly clicked on the link and read through the page. Parnell's testimony, as well as the gold he had on him when he was arrested, became the subject of much speculation in the years following the trial. UVT members had sold off their personal possessions and transferred the proceeds to the bank account Gibbons had set up, but the numbers didn't add up. Gibbons had drawn on the account and converted the cash into gold, but estimates put it well above the amount of gold he had been carrying with him. His tales of the old mine inspired more speculation. There were rumors of a secret hiding place in the mountains, a designated safe spot where the UVTs would wait for the looming arrival of their alien brethren. There were documents found at the scene indicating the members were planning on leaving, and a list of items with each member's name above it had been found at the communal table. They'd been used as evidence by Parnell's defense team, who suggested the UVTs knew exactly what they were doing when they drank the fatal doses of cyanide.

Rolly's mother called to him from the kitchen. 'Your tea is ready,' she said.

Rolly got up from the table and walked into the kitchen. His mother had laid out a plate of cookies to go with the tea. They looked like cookies anyway – a chocolate color pressed into round cookie shapes. Rolly could never be sure what his mother had brought home from the natural food stores. He tried one of the cookies. It tasted like raw honey mixed with an indeterminate root vegetable, perhaps beets. It wasn't bad, but it wasn't anything like chocolate.

He sat down at the table and stared at the steam from his tea mug, waiting for it to cool.

'You look tired, dear,' said his mother.

'I guess I am.'

His mother picked up the plate and offered it to him. 'Have another one,' she said. He took one of the not-chocolate round things and chewed on it. It gave him something to do while he stared at his tea.

'That man, Parnell Gibbons,' he said. 'The leader of the UVTs?'

'He wasn't really their leader,' said his mother. 'Not spiritually. There was that woman. I found her quite fascinating. It was really her theories, you know, about the tones and the frequencies. She came up with the original vibration technologies. I found the precepts quite compelling. If it hadn't been for that horrible man I might have stayed.'

'What did she look like?'

'Beautiful corn silk hair and a radiant smile. She was wearing a long purple dress the day I went up there.'

The so-called cookie felt like sawdust in Rolly's mouth. He swallowed it and looked over at his mother. 'Do you remember her name?'

'D something, I think it was.'

'Dorothy Coasters?'

'No, that wasn't it. It was similar.'

'Dotty? Did anyone call her Dotty?'

'Now that you mention it, I think they did.'

Rolly nodded and blew on his tea. It was still too hot to drink. His phone rang. It was Bonnie.

'It's a pay phone,' she said.

'What?'

'That number you were asking about, the one that keeps calling you. It's a pay phone.'

'Where do you find a pay phone these days?'

'Out in the desert. That's where. 17817 California Route 111. It's in Coachella. I checked the satellite maps online. It's outside a 7-Eleven, right on the highway.'

Rolly walked into the living room and jotted the address down. Coachella was where Macy gone to attend the music festival with Randy Parker.

'Any sign of Macy or Parnell or Dotty yet?' he asked.

'Nothing yet. We're working on it.'

'Can't you put out one of those amber alerts?'

'Those are for kids. She's an adult. We don't know for sure she didn't dump you.'

'I told you what happened.'

'You didn't actually see anyone force her, though. I'm working on it.'

'Listen, Bonnie – that UVT thing, twenty years ago. How much do you know about it?'

'More than I did two days ago. I'm going through the case files.'

'I was looking at Randy Parker's blog. He said there was a woman named Dorothy Coasters who testified against Gibbons.'

'Sounds familiar. Give me a second.'

Rolly heard Bonnie rustling through things on her desk and other voices in the background. She was at the office, not in her car.

'Dorothy Coasters,' she said, coming back on the line. 'Yeah, she's listed here. They gave her immunity for testifying against Gibbons.'

'Is there a description?'

'Let's see. White. Long blonde hair. Five foot two. Founder of Universal Vibration Technologies and alleged companion of Parnell Gibbons.'

'I think it's her. Dotty. The woman at the shop.'

'You mean the old lady who locked you in?'

'Yes. They're in this together. She and Parnell.'

'Why would he hook up with her after she testified against him?'

'They're looking for something. Randy Parker was looking for it too. And Daddy Joe. They were trying to find it before Parnell got out of jail.'

'What are they looking for?'

'I don't know. But it's got something to do with Macy.'

'You think she knows something?'

Rolly saw Macy's face in his mind. He saw her dirty-blonde dreadlocks and her gold eyes. He saw the necklace, the gold tube hanging above her lovely jugular notch. He remembered what the birdman in Slab City had said.

The Macy has the key.

TWENTY-SIX
The Number

Rolly pulled up to the corner of the street next to the Villa Cantina. Marley Scratch stood outside the cantina's front door with a takeout container in one hand and the Astral Vibrator schematic in the other. Rolly opened the door of the Tioga and let Marley in.

'Where'd you get this beast?' said Marley, climbing into the cabin.

'Borrowed it from my dad.'

'Where you headed?' said Marley.

'Not sure yet. Someplace I can stay out of sight for a while.'

'Going underground, huh? Where you want this?'

'On the table,' said Rolly, nodding towards the back.

Marley placed the items on the dining-room table and glanced around the interior.

'Sir Roland's rolling crime lab,' he said. 'Stylin'!'

One of the drivers behind them started leaning on the horn. The Tioga was blocking the lane.

'Just remember,' said Marley as he headed back to the door. 'It's a sequence of specific frequencies – nine, I think. That's how it unlocks whatever it unlocks. I left you my notes.'

'Got it. Thanks.'

The car behind them honked again. Another one joined in. Marley descended back down to the street.

'I owe you one, buddy,' said Rolly.

'Good luck, bredren,' said Marley. He flashed Rolly a peace symbol and shut the door.

Rolly put the vehicle into gear and turned down Tenth Avenue. He hadn't completely worked out his plan yet, but until he knew why Gibbons was looking for the diddley bow and the Astral Vibrator, he would stay on the move. He drove to the end of Tenth Avenue and turned onto Harbor Drive. There was a public parking lot behind the Convention Center that might be empty at this time of night, assuming you were allowed to park there this late. He circled around the Convention Center and found the lot. It was open, mostly vacant. He steered the Tioga to the emptiest section of the lot, parked and ate his dinner. Then it was time to go to work.

He placed the black box, the box Cool Bob had given him, on the dining-room table, opened up the schematics plan for the Astral Vibrator and reviewed Marley's notes. The word was there in the bottom corner, just like it was on the whiteboard at Daddy Joe's house. The birdman's call. TEOTWAYKI. Maybe it did mean the end of the world, but it meant something else too. It was a code. It was a clue.

He unwrapped the diddley bow, slipped a clip-on tuner to the bridge and adjusted the peg until the tuner indicated he'd found the right note – 440Hz, concert A, the answer to one of the questions Cool Bob had asked him when they met in Slab City. He pulled the tuner off, connected one end of his guitar cable into the diddley bow and the other end into the black box. He pulled out a guitar pick and his slide and played a few notes. The slide was a metal tube, not unlike the gold tube on Macy's necklace. He was ready.

The Astral Vibrator is a locking security device utilizing a pitch interval based system for encoding and decoding physical locking mechanisms via vibration-tuned tumblers.

An hour later he was still there, contemplating defeat. He'd run out of ideas. His phone rang. He picked it up and checked the caller's ID. There was no name but he knew who was calling. It was the beeper's number. He answered. The same pattern of tones played on the other end of the line.

'Why do you keep calling me?' Rolly said. The tone pattern stopped. Rolly could hear the other man breathing.

'Teotwayki,' said the man. He played the tone pattern again. Rolly hung up and placed his phone on the table. The digital keypad stared up at him. There were three letters listed under each number on the keypad. It gave him an idea. He grabbed his composition book and a pencil and jotted the numbers down. 'T' was an 8. 'E' was 3. 'O' was 6. He wrote the whole word down as numbers. It was the numerical equivalent of *Teotwayki*, if you spelled it out on a phone's keypad. The numbers were the same as the ones on Macy's gold charm. He had the combination. He knew how the lock opened. He felt sure of it.

Notes in a musical scale could be represented by numbers. Each number indicates the distance from the root, or key note. The root was the one. Other notes could be thirds, or fourths, or fifths – any whole number. Using his pencil, Rolly marked the positions of each of the notes in the sequence on the diddley bow, assessing the accuracy of the position by ear. The first note was easy. Eight was an octave above the root, exactly halfway up the neck. He could recognize the sound of an octave in his sleep. The other notes were more difficult to nail down, especially the nine, but he felt sure he had them all now. He practiced playing the whole sequence of notes. Nothing happened. He played it again. He tried it a dozen times, but still nothing happened.

Frustrated and fatigued, he decided to take a break and set the diddley bow down on the table. Assuming the numbers represented standard intervals in a major scale, he knew he'd played the correct sequence of notes. The concert pitch he'd tuned to was the standard frequency that everyone tuned to, be it guitar duos or ninety-piece orchestras.

He climbed out of the booth, went to the bathroom, turned on the faucet in the tiny sink and looked at himself in the grimy mirror. The man he saw looked like he hadn't washed his hair in a week. The man needed a shave. He suspected the man in the mirror had started to smell funny, too.

Returning to the cabin, he grabbed a Coke from the refrigerator, seated himself at the table again and reconsidered his plan, wondering where he'd gone wrong. It came down to two things: the sequence of notes was incorrect or his execution of them wasn't accurate enough. He picked up the diddley bow and thumped out a funky rhythmic figure, singing along with it, trying to clear his mind.

She sells black honey,
She sells black honey,
She sells black honey in Tupelo

Few people realized it, but almost all of the music they listened to, be it live or recorded was built on an arbitrary system, a series of compromises musicians had worked out over hundreds of years. A protocol had been agreed upon, one that made it easier for instruments and their owners to play together in harmonious ways. As frequencies went, an octave note was twice the frequency of the original. The octave for A440Hz was A880Hz. The octave to that note was 1760Hz.

The songs you played on your guitar, or your piano, on almost any instrument of European origin used twelve equal divisions for the notes between the octaves. But you could break the space between them into any number of frequencies. There were other types of scales, other divisions of the frequencies musicians could use. They could be found in some non-Western countries, in avant-garde experiments, in the Indonesian Gamelan scales, Wendy Carlos's electronic temperaments or Harry Partch's homemade instruments. When you considered the whole range of frequencies, a single stringed instrument, one without frets like the diddley bow could play any number of notes in-between the standard divisions of the twelve-tone scale. If the UVTs really thought they were aliens, they might have used some sort of alternate tuning and scales.

He picked up the diddley bow and looked at the marks he'd made on the neck. None of them matched up with the dots of gold filigreed into the neck. Norwood had remarked on the filigrees when Rolly first showed him the diddley bow – how they looked out of place. He and Norwood had both assumed they were decorative, but that was because he and Norwood had been playing the same guitar their whole lives. Their guitars came in different colors and shapes, with variations in the pickup configurations, and they were constructed from different types of wood, but they were all the same guitar in one important way. The position of the frets on each of them was based on the twelve-tone scale. The relative position of the frets and fingering guides was always the same.

He laughed. He understood now. The diddley bows were so simple he'd completely missed the meaning behind their design. They'd been built for beginners, people who'd never played a guitar in their life, not experts like Norwood and he. There were exactly nine gold dots on the diddley bow's neck, a filigreed inset for each note in the sequence. It was the Solfeggio frequencies, the New Age tones he'd read about in Marley's loft. There were nine of them, and nine dots on the diddley bow's neck. It was like painting by numbers. He rubbed his forehead and closed his eyes. It just might be that simple.

He pulled out his slide again and plucked the string nine times, matching the position of his slide to the proper dot on the neck of the diddley bow. He played the notes slowly, making sure to match his position with each dot before he plucked the note. When he played the last note the bolts locking the front panel of the vibrator box clicked open. He stared at the box, almost afraid to look at what was inside. He tugged on the guitar cable where it connected to the box. The front panel fell off. There was something inside. It was a postcard of the Desert View Tower. It was blank on the back. He felt cheated.

He grabbed his phone, found the beeper's number and tapped it. If the man answered, he was going to give him a piece of his mind. The pay phone at the other end of the line rang four times, then five, six, seven. He let it keep ringing. He was going to stay on the line until someone answered. He didn't care who it was.

'Hola?' said a voice at the other end of the line.

'Hello,' said Rolly. 'Who's this?'

'Manuelito.'

'Manuelito, can you speak English?'

'Sure. I speak English.'

'Did you call me just now, Manuelito?'

'I no call you. I hear the phone ring. It rings a long time, so I answer.'

'Where are you?'

'By the 7-Eleven. I ride my bike here. Get some Takis and a Monster drink.'

'Was there anyone else using the phone just a minute ago? Did you see anyone?'

'There was this old guy in the parking lot. The one with the crazy car. I seen it sometimes. That car.'

'Why do you call it crazy? The car?'

'He's got all this stuff on it. Flying planets and wings. I seen him before. He's kind of loco, that guy.'

'What kind of car is it?'

'It's like one of those hippie things. You know?'

'A van? A Volkswagen Van?'

'*Si*. That's it.'

'Is the man still there?'

'No. He is gone. He drive away.'

'You've seen him before? Using the pay phone?'

'I seen the van before, in the parking lot. On the street.'

'All right. Thank you, Manuelito.'

'You want me to tell the man something? You know, if I see him?'

'Tell him to call me,' said Rolly. 'Tell him Golden Eyes is in trouble. Tell him the Waters needs his help.'

'OK,' said Manuelito. 'I tell him, if I see him. I hope he helps you.'

'I hope so, too, Manuelito.'

'You buy me some Takis if I get him to help you?'

'You bet. I'll buy you a whole case of them.'

'OK,' said Manuelito. '*Adios.*'

'*Adios,*' said Rolly. He hung up the phone. He had to drive to Slab City. Tonight.

TWENTY-SEVEN
The Constant

By the time Rolly pulled into Slab City and parked the Tioga he couldn't remember what parts of the drive had been real and what parts he'd only imagined. Driving through the early morning darkness – the looming shadows of the East County mountains, the heavy canopy of stars over the desert, the ghostly green streetlights of Brawley and the silhouetted cross above Salvation Mountain – had been like one long, disjointed dream.

An icy blue line hung over the eastern horizon, the cold gleaming before sunrise. He knew it would be safer to wait for the sun to break above the desolate landscape but he'd abandoned all sense of caution. He would find his way to Cool Bob's trailer in the half-light.

He grabbed the diddley bow from the dining booth, stepped down from the vehicle, locked the door and set out for Bob's trailer. His leg still hurt. He could walk without crutches now, but he still limped. He'd figured it out, almost to the finish line, but there'd been no prize at the end. There was only an empty metal box with a fancy lock he could open by playing the diddley bow. There had to be more.

He trudged down the dirt road. Clumps of creosote bush and mesquite rose up in gnarled bunches around him, interrupted by single tall spires of desert agave and spiky explosions of ocotillo plants. Finches and flycatchers twittered from inside the bristly shrubs. A family of quail marched across the road in front of him, returning home from a night's foraging. He stopped so as not to disturb them then turned his head at the sound of footsteps behind him.

'Hello,' he called. 'Is someone there?'

There was no answer. He started off again, listening to the night air. The sound of other footsteps returned. Cool Bob's trailer was close, no more than fifty yards or so by his figuring. He'd be safe once he got there, after he'd knocked on Bob's door. Unless it was Bob following him.

'Stop right there,' said a voice from behind him. Rolly kept walking.

'If you don't stop, I'll sting you,' said the voice.

Rolly stopped. The man walked up behind him and stood so close that Rolly could feel the man's breath on the back of his neck. The guy was a serious mouth-breather.

'Where are you going, jerkoff?' said the man.

'I'm going to see Bob. Cool Bob.'

'What for?'

'I just want to talk to him.'

'What's that in your hand?'

'I don't know. What do you think it is?'

'I think it's a funny-looking guitar with only one string.'

'Sorry, it's a machine gun.'

The man chuckled. 'Little Roland Waters. Always a smartass; always acting like he's the coolest shit in town.'

'Do I know you?'

'No. But I remember you. Snotty-nosed little bastard.'

'Are you Buddy Meeks?'

The man laughed. 'You would remember Buddy, wouldn't you? Yeah, of course. Buddy would've done anything for you.'

'I don't know what you're talking about.'

'Buddy fell for your bullshit. He thought you were his pal, the way you talked to him.'

'I liked Buddy. I learned a lot talking to him.'

'I spent twenty years in prison because of that little shit.'

'Buddy's here in Slab City, isn't he? Randy Parker was looking for him, wasn't he?'

'Randy Parker was a little shit, too.'

'Did you kill him?'

'Shut up,' the man said, kicking Rolly's legs out from under him. Rolly ate dirt. The man stepped on Rolly's bad leg. Rolly screamed and let go of the diddley bow. He reached for his ankle as a nauseous bolt of pain shot up the side of his leg. The man applied more pressure. Rolly squirmed. He broke loose and crawled away. The man followed and crouched down next to him. He grabbed Rolly's collar and shoved his face behind Rolly's ear.

'It's been fun, Roland Waters,' he said. 'I could do this all day. But it's time for me to go. My prize is waiting.'

'I know who you are. You're Parnell Gibbons.'

'What's in a name?'

'I met you at the Alien Artifacts shop. You pretended to be Randy Parker.'

'We met a long time ago, Roland Waters. I recognized you right away when I came in to the store, even with you being old and fat. You know what I said to myself when I saw you?'

'I have no idea.'

'Look who's a big fat loser now. That's what I said to myself. Roland Waters, the skinny little kid with the fast fingers and the big mouth.'

'I don't remember you,' said Rolly.

'You insulted me.'

'Sorry.'

Gibbons shoved Rolly back into the ground and stood up. 'Fuck you, Roland Waters,' he said.

Rolly rolled onto his side. He watched Parnell pick up the diddley bow and walk away.

'I know how to open it, the Astral Vibrator,' said Rolly. 'I have the key.'

Gibbons stopped. 'I have the key, too,' he said, turning back to Rolly. 'And I have the Sachem.'

'Let her go,' said Rolly.

'Who?' said the man.

'You know who I mean. Macy Starr. What have you done with her?'

'What have I done with her? What kind of question is that?'

'I know it was you. When we came back to the shop. It was you that locked me in the shop, wasn't it? After I found Daddy Joe.'

'That was unfortunate, having to leave the false witness behind. He's a tough old bird.'

'Daddy Joe told me everything,' said Rolly. It was a lie. The paramedics had taken Joe Harper away while Rolly was still talking to the police.

'Did he tell you what I was looking for?'

'Yes.'

'Did he say where it was?'

'Desert View Tower.'

Gibbons laughed. 'A decent guess, Roland Waters, but not the correct one.'

'I talked to the police. They know about Dotty.'

'I'll take care of that bitch when I'm done. I've waited a long time for this.'

'I want to see Macy.'

'Don't tell me you're in love with that little mongrel?'

'I don't like to lose clients.'

'You're too old for her. That would be my concern.'

'I feel like I owe her something.'

'She's done with you. You're fired. She knows her true destiny now.'

'I'd like to have her tell me that.'

Parnell took a step towards Rolly. 'Macy told me all about you,' he said. 'You're an even bigger fuckup than I thought.'

'The police are looking for you.'

'Rolly Waters is one sad sack of shit. Not the kind of man I would approve of.'

Rolly climbed to his feet and shifted his weight to his good leg. Parnell retreated two steps.

'This is mine,' he said, indicating the diddley bow. 'No one will press charges. They owe me. I can put them in jail.'

A light blinked on from a trailer nearby.

'Who's out there?' someone called. Gibbons glanced towards the trailer.

'The aliens are waking,' he said. 'Gleep, gleep. Time to go.'

'I want to see Macy.'

'She needs to spend some time with her people. Not losers like you.'

'Wait,' Rolly said, taking a step towards Gibbons. 'Are you her father?'

'Who's to say? It was so many years ago. I get confused sometimes, all those stupid, eager women. I'm sure you know how that is. You were the rock star. Oh, wait, I forgot. That never happened, did it?'

Rolly wanted to throw something at Gibbons. 'Is Macy your daughter?' he said.

'She never came to visit me. All these years. We have a lot to catch up on.'

Rolly took a wobbly step towards Gibbons. The voice from the trailer called out again.

'You'd better scram. I've got a shotgun.'

Gibbons put one finger up to his lips, turned on his heel and walked away. Rolly watched him go. Did Macy think Gibbons was her father? Had she suspected it? Growing up on the reservation, surrounded by Daddy Joe's UVT obsession, she might have read about Gibbons, seen his photograph. It was something she might have clung to, a fantasy about her bad boy father, a killer. It explained her strangeness, her separateness from the tribe. It explained the outlaw blood in her veins.

Everyone was an outlaw in Slab City. On the run. They'd come to escape from themselves, to relieve the pressure and pain in their lives, away from the traffic and TV, the lost jobs and unpaid mortgages, the soul-killing demands of just staying upright in the modern world. There hadn't been enough money, or love, or purpose in that world to sustain them. They came to Slab City because it was cheap, because it was free, because no one would bother you if you didn't want to be bothered, because your time was your own instead of your company's. You could see where you stood in the universe, living under the stars. You came to Slab City to be born again, just like the man who'd built Salvation Mountain.

The UVTs had tried to escape even farther. They'd tried to escape to the stars. Their true nature was with the aliens, above and beyond the debasements of earthbound humanity. But it was a false promise, a swindle. Gibbons took their money. He cheated them. Twenty years after they'd died and he'd gone to jail he would still get to pick up his check. Rolly couldn't believe Macy would go along with it, even if Gibbons was her father. He wouldn't believe it until he'd heard Macy say it – until he looked her straight in those bright gold eyes and heard the words from her mouth.

'Help!' he shouted, breaking into a clumsy trot. Electric jolts of pain shot up his left leg. Gibbons looked back and hastened his pace, revealing a similar limp in his gait. Neither of them gained any ground on the other.

'Help!' shouted Rolly again, trying to rouse the Slab City denizens. 'He's getting away.' He didn't care who came after them or what kind of guns they might brandish. He needed to stop Gibbons. A loud blast filled the air, a warning shot from one of the trailers. Other lights went on. Gibbons ducked off the road, into the bushes. Rolly followed him. Prickly branches tore at his clothes. He crossed an open space near a trailer camp. A light went on outside the trailer, illuminating the area. Gibbons scuttled into the shadows like a big cockroach. Rolly ran to the end of the trailer and looked behind it. He couldn't see anyone. He heard a grunt from inside the trailer.

'Who's there?' someone called.

'Call the police,' Rolly yelled back.

'Who's there?'

'He's trying to kill me. Call the police.'

Rolly spotted a break in the brush on the other side of the trailer. He stepped through the break onto a new road. A dark figure moved away from him. He set out after it. Gibbons had put more space between them. Rolly had to keep Gibbons in sight and rouse the Slab City regulars. If enough people started looking, they'd find him. Gibbons couldn't taser them all.

The dark figure climbed a small hill at the end of the road. Rolly kept after him, stumbling up the slope. He paused at the crest and searched for movement below. There was an open expanse of manicured desert below him, filled with large, irregular shapes. It was East Jesus, the sculpture garden. Deep orange broke on the eastern horizon, the first curve of the sun. Rolly looked back to the Slabs. A dozen encampments now had their lights on. He shouted down to them from the summit, like an Old Testament prophet exhorting the wandering tribes.

'East Jesus,' he called to them. 'He's over here, in East Jesus.'

A shadow rose up towards him. It made a tapping sound and jolted his body with a painful shock. He wrenched away from the pain, dropped to one side and rolled down the hill into East Jesus, coming to rest against the half-buried tire perimeter. He lay on his back and stared up at the sky. He saw stars in the firmament but they might have been stars in his head. It was confusing. A shadow moved over him, an evil alien who shot people with ray guns and filled them with poisonous gold liquid.

'Help,' Rolly said.

'Shut up,' said the alien. He lifted his arm and swung something at Rolly, as if striking a kettle drum. A dissonant orchestra exploded in Rolly's brain. It faded away and he heard only ghost notes, the notes no one plays.

TWENTY-EIGHT
The Trailer

Rolly opened his eyes to a dim yellow light and saw the particle board underside of a Formica table. He lifted himself up and took in the rest of his surroundings. It was the interior of an old trailer, small and cramped. Steam drifted up from a small pot on the stove. His head pulsed in a languid jackhammer of pain. He put his hand to his face. His left nostril had been plugged with a large wad of cotton. He sat up to the table, squeezed his eyes shut and rubbed his temples.

Something rattled in the back of the trailer. He opened his eyes and looked for the exit, wondering if he should try to escape. The trailer didn't seem to be moving. They weren't on the road. He didn't have the energy to make a run for it. He hoped some Good Samaritan had delivered him here.

'Hello?' he said.

Cool Bob stepped into view. 'Hey,' he said. 'How you feeling?'

'I'm OK, I guess.'

'You want to go to the hospital?'

'You think I need to?'

'Dunno.' Bob shrugged. 'You sure got a gift for getting messed up.'

'Yeah. I'm pretty good at that. How'd I end up here?'

'Me and some of the guys found you. That was you, right, screaming for help?'

'Did you catch the guy?'

'People heard you ragin'. They thought you were baked on meth or something. I remembered what Macy said, though, about you being so orthodox.'

'Did anyone call the police?'

'As a general rule, we don't invite the authorities into our domain unless it's absolutely necessary. Only if there's some misdeed we can't handle ourselves.'

'Like Randy No Pants in the hot springs?'

'Yeah, that'd be the kind of singularity where we engage officers of the law.'

Rolly nodded. 'The guy stole my diddley bow,' he said.

'Oh, man. Odious.'

'I was coming to see you.'

'Double odiferous. You know who did the deed?'

'His name's Parnell Gibbons.'

'Not a moniker with which I'm familiarized. Definitely not native. Is he Canadian?'

'Not that I'm aware of.'

'The first blast of Mounties rolled in today. That's why I was asking. They like to set up their own section before the winter season.'

'He said he was Macy's father,' Rolly said. 'He just got out of jail.'

'Macy's dad did this to you? Dude, you need to work on your relationships.'

Rolly put his hand to his nose again, felt the cotton stuffing.

'You can probably take that out now,' said Bob. 'You were dripping pretty good when we found you. Going to have a nice shiner, too. That eye's starting to turn.'

Rolly tugged the cotton from his nose and took a look at it. It was soaked with blood but most of it had dried. He touched his nose. It felt swollen. He hoped it wasn't broken.

'Hey,' said Bob. 'Why were you looking for me?'

'I need to talk to that guy. The gold guy, the guitar maker.'

'He's not usually agreeable to conversational ambitions.'

'He's the only one who can help me.'

'He's seriously inauspicious.'

'What's his name?'

'We just call him Goldhands.'

'Listen, Bob, you care about Macy, don't you?'

'Macy's profound. Sexy with a semi-automatic, too.'

'You'd want to help her, then, if she was in trouble?'

'Irrefutably.'

'This guy that hit me, Gibbons, the one that says he's her father. I think he killed No Pants.'

'Now that's consequential,' said Bob.

Rolly nodded. 'Tell me about the other time No Pants was here,' he said. 'When he brought the other lady, the one with the white hair who talked about aliens.'

'That chick tripped me out seriously.'

'What did she say?'

'She was expounding, you know what I mean? On how we're part alien, like it's part of our heredities. She was saying everybody's got this alien blood in them – it's in their DNA or something. Some people have more than others, you know, they're closer to being full aliens. She said you could recognize people sometimes, the more alien ones. You can recognize them by certain signs.'

'What were the signs?'

'Gold was one of them. She liked to talk about gold.'

'What'd she say?'

'Well, you see these aliens, you know like the full aliens, she said they have gold in their blood, I mean it's not really blood, 'cause they're not us, but it acts like blood does in humans. She said that's why there's always gold being used in religions, because religions are always about higher powers. It's just that most people don't understand that the higher powers are aliens. She got really turned on about it. They were looking for aliens.'

'Were they looking for Goldhands?'

'I think so. They were kinda general in their questions. They wanted to know if I knew anyone who showed the signs.'

'The gold signs?'

'Yeah. Like in their eyes. They said if you saw somebody with gold eyes or gold hair that was a real connection. I asked No Pants if he thought Macy was alien.'

'What'd he say?'

'He got kinda obtuse.'

'What do you mean?'

'He pretended like he didn't know her, said I must be confusing him with someone else. I think it was 'cos of the other lady being with him, like maybe he didn't want her to know. I backed off.'

'Anything else?'

'They asked if I knew any alchemists. They said people who worked with gold, that they had some kind of connection to the aliens too. I guess they were looking for Goldhands, now that I think about it.'

'I need his help, Bob. It's important.'

Cool Bob twisted his lips to one side of his mouth. He looked out through the front of the trailer and scratched his beard.

'We got a code around here in the Slabs,' he said. 'We protect our own. If a guy doesn't want to be found, we're not gonna give him away as long as he contributes positively to the citizenry. Not a disgruntler, or something.'

'Why do you call him Goldhands?' Rolly asked.

Bob stared out the front window. His eyes moved, as if watching something outside.

'He knows how to make gold from old electrical stuff, like computers. He collects parts, stuff he finds, or people trade with him, for his help with electrical stuff. It's mostly old computer boards and electrical things. He's got chemicals and burner stuff too.'

Something rattled against the back window of the trailer. It sounded like gravel.

'It's him, isn't it?' Rolly said. 'It's Goldhands?'

Cool Bob walked to the front of the trailer, opened the door and stepped outside. He shut the door behind him. Rolly heard muffled voices, but he couldn't make out any specifics. The door to the trailer opened. Cool Bob stuck his head inside. 'Goldhands wants to talk to you. Outside.'

Rolly slid from the booth, walked to the door, stepped down onto the sand and planted himself next to Bob. The other man, Goldhands, stood about twenty feet from the trailer, just inside the shade of the overhanging canopy. He wore heavy black-rimmed glasses. The hair he had left clung to his head like a shriveled badger.

'Do you remember me?' Rolly asked.

The man nodded. 'I remember the Waters.'

'I remember Buddy Meeks, the best guitar tech in town. He and I used to talk a lot.'

'That man is in here,' said Goldhands, tapping his right hand with its gold fingers to his temple. 'I remember him. Before the Conjoinment.'

'Can I still talk to him? To Buddy Meeks?'

'The Waters can talk to him. Only the Waters.'

Rolly smiled. There was enough of Buddy Meeks in the man to bring back his own memories. Buddy, the nerd, behind the shop counter at the Guitar Trader, his glasses slipping down his nose, going off on a tangent, giving long, detailed explanations of what made your guitar imperfect and how he could improve it. Sometimes the boss would interrupt them, remind Buddy that he didn't pay him to stand around talking with customers all day. Rolly had enjoyed talking to Buddy. He'd learned a lot from him.

'I figured it out,' Rolly said. 'The combination. I opened the box. It was empty.'

'The box is empty. Yes. The vibrator box is only for practice.'

'What do you mean?'

'The Waters must practice. Practice makes perfect.'

'Why do I need to practice so much?'

'The Waters must be perfect. He must play the Astral Vibrator.'

'Isn't the box the Astral Vibrator?'

'The box is for practice. The Astral Vibrator is for The Conjoinment.'

Rolly thought for a moment. The real Astral Vibrator was somewhere else. It was wherever Gibbons was going. 'Parnell Gibbons has the diddley bow,' he said. 'He stole it from me. He's got Macy, too. And the key.'

Buddy Meeks looked up at the sky and screamed. 'Teotwayki!' He paused then howled again, three times.

Rolly looked at Cool Bob, gauging his reaction. 'Why does he do that?'

'Three times like that,' said Bob. 'He's calling the Rockers.'

A response to Buddy's call echoed through the air, then another. They sounded close by, within the area inhabited by the year-round Slabbers.

'That's the Rockers,' said Bob. 'They're echo-locating, so he knows where they are. It shows that they're ready and listening.'

Buddy Meeks howled again, this time with a stop and start rhythm, short, long, short.

'Whoa,' said Bob. 'SOS call.'

Cool Bob joined the chorus, repeating the start and stop rhythm, the SOS call. Calls came in response. They sounded closer than before. It was like being part of a wolf pack. Someone ran in from the road. Rolly recognized the drummer from the band. Soon others had arrived. They were all members of the band – the drummer, the bass player and the man who played saxophone and piano.

'What's up?' said the drummer, catching his breath.

'You all remember this guy?' said Bob, indicating Rolly. 'Guitar player who sat in with us at The Range a couple nights ago?'

The band members nodded and greeted him.

'Somebody slugged him and stole his diddley bow. Somebody in camp.'

'What's the plan?' said the keyboard player.

'Goldhands made the SOS call,' said Bob. 'It's up to him.'

All eyes turned to Buddy Meeks – Goldhands. He signaled to Bob with his hands.

'Road trip,' said Bob.

The band members cheered.

'Where we going?' said Bob.

'The Conjoinment,' Buddy said.

Bob looked over at Rolly. 'You know where that is?' he said.

'Yes, I think so,' said Rolly. It all made sense now. And it made no sense at all. 'We can take my RV.'

'OK, boys,' said Bob. 'Let's saddle up. Me and Goldhands will go with this guy. You guys get the rocket ship and meet us at the guardhouse, follow us from there.'

'Electric or acoustic?' said the bass player.

'Fully loaded,' said Bob.

'Holy shit, Bob,' said the drummer. 'You mean it?'

Bob turned to Rolly. 'This guy's dangerous, right? Him taking Macy and all.'

'He's got a stungun,' said Rolly. 'He just got out of prison.'

The men stared at Cool Bob for guidance. Bob raised his arm and clenched his fist.

'Locked and loaded,' he said. The men cheered.

'Does that mean what I think it does?' said Rolly.

'That's right,' replied Bob. 'We're packing heat.'

TWENTY-NINE
The Ascent

As soon as they hit the main road and the signal was strong enough, Rolly put in a call to Kinnie Harper. She didn't answer, so he left her a message. He told her about Parnell Gibbons and said he was headed her way. He warned her that a group of long-haired freaks bearing firearms were coming her way, driving his Tioga and a Volkswagen van that looked like a spaceship. He hoped Kinnie got the message. With any luck she and her deputies would have Parnell Gibbons locked up by the time Rolly arrived. And the Rockers could put away their guns.

Buddy Meeks sat next to Rolly in the shotgun seat. Cool Bob sat in the dining booth, looking over Rolly's shoulder. The freeway split as they started up into the mountains. The grade became steeper and the Tioga slowed as they hit the first switchback. Rolly moved to the truck lane. He checked his rearview mirror. The rocket ship, filled with the rest of the Rockers and their guns, moved into the truck lane as well. Neither vehicle had been built for climbing mountains, let alone high-speed pursuit. The Rockers and their ordnance were a mixed blessing. There was some protection in numbers, but a lot less control. He wasn't sure how desperate Parnell Gibbons might be.

The sky grew more overcast as they climbed up the mountains. Rain would bring out the wildflowers in the desert but it wouldn't make his job any easier. The backcountry roads would become slick with thin layers of oil, squishing mud. Flash floods might block off their access entirely.

Buddy Meeks mumbled something.

'What's that?' said Rolly.

Buddy stared out the window and mumbled again. Rolly glanced down at Buddy's hands, the gold stains on Buddy's fingers. He wondered if the stains were permanent or if Buddy just needed a cleaning regimen. Of the three men traveling in the Tioga, Buddy was the ripest, but all of them could use a little freshening.

'What's he looking for?' Rolly said. 'What's Parnell Gibbons looking for?'

Buddy mumbled something unintelligible. He traced his index finger on the window – quick little motions, as if he were playing invisible tic-tac-toe or solving equations on a chalkboard. Rolly glanced in the rearview mirror at Bob.

'Do you know what he's doing?' he asked.

'Cogitating,' said Bob. 'He gets like that sometimes. Serious internals.'

Buddy continued with his calculations. He paid no attention to them.

'Do you know why his fingers are gold like that?' Rolly asked.

'He makes gold. From old computer parts. The circuit boards have gold in them, the connectors and stuff. That stuff's too chemicalized for me, working with that stuff.'

'Can you make money doing that?'

'I don't know if he makes any money.'

'Can you make enough to get by in Slab City?'

'You don't need to make much to survive in the Slabs,' said Bob. 'He showed me how to do it once, had this big pile of old circuit boards somebody gave him. He cut off the gold parts, the connectors, then melted them down and mixed in some chemicals. Ended up with a nice little chunk of gold. Too toxic for me to mess with. They use cyanide, you know.'

'How long's he been doing this?' Rolly asked.

'As long as I've been at the Slabs.'

'How long is that?'

'It was maybe five years ago I set up my trailer. I didn't meet Goldhands for a while, though, him being so singular. People don't tell you about stuff at the Slabs unless you've been around a while, when you're one of the regulars. Don't bother people when they don't want to be bothered. That's the standard. You got to be trusted first. Don't look for people who don't want to be found.'

As a general life rule it was a good one to follow, but Rolly got paid to find people who didn't want to be found. That's why people hired him. People like Macy. There were ghosts in his clients' lives, people missing. He wondered how many of the regulars living in Slab City had become ghosts, haunting the minds of the people who used to know them, people who loved them, people who hated them. Buddy Meeks had been a ghost, a haunted spirit from Rolly's past. Now he was a real person again, a weird and distracted one, but real, not a ghost.

'You say he used cyanide for the gold,' Rolly said.

'Yeah,' said Bob. 'That's nasty shit. They use that stuff to kill rats.'

'And people too.'

'Yeah, I guess. I worked for an exterminator one summer, back in Tennessee. We used it for rats.'

Rolly remembered something Gibbons had said to him. *I spent twenty years in prison because of that little shit.* He wondered if Buddy Meeks, the crazy man with gold fingers, had somehow been responsible for the UVT deaths twenty years ago. They'd been poisoned with cyanide. Was Gibbons innocent? Was he looking for revenge?

He checked the speedometer as the Tioga lumbered up the grade. Their speed had dropped to forty miles an hour. He checked the side mirror. The guys in the van had fallen even further behind. Four men and their weapons were too much for an old Volkswagen to haul up a mountain. He thought about Macy, if she would become a ghost, lost in his memory as the years went on, just like Buddy.

'He makes gold paint too,' said Bob. 'I've seen him do that.'

'Hmm?'

'That might be how he gets the gold fingers. He pulverizes this foil stuff, adds some kind of chemicals and water.'

'What does he do with the paint?'

'He made this sculpture in East Jesus – gold dolls, a pile of them.'

'I didn't see any gold dolls.'

'They disappeared about a week ago.'

'He painted the dolls?'

'Don't know for sure, but that's what I heard.'

Buddy turned from the window and looked at Rolly. 'Gold is

an electrical conductor,' he said in a flat tone. 'Very high conductivity. Seventy percent.'

'People are always trying to sell me guitar cables with gold connectors,' said Rolly.

'Silver and copper are better conductors,' said Buddy. 'Gold is better for corrosion, more durable.'

'I didn't know that,' said Bob. 'This dude is awesome.'

'Awesome,' said Rolly.

'Gold is a noble metal,' said Buddy. 'The Ancients have gold in their veins.'

'Totally engrossing,' said Bob.

Rolly held the steering wheel tight as they curved through the second switchback and headed up another long slope of asphalt.

Buddy did some more calculations on his fingers and pointed up the hill. 'Sluggish,' he said.

'Yeah, sorry,' said Rolly. 'Tell me about the Ancients. They're supposed to be aliens, right?'

'From the Oort,' said Buddy.

'What's that?'

'It's the cloud where comets come from. The Ancients.'

'Oort, oort, oort,' said Bob.

Rolly fought back an impulse to tell Bob to shut up. He might never have found Buddy if it hadn't been for Bob.

'It is time for the Conjoinment,' said Buddy.

'What's that?'

'When the planets align. When the Ancients are closest. We will call them.'

'How do you call them?' said Rolly. He had a pretty good idea of the general concept, but was still unclear on the specifics.

'The Astral Vibrator.'

'What is the Astral Vibrator? What does it do?'

'It calls the Ancients.'

'Is that why I have to practice? So the Ancients will show up?'

'Yes. The Waters must play it. So the Ancients will see.'

Great, thought Rolly. This would be the weirdest gig he'd ever played.

'The Waters must play the Astral Vibrator so the Gentlings may join with the Ancients,' said Buddy. 'They will speak through the Sachem.'

'Whoa,' said Bob. 'He's starting to sound like that lady, the one with No Pants.'

'That lady with No Pants, I think she knows Goldhands from a long time ago. That's right, isn't it, Buddy? You know Dotty, Dorothy Coasters? You were there with her, and Gibbons, with all the UVTs.'

'UVTs?' said Buddy.

'What's a UVT?' said Bob.

Rolly realized that UVT was a term Buddy might never have heard before. It was a shortcut the police and press had started using after the event.

'The Universal Vibration Technologies. You lived with them, didn't you, in that house?'

'Meeks implemented the frequencies,' said Buddy.

'Sounds formidable,' said Bob. 'You know what he's talking about?'

'Not exactly.'

'I'm totally Kenneth, what is the frequency right now,' said Bob.

'It's an alternate scale he worked out,' said Rolly. 'Somebody worked it out, anyway. Nine tones. The Solfeggio frequencies.'

'You mean the Do, Re, Mi?'

'It's different. They claim it's the original scale of the Ancients.'

'Primordial,' said Bob.

'Exactly,' said Rolly.

He guided the Tioga through the next hairpin. They'd made it halfway up the mountain, holding steady at forty. He remembered what Kinnie had told him about the UVTs, how they paired up together, playing the diddley bows at sunrise and sunset. They'd been practicing for the Conjoinment. He took a deep breath and looked over at Buddy, who was doing his calculations again. Rolly didn't know what would happen once they got to the gold mine. With all the heat the Rockers were packing, it would be a wonder if anyone survived. He had to ask now.

'Buddy,' he said, 'can you think back for me . . . those people you were with, when you implemented the frequencies. Did you know a girl named Betty? Or Beatrice? Her mother was there too. Wanda Ozzie. Do you remember either of them?'

'Betty,' said Buddy. It didn't sound like a question. Rolly held his breath.

'Betty's gone,' said Buddy. 'Betty fell down in the hole. Couldn't get out.'

'Was there a baby?' said Rolly. 'Did Betty have a baby with her? A little girl with gold eyes?'

'The Sachem,' said Buddy.

It was the closest Rolly had come to a confirmation. Macy had been there, with the UVTs, as a baby. Bob was silent. He seemed to sense the weightiness of the situation. Rolly took the last hairpin. They were almost at the summit and the In-Ko-Pah exit. Rolly had no idea what they would find when they got to the Astral Vibrator. He took a deep breath. One more question.

'Buddy, what happened to those people?' he said. 'The UVTs?'

'The Waters must play it,' said Buddy. 'The Waters will free them.'

THIRTY

The Mine

The sky had darkened considerably by the time they reached the In-Ko-Pah exit and turned off the freeway. Rain was a rare occurrence on this side of the mountains, but the slate-colored clouds above them looked menacing and heavy, as if they would open up any minute. Trees and bushes by the side of the road trembled in the rising wind. Rolly drove towards Desert View Tower while Buddy ran calculations with his fingers.

'Left turn,' said Buddy.

Rolly stopped the Tioga and spotted an access road that Buddy apparently wanted him to take. It didn't look like much. When the rain came, it would get muddy. The Tioga would slide around in the ruts, or, even worse, sink its tires into a wet spot. It was the same road he'd seen the blue Toyota exit from two days ago when he and Moogus were stranded. Daddy Joe's Toyota had been found in the area. He wondered if Daddy Joe had been driving it that morning.

A splatter of raindrops hit the window, as if warning him.

'I don't know if I can drive in there,' said Rolly. 'We might get stuck.'

'The rocket ship can handle it,' said Bob. 'Let's wait for the Rockers.'

Rolly pulled over to the side of the road. Soon the others arrived and pulled up behind them. More splatters of rain hit the ground as the three men left the Tioga behind and climbed into the van. The VW wasn't much of an off-road vehicle, either, but it was a lot lighter than the RV. Three men could lift the van out of a rut if they needed to.

They headed down the side road, packed in like sardines. Rolly looked at the faces of the Rockers. They looked calm, almost bored, as if carrying guns along with them was an everyday experience. Nobody seemed to be in a hurry; no one was amped up for a shooting. That was good. He looked out the side window, surveying the scenery. They passed behind the boulder field where the stone animals lived. The van lurched to the right then came to a stop.

'Looks like the cops are here,' said the driver.

Rolly looked out the front window. A tribal police truck was parked at end of the road in front of the guardrail. There was another car next to it, a cheap-looking Suzuki.

'Let me find out if she's around,' Rolly said, not wanting to disgorge a gang of gunslingers on Kinnie without some discussion of their proper employment. He opened the sliding door and walked to the police truck. There was no one inside. He checked the Suzuki. It wasn't locked. He looked in the glove compartment and found the registration slip listing Randy Parker as the owner. Parnell Gibbons was here already. Kinnie had found him. Or followed him into the canyon.

Two mesas jutted out from the other side of the canyon, a solitary house located on each of them. The first one was Daddy Joe's house. The other was Beatrice House, with the UVT memorial park out on the point. They looked closer together from this angle, more like neighbors than they'd seemed before. Below them, the canyon widened out into a flat plain. There were signs of an old settlement in the canyon, ruins of wood structures.

Buddy walked up beside him. 'The Waters must play it,' he said. He walked around the end of the guardrail, stepped off the ledge and disappeared into the canyon.

'Hey!' Rolly called. He hastened to the end of the guardrail and looked down. Buddy stood on a ledge ten feet below. He pointed up at a skinny path leading to his location. Rolly looked back towards the van. Bob stood outside, watching him.

'Stay here,' said Rolly. 'Don't let anyone get by you until I get back.'

Bob nodded and waved.

By the time Rolly turned back, Buddy had disappeared again. He walked down the path to the ledge where Buddy had been and looked around. Buddy appeared again, twenty feet further down the canyon.

'Wait!' Rolly called. Buddy stopped and looked back at him. He pointed at a break in the rocks below the ledge to Rolly's left. Rolly climbed down through the break, slid around the side of a large boulder, found the trail again and followed it until he'd caught up with Buddy. The rest of the trail was an easier trek, gentle switchbacks leading into the flat part of the canyon. Shrubs clumped thickly as they got to the bottom, but a narrow break let them through.

As they hiked along the canyon floor, broken-down structures of wood appeared by the side of the trail, the remains of old cabins and fences, skeletal wood grids that looked like they might have been planters or sorting bins. Three rusted train cars stood on railroad tracks next to a smashed water tower. Someone had spray-painted the word *TEOTWAYKI* on one of the cars. A steady drizzle began to fall.

The trail became wider. Buddy turned off and headed back up the slope they'd come down, but farther along, in the direction of the Desert View Tower. Rolly looked back to find the spot where they'd parked. He could see the front grill of Kinnie's truck and Randy's Suzuki, but they soon passed out of sight.

They climbed the hill a short way before Buddy stopped and cogitated for a moment. Using two of his golden fingers, he pointed at something farther up the hill, a large black hole in the side of the earth covered by a steel gate. It was the bat gate Kinnie had told Rolly about, designed to keep people out, allowing the bats to come and go as they pleased. Buddy climbed up to the gate. Rolly joined him. The edges of the hole had eroded over time, leaving gaps on either side of the gate. They squeezed through the right side of the gate and entered the hole in the mountain, just as the rain began falling in sheets.

The inside of the mine looked like Rolly had expected – an earthen tunnel braced by crisscrosses of splintery pillars and beams. It got darker as they hiked further in. Soon he wouldn't be able to see his hand in front of his face. Buddy pulled a flashlight out of his pocket and turned it on. They continued on into the mine, snaking through the tunnels, following Buddy's light. Buddy stopped.

Rolly bumped into him. 'What is it?' he whispered.

Light blazed through the room, a string of safety lights running along the edge of the cavern. It was too much light, too soon.

Rolly covered his eyes with one hand. 'Yah!' he said.

'Grmmph,' someone grunted.

Rolly looked towards the grunt, still shading his eyes. Someone lay on the floor.

'Kinnie?' he said.

'Grmmph,' said Kinnie. It was all she could say. She'd been gagged, with a red bandana tied over her mouth and her hands pulled behind her. Rolly stepped towards her.

'Hold on, Roland Waters,' someone said. Rolly turned towards the voice. It was Parnell Gibbons. He had the diddley bow with him. Dotty stood next to him. She had an automatic pistol in her hand, pointed in Buddy and Rolly's general direction.

'Hello, Buddy,' said Dotty. 'It's good to see you again.'

Buddy Meeks made a strangling sound in his throat. His body went rigid, almost as if he were having a seizure.

'Grmmph,' said Kinnie.

Rolly looked back at her. 'Are you OK?' he asked.

Kinnie nodded. 'Grmmph.'

'Well, everyone's here now,' said Gibbons. 'All the liars and freaks and criminals, back together again. The Conjoinment, round two.'

'Where's Macy?' said Rolly.

'A stand-in for the old chief, of course,' said Gibbons, nodding at Kinnie. 'But his daughter will have to do.'

'Where's Macy?' said Rolly again.

'Down there,' said Gibbons, pointing to a hole in the ground.

'What did you do to her?'

'She's retrieving something valuable.'

'He figured it out, Buddy,' said Dotty. 'What you did with the gold.'

'Twenty years, Buddy,' said Parnell. 'I thought about you a lot. Weird little Buddy, with his puzzles and numbers, his anal-compulsive oddities.'

'I want to see Macy,' said Rolly. 'Where is she?'

A beam of light shot up from the hole in the ground between Dotty and Gibbons.

'I'm coming up,' said a voice from inside the hole.

The flashlight beam bounced around the walls of the cave. Macy climbed out of the hole. She turned off the light that was strapped to her head, reached back down and hauled up a rope. A plastic crate appeared at the end of it. There was a metal box inside the crate.

'Is that it?' said Rolly. 'Is that the Astral Vibrator?'

'Hey, Waters,' said Macy, 'what're you doing here?'

'Trying to find you,' Rolly said. 'Among other things.'

'Well, you found me. Sorry.'

'I'm sorry too.'

'Guess this'll teach me to go chasing after old ladies.'

'Shut up,' said Gibbons. 'Let me see it.'

'Yes, boss,' said Macy. She reached into the crate, lifted out the metal box and placed it on the floor. Gibbons leaned down and inspected the box.

'The Waters must play it,' said Buddy. He seemed to have come out of his spell.

'The what?' said Gibbons.

'The Waters must play it,' said Buddy. He sounded like a five-year-old kid, as if he'd start screaming or crying. 'The Waters must play it.'

'Screw that,' Gibbons said. He grabbed the other end of the guitar cable and plugged it into the box.

'No, no, the Waters,' pleaded Buddy.

'You heard him,' said Macy. 'Let Waters do it. Waters is the shit.'

'Fuck Roland Waters,' said Gibbons. 'I spent twenty years waiting for this.'

Gibbons sat down on a rock and placed the diddley bow on his knees. He pulled out a slide and played a sequence of notes similar to the ones Rolly had played. Nothing happened. Gibbons turned the volume knob all the way up and played the notes again with the same results. He jiggled the cable, made sure it was seated properly. He played the notes again. Again there was nothing.

Buddy giggled. 'The villain sucks,' he said. 'Teotwayki!'

'Shut up,' said Gibbons. He played the notes again, with still no result. 'I know I'm playing it right.'

'The Waters must play it,' said Buddy.

'Fuck you.'

The diddley bow clattered to the ground as Gibbons jumped up from his seat. He pulled something out of his back pocket as he rushed towards Buddy. Rolly saw an arc of electricity and heard the woodpecker sound as Gibbons jabbed the prongs of his stungun into Buddy's waist. Buddy yelled and jerked backwards. He fell to the ground.

'Stop it,' said Rolly.

Gibbons turned on him. 'You want some?' he said.

Rolly held his hands up in front of him. 'No, thanks. I've had my share.'

'What does he mean?' Gibbons said. 'Why does he want you to play it?'

'I can open the box,' Rolly said. 'I've got one just like it in the RV. I opened it.'

'Was there anything in it?'

'A postcard.'

'You're a liar.'

'I'm not lying.'

'Where did you hide it?'

'I didn't hide it. You can come take a look if you want. I've got it with me, in the Tioga. There wasn't any gold, just a postcard of Desert View Tower, no writing or anything.'

Dotty walked over to Buddy, leaned down and stroked his hair with her free hand, the one without the gun. 'Buddy,' she said, 'it's almost time. What should we do?'

'The Waters must play it,' said Buddy. 'Teotwayki!'

'It's a trick,' Gibbons said.

'For God's sake,' Dotty said, turning on Gibbons. 'Just let him play the damn thing.'

The look on Parnell's face turned to pure loathing, as if he remembered every day he'd spent in prison, every hour he'd spent planning his triumphal moment. He hadn't expected to argue with half-a-dozen people about it. He waved the stungun at Rolly.

'No tricks,' he said. 'I'll fry your ass like bacon if this is a trick.'

'Understood,' said Rolly. He picked up the diddley bow, reached into his pocket and pulled out his slide, then sat down on the rock. He laid the diddley bow on his lap and rehearsed the sequence of notes in his head. He stopped and looked at the slide on his finger. It wasn't right. He put it back in his pocket. 'Macy?' he said, looking over at her.

'Yeah?'

'Give me the key.'

Macy looked blank for a moment before recognition came into her eyes. She undid her necklace, slipped the gold tube off the end and handed it to Rolly.

'Rock my world, Waters,' she said. 'I don't want your ass getting fried.'

'Yeah. Thanks,' said Rolly. He closed his eyes and visualized the positions on the diddley bow's neck. He opened his eyes, took a deep breath, locked in and played the notes. The bolts popped on the front panel of the box.

'You did it,' said Macy. 'Right?'

'I think so,' said Rolly.

'Let me see,' said Gibbons, shoving Rolly out of the way. He picked up the box, reached inside and pulled something out. It looked like a Barbie doll, a blonde Barbie doll covered in gold paint.

'What the hell is this?' he said.

'Teotwayki!' cried Buddy.

No one else said anything because the lights had gone out.

THIRTY-ONE
The Conjoinment

The stungun spit out an electrical arc. Rolly saw Gibbons' face in a halo of light, cramped and contorted in a rictus of pain. The arc light went out. Pure blackness covered their eyes again. Rolly smelled ozone. Someone moved in the darkness. There had been someone behind Gibbons, a cave monster hidden in shadow. Rolly held his breath, listened to the soft rustling sounds. Someone groaned.

'Who's there?' he said.

A flashlight beam danced on the walls. Macy had turned on her headlight. The beam settled on Gibbons. He lay prostrate on the ground, his hands tied behind him. They could see a man's boots next to him. Macy swiveled the light up the other man's body. He turned away from the light.

Gibbons screamed, 'Shoot him!'

Macy's light went out. A deafening explosion burst from the darkness. Rolly ducked into a fetal position, hugging the rocky floor. The gun went off again, three more shots. Bullets pinged through the cavern. The room went silent. He lifted his head. There was a loud smack, like a slap. Something metallic clattered onto the rocks. Someone began crying. The cave was still dark.

'Macy?' said Rolly.

'Yeah?'

'Are you OK?'

'Yeah. What happened?'

'I don't know.'

'Where's your flashlight?'

'It fell off when I ducked.'

Someone groaned in the darkness.

'Here it is,' said Macy. She turned on the light and blasted it in Rolly's face.

'Not on me,' he said, squinting his eyes. 'Over there.'

Macy turned the light towards the center of the room. Gibbons lay face down on the floor, trussed up like a hog.

Dotty lay near him, flat on her back. She was sobbing. 'I am blameless,' she said. Someone grunted, off to the right. Macy swung the light over and found Kinnie.

Rolly stood up and walked over to Kinnie. He leaned down and pulled the gag from her mouth.

'Find my gun,' she said. 'That was my gun.'

Macy turned the light and walked to the middle of the room. Rolly followed her. They looked down at Gibbons and Dotty.

'Where'd he go?' said Macy.

'I don't know. We need to find Kinnie's gun.'

'Shit,' Macy said. 'Is that blood?'

Rolly saw it as soon as Macy did: a wet red puddle.

Kinnie called over to them. 'Turn on the lights.'

'Where are they?' said Rolly.

'By the ladder. Watch for the hole.'

Macy swiveled her headlight around the room and found the hole in the floor. She tilted the light up to the wall.

'There,' Rolly said.

Macy walked to the wall and flipped the switch. The lights came back on. 'Shit,' she said.

'What?'

'There's more blood here. On the ladder. Hey, lady!'

Rolly turned back to the room. Parnell lay trussed up on the floor, but Dotty had risen. She stood at the edge of the tunnel with Kinnie's gun in her hand.

'Put the gun down, Dotty,' said Rolly. 'You can't get away.'

'I did before,' she said. 'I can do it again. I am blameless.'

Gibbons laughed. 'Stupid bitch,' he said. 'You're not blameless. All of this is your fault.'

'Shut up, Parnell,' she said. 'I had to testify against you. I had to protect myself and my work. You ruined me.'

'Those people got what they wanted. They did it for you.'

'That's a lie. You were unfaithful to me.'

'I'm more faithful than anyone.'

'Stop it. Stop your lies.'

'What do you think would have happened if the Conjoinment had passed and nothing changed, everyone sitting around waiting for something to happen? You made it so easy, you and your stupid rituals. Everyone synchronized, like the music, taking a drink at the same time. That's how it worked. Once the poison was in the pot, they were all done for.'

'You put the poison in there.'

'That stupid girl did it. She made the soup.'

'You gave the poison to her. You told her to do it.'

'You don't have any proof of that. No one does.'

'They were believers,' said Dotty. 'They were my disciples.'

'They knew exactly where you were leading them. They wanted to die.'

'You treated them like vermin. I made them gods.'

'They were cattle. Stupid, dumb sheep. They wouldn't have died without you taking them in, leading them on.'

Dotty moved towards Gibbons. Her voice shook. 'You left me with nothing, Parnell. I had to sell my house. I had to leave town. I had to change my name and scrape along, reading auras in Sedona. Then Randy found me. He knew my work. He believed in the universal vibrations. He seduced me. But it was you, all along, leading him on. You fed him stories. You gave him ideas. And then you killed him.'

'That was an accident,' said Gibbons. 'The little shit tried to cheat me. I knew what he was up to. Looking for Buddy, so he could get here first.'

'Can't you see, Parnell? It's not here. Buddy used it all up. It's gone.'

Rolly looked around the room. Buddy was missing.

'It's here,' Parnell replied. 'I know it is.'

'You lie to yourself, like you lied to Randy, like you lied to me.' Dotty's hand quivered. She pointed the gun at Parnell.

'Don't do it, Dotty,' said Rolly. 'He's not worth it.'

She looked over at Rolly and dropped the gun to her side. 'I have to go,' she said.

'There's a posse out there,' said Rolly. 'Friends of mine from Slab City. They've got guns. They won't let you leave.'

Dotty stared at Rolly a moment. 'All men are liars,' she said, and ran out the tunnel.

'Holy shit, Waters,' said Macy. 'That was screwed up.'

'Now that you both screwed things up,' said Kinnie, 'you think you could find the key to my handcuffs and set me loose?'

'Where are they?' said Rolly.

'Check his pockets.'

Rolly walked over to Gibbons, knelt down and began searching him.

'Think you won again, don't you, Waters,' said Gibbons.

'I don't care about winning,' said Rolly.

'You used to.'

'What are you talking about?'

'The jam contests. At McP's on Sundays. You remember when you won?'

'I won a lot of those things,' said Rolly.

Gibbons snickered. 'Asshole. I mean the first time. When you were in high school.'

Rolly found the key in Gibbons front pocket. He grabbed it and stood up. 'Sure, I remember,' he said. 'Some guy made me give back the prize money. He said I was too young because I used a fake ID to get in.'

'I was that guy,' said Gibbons.

'That was you, huh?'

Rolly walked over to Kinnie and unlocked her handcuffs. Kinnie sat up and rubbed her wrists.

184 Corey Lynn Fayman

'Where's Buddy?' said Rolly.

Gibbons laughed. 'The bitch shot him,' she said.

Kinnie stood up, walked over to Gibbons and slapped her handcuffs on him to make sure he didn't slip out of his knots.

'Somebody tied you up pretty good, didn't they?' she said. 'Who was it?'

'You know who it was,' said Gibbons. 'He's part of this too.'

'Hey, Waters,' said Macy, 'the blood. I think the bird guy went down the ladder.'

'Show me,' said Kinnie. She pulled a flashlight from her belt and walked back towards Macy. She pointed the light at the top of the ladder.

'That's fresh blood, all right,' she said. 'What's the guy's name?'

'Buddy Meeks,' said Rolly.

Kinnie leaned down into the hole. 'Mr Meeks! Buddy Meeks! Are you down there?'

No one answered.

'Let me go down,' said Macy.

'You don't know what he's got down there,' said Kinnie. 'It could be dangerous.'

'You gotta go down, then.'

Kinnie squatted down by the hole. She sighed. 'Shit,' she said. 'I'm off the rez. That lady's got my gun. I shouldn't even be here.'

'I can do it,' said Macy. 'I went down there before.'

'How'd you find this place, Kinnie?' said Rolly. 'The message I left just said we were going to the tower. How'd you end up here?'

'We can talk about that later, Mr Waters,' said Kinnie. 'I better call in support, get the sheriff on this. They can helicopter the guy out of here.'

'It's too bad about your gun, Chief Harper,' said Gibbons.

'Shut up, asshole. You're getting kicked back to the big house for a long time.' Kinnie stood up. 'My radio won't work in here,' she said. 'I'm going outside to call in support.'

'What about him?' Rolly said.

Kinnie kicked Parnell's boot. 'This asshole ain't going anywhere,' she said. 'Macy, you do whatever you want. I warned you. If you find that Meeks guy down there, if he's bleeding serious, apply pressure,' she said. 'Stuff your shirt in his wound or something, whatever you got. Try not to let him bleed out. I'll get the paramedics in here as soon as I can.'

Kinnie stomped away down the tunnel.

'Waters, I'm going in,' said Macy. She adjusted her headlight, climbed onto the ladder and stepped halfway down into the hole.

'Macy?' said Rolly.

'What?'

'Be careful.'

'Don't believe in careful. Hey, Waters?'

'Yeah.'

'In case something happens, just so you know.'

'What?'

'Best date ever! Awesome!' Macy disappeared into the hole.

Rolly turned back to Parnell. 'Got anything you want to tell me?' he said. 'You know, just between us.'

'Suck my dick,' said Gibbons.

'Oh, come on now. You know I like girls,' Rolly said. He looked back at the ladder. 'Crazy girls.'

'I was framed,' said Gibbons. 'I didn't kill them.'

'Who did then?'

'That girl. The stupid one. Stupid bitch put that stuff in the soup. Thought it was salt or something. All Buddy's fault, leaving it out on the counter.'

'You're telling me it was an accident?'

'It looks just like salt, you know. Buddy Meeks, smarter than shit but no brains at all, left that shit on the counter.'

'You bought the stuff. Your name was on the receipt.'

'Buddy asked for it. We were looking for gold. We found some here, in the mine.'

'What happened to the girl?'

'Big chief. He took her. Lied on the witness stand. Who's the jury gonna believe, me or some noble Indian chief bullshit?'

'It was Betty, the girl, wasn't it? Her name was Beatrice Ozzie?'

'Black girl. Nice piece of ass. Stupid girl had a baby.'

'Maybe somebody else was stupid, too.'

Gibbons chuckled. 'Yeah. Maybe.'

'Is she your daughter? Is Macy your daughter? You and Betty?'

'Ungrateful bitches, all of 'em.'

'Yeah, it's weird how women get like that. All you did was poison everyone and take their money.'

'Fuck you, Waters. All that tired blues stuff you play. It sucks.'

'What?'

'That's how you won. All those cliched licks. That's how you won all those contests.'

'Yeah, well, play what you know.'

'You don't know shit.'

Rolly decided to lay off for awhile. Gibbons might get chatty later and tell him more.

'Hey, Waters!'

It was Macy, popping up out of the hole like a gopher. She was naked to the waist.

'Where's your shirt?' he said.

'Shit, Waters. It's not like you haven't seen 'em before. I stuffed my shirt in the guy's wound just like Kinnie said I should. There's a lot of blood. He asked for you.'

'Buddy asked for me?'

'He wants you to play that thing again.'

'He wants me to bring the diddley bow down there?'

'Yeah. There's something down here. It's just like that box thing I brought up before.'

Rolly looked down at Parnell.

'I knew it,' said Parnell. 'I knew it was here.'

'Jesus shit, Waters. C'mon. This could be the guy's dying wish or something.'

Kinnie was right. Parnell wasn't going anywhere – not before she got back, anyway. Rolly grabbed the diddley bow, wrapped the cable around it and handed it to Macy. She disappeared back into the hole. He grabbed the first rung of the ladder. The blood was still wet. Buddy's blood. He lowered himself down into the hole.

They walked through the lower tunnel. Macy's light bounced off the walls.

'You're not going to believe this shit,' Macy said. 'There's something crazy down here.'

'What is it?'

'I'm not sure exactly. There's a grotto or something, this big room. There's one of those boxes stuck in the rocks, farther back than that first one I found.'

Macy stopped and aimed her headlight down at the floor. Buddy lay there, covered in blood, with Macy's T-shirt stuck in his gut. His head lolled to one side. Macy squatted down and cradled the back of Buddy's head against her small breasts. He opened his eyes and spotted Rolly.

'The Waters,' Buddy said, raising one gold finger.

'Plug the guitar thing in there,' said Macy. She pointed her light at a black box embedded in the rocks. The top of the box was covered in concrete. There was a quarter-inch input on the front of the box, just like on the others. Unlike the first two boxes, there was a thick black cable running out of the back. Rolly plugged in the diddley bow.

'The Waters must play it,' said Buddy, his eyes glazing over.

Rolly took Macy's gold charm out of his pocket. 'I need more light,' he said, indicating the diddley bow. Macy gave it to him. He took a deep breath then played the notes again. A switch clicked. Lights went on in the cavern.

'Holy shit,' said Macy. 'What is it?'

The cavern was burnished in gold, its walls covered in gold paint. There were diddley bows arranged in a half circle, a dozen or more, with gold filigrees. A doll had been placed in front of each diddley bow – all kinds of dolls, Barbies and GI Joes and baby dolls. The dolls were all covered in gold, with gold-painted skin and gold eyes. A flat rock slab rose in the center of the room. A human skeleton lay on the slab.

'It's a tomb,' said Rolly.

'The bones,' said Macy. 'He painted them gold.'

Buddy Meeks gurgled. 'The Conjoinment is done,' he said. 'The Gentlings are free.'

His eyes went still. Buddy Meeks was released.

THIRTY-TWO
The Rockers

Rolly and Macy stood just inside the entrance to the mine, watching the rain. Two deputy sheriffs had picked up Gibbons and escorted him back down the trail. A helicopter had arrived and taken Buddy away. The paramedics pronounced Buddy dead where they found the body, propped up against the base of the ladder where Macy and Rolly had placed him. Neither the paramedics nor the deputies questioned their story. Kinnie had explained the situation to the deputies outside. They took her at her word. She was a cop, one of them. The details could be sorted out later. The bad guys had been identified – a man and a woman. The man was in custody. The woman had escaped with the officer's gun. No one but Rolly and Macy had seen the gold room. The lights inside it had gone out before the others arrived.

Macy shivered. The paramedics had given her a blanket to cover up when they arrived. The blanket had been replaced by Kinnie's jacket, which was at least twice the size Macy would normally wear. She'd rolled up the sleeves. The jacket came to her knees.

Kinnie came in out of the rain, along with a county sheriff who seemed to be in charge of things. 'We got a situation,' said Kinnie.

'What's that?' said Rolly.

The sheriff spoke. 'I need you to call off your guys,' he said. 'They're interfering with my operation.'

'My guys?'

'Some long hair types in a VW van up at the lookout are refusing to cooperate. My deputy says they're armed and unfriendly. I hear you're the boss. They need to stand down and let us remove the fugitive to the patrol vehicles.'

'You mean Gibbons?'

Kinnie nodded.

Rolly turned back to the deputy. 'I asked them to stop anybody that came through,' he said, 'until I came back.'

'Are you willing to go up there and talk to them?'

'Yes,' said Rolly. 'Anytime.'

The sheriff spoke into the radio clipped to his vest. 'David, listen, have everybody stand down up there. Back off. Tell them we'll have the guy up there in ten minutes so he can talk to them.'

'Roger,' came a voice over the radio.

'All right, Chief Harper,' said the deputy. 'You have charge of your prisoners. I'll meet you back at the top.'

The deputy walked down the hill and climbed into a waiting helicopter. It lifted off, leaving the three of them alone.

'Who's up there, Waters?' said Macy.

'Cool Bob and the Rockers,' said Rolly.

'Sounds like a band,' said Kinnie.

'Yeah,' said Rolly. 'It is.'

'These guys'll do what you say?' Kinnie asked.

'They have so far,' said Rolly.

'Count on it, Kinnie,' said Macy. 'The Rockers totally dig on Waters.'

'All right, let's go.'

They headed down the trail, turned up the valley and headed back to the overlook. Rolly walked in front with Macy behind him. Kinnie brought up the rear.

'Why did that guy call us your prisoners, Kinnie?' said Macy.

'I'm taking you back to the rez for your own protection.'

'Are you going to put us in jail again?'

'Not if you tell me what happened down there.'

'We already told you once. I found the guy. He was bleeding. I tried to bandage him up with my shirt, just like you told me.'

'He was the one made those bird calls?'

'Yes,' said Rolly. 'It's just like I explained before, to you and the deputies. His name's Buddy Meeks. He lives . . . lived in Slab City. He was one of the UVTs. Twenty years ago. All three of them, there's some kind of bad blood between them. About the money, the gold. You heard them talking.'

'Why was he doing that, making that sound?'

'It's hard to explain. It's some kind of code.'

'You really think he's the one took down Gibbons?'

Rolly and Macy were silent. They'd reached the spot where the trail started up to the outlook. They stopped and looked at each other.

'Yeah, I didn't think so either,' said Kinnie. She stopped too and waved to the deputy standing guard above, at the overlook.

'I started thinking about it,' said Kinnie. 'While I was out there waiting for the chopper. Those chirps he was making. It's that word, isn't it? On Daddy Joe's whiteboard?'

'Teotwayki,' Rolly said. 'Yes.'

'What else did you see? How did that Gibbons guy end up hogtied like that? I don't figure it was you.'

'No,' said Rolly. 'It wasn't me.'

'And it wasn't the birdman.'

'No. There was a big man, bigger than Gibbons,' said Rolly. 'I couldn't see his face. He had cowboy boots.'

'There's only one way this makes sense,' said Kinnie.

'I thought he was in the hospital.'

'I brought him home yesterday.'

'You think it was Daddy Joe who kicked that guy's ass?' said Macy.

'And saved ours,' said Kinnie. 'It's the only thing that makes sense.'

'Where did he go?' said Rolly. 'Why didn't he want us to know it was him?'

Kinnie gave them both a severe look. 'Listen,' she said. 'We gotta be careful about this. We don't know for sure yet, and I don't want him getting involved if we can help it. It was dark and you didn't see what happened. Right now, they think it was the birdman that took Gibbons down and got himself shot in the process.'

'Gibbons knows it was Daddy Joe, doesn't he?'

'That's why I'm taking you back to the rez,' said Kinnie. 'So I can get you both out of here before he starts squawking.'

'I have to talk to the Rockers first,' said Rolly.

'Let's go,' said Kinnie.

They hiked through the switchbacks, up to the guardrail at the edge of the outlook. A deputy stood behind the guardrail, waiting for them.

'Come with me,' he said. Rolly followed. Macy started after him but Kinnie grabbed her arm and held her back. The deputy led Rolly between the two cars and stopped. Two deputies stood at the rear of Kinnie's truck with Parnell Gibbons between them, in handcuffs. Cool Bob had placed himself in their path, twenty feet down the road, in front of the VW van. He had his rifle strapped to his back. One of the Rockers, the bass player, stood next to the van. The side door was open. He rested his gun in his arms.

'Hey, Bob,' said Rolly. 'What's happening?'

'We did just like you said. Nobody passes.'

'I can see that.'

'It got kinda tortuous, with the cops showing up and boxing us in,' said Bob. He pointed to the rocks off to his right. 'I got two guys up there. That slowed 'em down. I told 'em no prisoner release unless I got the word from you.'

Rolly looked up into the rocks. He saw the two other band members holding their guns. He looked down the road, past the van. Three sheriff's vehicles blocked the road. The helicopter had landed behind them. The rotors spun down in slow motion.

'I'm here now,' said Rolly. 'This guy they arrested, he's the one who took my diddley bow. We'll let the police take care of him.'

'Everything's cool?' said Bob.

'Everything's cool. You can let them through.'

Bob looked up to the rocks. He shouted. 'Stand down, boys. We're letting 'em through.'

The men moved into the clear and leaned the butts of their guns on the ground. Bob checked the man outside next to the van to make sure his message was clear. The man nodded and leaned his gun against the van.

Cool Bob moved out of the way. 'All clear,' he said. 'Desecuritized.'

Rolly turned to the deputy. 'That enough?' he said.

'It'll do,' said the deputy. He motioned to the men with Parnell. They marched him down the road, keeping a wary eye on the Rockers.

'Where's Goldhands?' said Bob, walking over to Rolly.

'Goldhands is dead. Someone killed him.'

'Oh, man. Catastrophic.'

'I'm sorry.'

'This is gonna go down hard with the Slabbers. Debilitating. What're we going to do without Goldhands?'

As Parnell passed the Volkswagen, he turned to look at something inside. He sneered. It looked like he was talking to someone. The bass player with the gun stood outside the van. There were two other band members in the rocks, and Bob here. All four Rockers were accounted for.

'Bob?' said Rolly. 'Who's in the van?'

'Oh, yeah,' said Bob. 'Remember that alien lady I told you about?'

'She's in there?' said Rolly. 'Did she give you her gun?'

'I didn't see no gun on her. She was cool. Tranquility base.'

'You didn't search her?'

'She's an old lady.'

Someone shouted. A gun went off. Rolly turned to see the bass player diving towards the rear of the van. The deputies ducked down, fumbling at their gun holsters. Gibbons stood alone. He stepped towards the van, defiant and screaming. The gun went off again from inside the van. Gibbons tottered backwards. He turned and pitched face first into the road. The deputies rolled to their feet, guns at the ready. A pistol flew out of the van and landed next to Gibbons. The deputies drew a bead on the shooter inside. Dotty stepped out of the van, with her hands up.

'I'm done,' she said. 'We're all done now. It's over.'

THIRTY-THREE
The Chief

The tribal police truck bounced down the back road to Daddy Joe's house. Kinnie Harper looked in the rearview mirror at the two people in the backseat. She pulled up to the house and switched off the engine. She turned back to talk to them.

'What'd you see down there?' she said. 'When you went down the hole?'

'Not much,' said Macy. 'I found that box thing I brought up.'

'When you went down the second time, to look for the bird guy. While I was gone.'

'You know what I saw, Kinnie.'

Kinnie sighed. 'I'm sorry, Macy. I don't know how many times I gotta say it. I'm sorry.'

'You tried to kill me, Kinnie.'

'Excuse me,' said Rolly. 'Could one of you explain what's going on here?'

Kinnie rubbed her forehead. 'You know how I told you about the mine, how Daddy Joe had that gate installed so people wouldn't go looking down there?'

'Sure, because of the UVTs. Because there were people looking for gold all the time.'

'That was part of it. The real reason he did it was because I left Macy down there one day. I was pissed at her. I left her in the dark to teach her a lesson. I kinda forgot about her. Daddy Joe found out when he came home for dinner. He made me tell him what happened.'

'I spent the whole night down there,' said Macy. 'Until Daddy Joe found me the next morning.'

'How old were you?' said Rolly.

'Seven,' said Macy.

'You stayed down there all night when you were seven?'

Macy looked directly at Rolly. 'Kinnie and I both went in that hole. We were exploring. We both saw that old skeleton. Just like we saw it today. That's what we saw. Kinnie and me. An old skeleton in a mine.'

Macy's gold eyes stared into Rolly's as she spoke. Her eyes told him something different than the words that came out of her mouth. They told him to keep his mouth shut, to stop asking questions. Macy turned back to the front of the truck.

'Kinnie took the ladder away,' she said. 'Left me there. She told me that skeleton was how I was gonna look after the bats ate out my eyes.'

'I was disciplining you,' said Kinnie. 'Until you'd learned your lesson.'

'You know, Kinnie, fifteen minutes woulda been disciplining. All night's more like cruel and unusual punishment.'

'I said I was sorry.'

'Shit, it was easy going down there today,' said Macy. 'I've already seen what was down there. Couldn't have been any worse than when I was seven, in the dark with the bones and the bats.'

'Yeah, well, it didn't do me any good either,' said Kinnie. 'Daddy Joe never forgave me. He stopped talking to me after that, he got so mad. It seems like he started bringing home all that stuff on the UVTs after that, too.'

'After he went in the mine?' said Rolly.

Kinnie nodded.

'You think he found something down there?'

Kinnie opened her door. 'I think it's time we found out,' she said. 'It's time for some sleeping dogs to get kicked in the pants.'

Kinnie climbed out of the truck and opened the back door to let Macy and Rolly out. They walked to the front door. Kinnie knocked once then opened the door.

'Daddy Joe?' she said. 'It's me. I got somebody here who needs to see you.'

They walked into the living room.

'Daddy Joe?'

'Shit, Kinnie, what's that on the table?' said Macy.

Kinnie walked to the side table next to the sofa. 'There's blood on it,' she said, inspecting the stungun.

'Daddy Joe!' said Macy. 'It's Macy. Where are you?'

They heard a sound in the back. Kinnie led the way. Rolly saw drops of blood on the carpet. They found Daddy Joe in the study, slumped over the desk. There was blood on the back of his shirt. Kinnie rushed to his side and jammed two fingers into his neck.

'He's still alive,' she said. She pulled her radio from her belt and made an emergency call.

'I'll get under one arm, you take the other,' she said to Rolly after she finished the call. 'Let's see if we can move him. Macy, get the chair.'

Rolly watched Kinnie slide her neck under Daddy Joe's armpit. He did the same on the opposite side. They lifted Daddy Joe, straining under his weight. Macy pulled the chair away. Daddy Joe's head lolled to one side. He groaned.

'Where to?' said Rolly.

'Just lay him on the floor here,' said Kinnie. They took a few steps back, Daddy Joe's arms hanging over their shoulders. His dead weight made it hard to maneuver, but they managed to pull him away from the desk and lay him down on the floor. A flower of blood stained Daddy Joe's shirt just above his left hip.

Kinnie inspected the wound. 'Doesn't look like they hit anything vital,' she said. 'Stupid old man. Walking all the way back here after getting yourself shot.'

Daddy Joe groaned again.

'That's right, Daddy Joe,' said Kinnie. She leaned in closer to his face and lifted his eyelids. 'You're a stupid old man, chasing after ghosts and aliens when you can't even make peace with the living.'

Daddy Joe's lips moved as if he were trying to say something.

'Macy's here,' said Kinnie. 'She found something, down in the mine. This other guy here, her friend, he figured out how to open it with that guitar thing. There was just some old doll inside, painted gold. Maybe you knew that already, maybe you didn't, but that's what it came down to. Nothing. All those years trying to figure it out. All that sneaking around. There's no gold. Nothing.'

'Cut it out, Kinnie,' said Macy.

'Macy,' said Daddy Joe.

Macy sank down to her knees and took Daddy Joe's hand. 'I'm here, Daddy Joe.'

'Tell her what happened,' said Kinnie. 'You don't have much time left. No more sleeping dogs. She needs to know. I need to know.'

Daddy Joe's lips parted again, as if he might say something, but he didn't speak.

'He's too weak to talk,' said Rolly.

'He'll just have to listen, then,' said Kinnie. 'Daddy Joe, you listen to me. I'm going to tell you a story. You just nod if I get it right. Shake your head if I'm wrong. This might be your last chance to do right by Macy. You understand me? Shake your head if you understand me.'

Daddy Joe gave an almost imperceptible nod of his head.

'That time when I left Macy in the mine, when you got so mad at me, when you found the body down there, the skeleton. You knew who it was, didn't you? That's why you closed down the mine, wasn't it?'

Daddy Joe nodded.

'You knew who it was because you found the necklace there, on the body. You found it with the bones. That's how you knew it was her. You knew it was Betty.'

Daddy Joe nodded again. His bottom lip quivered.

'Then you got them to put that gate in to keep people out. Because you knew someone else might find the body. And if they found it, the sheriff would have to investigate, try to identify who the body was. They'd find out it wasn't that old. And they might find out what you did. How you lied on the witness stand. Then they might have to let that Parnell guy go free. You perjured yourself. You told the jury he was by himself when you arrested him. But he wasn't, was he? There was a girl with him, a black girl with a little baby. You brought that girl home with you, and her baby.'

Kinnie paused, waiting for Daddy Joe's acknowledgement. Rolly could see him still breathing. He nodded.

'That's what happened, isn't it, Daddy Joe?' said Kinnie. 'Nobody else ever knew. Not even me, not until after Macy ran away and I started thinking about things, trying to figure it out. What happened to her, Daddy Joe? What happened to Betty?'

Daddy Joe nodded. His lips moved.

'What'd he say?' said Macy.

Daddy Joe spoke again, barely audible. 'Birdie,' he said.

'What's that mean?' said Macy.

A thumping sound floated through the air. A shadow passed across the sunlight pouring from the window.

'The paramedics are here,' said Kinnie. She stood up. 'I'm going outside. Keep talking to him. Keep him responding.'

Kinnie left the room. Macy held Daddy Joe's hand up to her chest.

'Daddy Joe? It's Macy,' she said. 'What's the birdie?'

Daddy Joe's lips parted. It was almost a smile.

'The little birdie,' said Macy. 'What's the little birdie, Daddy Joe?'

'In the dark. Led me to you.'

'Yes, Daddy Joe. I remember that now. I told you about the little birdie that was my friend. The little birdie that stayed with me all night.'

'Wait a minute,' said Rolly. 'What did this bird sound like? Do you remember?'

Daddy Joe pulled his hand away from Macy. It wavered as he pointed two fingers up at the whiteboard, the word on the board. He gave his hand back to Macy. She looked at Rolly.

'It was him, wasn't it?' she said. 'He was with me, in the cave, when Kinnie left me there. That Buddy guy was there.'

The paramedics arrived, Kinnie leading them in. Macy and Rolly retreated into the living room. They walked outside with Kinnie and watched the emergency crew load Daddy Joe onto the helicopter. The helicopter flew away over the ridge.

'Kinnie,' said Macy, 'why did you lie about Aunt Betty?'

'Daddy Joe made me promise. He was going to give you that diddley bow thing and tell you the whole story when you turned eighteen. He was going to explain it all to you.'

'I remember him, Kinnie. The birdman. We would hear him sometimes. When you and I went exploring. He helped Daddy Joe find me, that time you left me in the cave.'

'I'm sorry, Macy.'

'Was it him? Did he kill my mother?'

'He didn't mean to. It was an accident. Your mom, Betty, heard the birdman calling one night. She tried to find him. She ran away. Daddy Joe didn't tell anybody because of the trial. Those bones that we found in the cave – that was your momma.'

'I know,' said Macy.

'He didn't mean for her to die, Macy. That birdman was your daddy. He loved your mama.'

'I know, Kinnie,' said Macy. 'I know he did.'

THIRTY-FOUR
The Homecoming

Rolly Waters stood offstage at The Range in Slab City. His Fender Telecaster hung from his shoulder as he waited to go on. It had been less than a week since he'd first played with the Slab City Rockers, a few days longer than that since he'd first met Macy Starr while eating Mexican food at two-thirty in the morning. Macy was here, sitting in the front row, the guest of honor in a beat-up reclining chair placed front and center in the audience. The Rockers would close out tonight's ceremony, a memorial service for the man the Slabbers called Goldhands: Buddy Meeks. The Rockers would play all night if they needed to. They would play until everyone in the audience felt that they'd done Buddy justice, until everyone had gone home, until they'd given the proper *adieu*. Until the sun came up, when the morning light told them it was time to move on.

The first part of the evening was for others to take the stage, a chance to express their personal feelings and appreciation. Cool Bob acted as master of ceremonies, introducing each person who offered a testimonial, poem or prayer. Many of the Slabbers told personal stories of how Goldhands had helped them, how they came to respect his eccentric ways. They talked about the weird birdman who had flitted through camp, the one who fixed their generators, hooked up their solar panels, restored old guitars so they played better than new. They talked about how they kept strangers away, protecting his privacy. One man displayed drawings of a sculpture he planned to build in East Jesus as a more permanent memorial, a large golden hand you could play like a harp, with guitar strings stretched between the various fingers.

Rolly and Macy had arrived early that afternoon in the Tioga, which they'd borrowed again from Alicia. Rolly's father had returned home from the hospital two days earlier. Macy had insisted on coming along to meet him. Her salty style seemed to amuse the old sailor. Rolly was glad to have her along to take up the slack. Their conversation remained civil, not strained. It helped Rolly avoid the big questions his mother had hoped he'd address with his father. Those questions were for another visit, one he'd make by himself when he screwed up his courage. He had enough on his plate now, keeping up with Macy and surviving a second trip to Slab City.

Sometime next week the DNA tests would come back, and Macy would find out for sure if Buddy Meeks had been her father. Then the coroner's office would honor her claim. Macy had a plan. She'd proposed it to Rolly earlier in the day. It was a crazy and reckless plan, but he'd have to give her an answer on the return trip.

After parking and setting up the Tioga, they went to meet Bob at his trailer. From there, Bob took them to Buddy's place, an old trailer parked further down the road from the East Jesus. Buddy had staked out a modest kingdom over the years, delineating his territory with a hodgepodge of barbed wire, old tires and corrugated tin sheets. A box had been set on a post at the entrance. There was a tuning fork set in the top of the box. According to Bob, anybody wanting to communicate with Buddy had to write out a message, set it inside the box and tap the tuning fork. An hour later, sometimes as long as a day, Buddy would show up at your campsite and take a look at the problem that needed to be addressed, tossing gravel and dirt at your window to announce his arrival. You could pay him in food or any discarded junk he found to his liking.

Buddy's property was covered in neatly arranged piles of junk, sorted by types. Computer parts, plastic dolls, metal wire and pieces of wood were all separated into individual piles. Two workbenches sat in the shade, close to the trailer. Bob showed them the table where he'd watched Buddy make gold, where Buddy melted down old motherboards with Bunsen burners and mixed in chemicals to separate the gold from the slurry. A half-finished diddley bow lay on the second bench, its roughed-out shape awaiting more passes with increasingly fine gradations of sandpaper.

The inside of the trailer looked surprisingly neat, even orderly, filled with papers and technical books. There were drawings and sketches taped to the walls, stacks of composition books filled with paragraphs of text and mathematical equations. There were cans of beans in the cupboards – white beans and black beans, pinto and red beans, baked, refried and barbequed. There was no identification to be found, no photos of Buddy, of any family and friends. He'd stripped away all vestiges of a personal life except for one item, a promotional flyer taped to the wall across from the dining table, a flyer for DJ Macy Starr.

Bob told Macy the trailer was hers if she wanted it. The police had already been through everything. Bob and the Rockers had set up a volunteer watch to discourage scavengers until Macy decided what she wanted to keep. He left Rolly and Macy alone in the trailer. They sat next to each other in the dining-room booth, going through papers and notebooks.

'How much you think I can get for this trailer?' said Macy.

'I don't know.'

'How much do I owe you?' said Macy.

'I haven't figured that out yet,' said Rolly.

'You think the trailer will pay for it?'

'It would more than pay for it, I'm pretty sure.'

'I might want to keep it a while.'

'We'll work something out.'

'This piece of ass don't come cheap, if that's what you mean by working it out.'

'That's not what I meant.'

'You're done with me, right, Waters? No more boning with Macy?'

'Would you stop it?'

Macy surveyed the trailer. She seemed nervous, even more twitchy than usual. 'It's weird,' she said. 'Having a dad.'

'Tell me about it,' said Rolly.

'Your dad's OK, not as bad as you made him seem,' said Macy.

'He wasn't drunk,' said Rolly.

'What's he like when he's drunk?'

'Louder. Likes to tell you what's wrong with you. All the ways you've failed to meet his expectations.'

'That did kinda piss me off, the way he orders your stepmom around.'

'I don't think she even hears it anymore.'

'Is that how you were? When you were a drunk?'

'I was very happy when I was a drunk. I liked everybody.'

'That doesn't sound so bad.'

'I didn't always make good decisions. About people.'

Macy laughed. 'Hell, Waters, you don't make good decisions when you're sober. How else do you explain me?'

Rolly smiled. He couldn't explain Macy Starr. He didn't need to. 'Have you called Eric Ozzie yet?' he said.

'No.' Macy sighed. 'I guess I should meet him.'

'He could tell you more about Betty. He's your uncle, after all.'

Macy scrunched her nose. Her dirty-blonde dreadlocks bounced off her shoulders.

'Does this mean I'm gonna have to start going over to his place for Christmas and stuff now? I don't know if I'm ready for that shit. I like being unattached.'

'Just meet him and see how it goes. That's all I'm saying.'

'Shut up and deal with it. That's what you're saying.'

'No, I'm not.'

'Aargh,' said Macy. She waved her hands in the air. 'I don't feel connected to any of this. The weird music and the alien shit. All those people that died. It seems like I should be freaking out or something. It's all kind of horrible. I mean, I've seen four dead people in the last week. My mom's a pile of bones and my daddy died in my arms. Shouldn't I be freaking out more?'

'We all process stuff differently.'

'You've seen people die before. How did you react?'

'Well, one time I threw up.'

'Yeah, that's what I'm talking about. Something more visceral.'

'It was pretty visceral.'

'You think anyone knows about it, besides us?' said Macy.

'What's that?'

'The room, with the gold.'

'Kinnie might know. She knows about Betty.'

'You think she was testing us?'

'What do you mean?'

'She didn't say anything about the gold. All she talked about was the bones.'

'I thought that was weird too. She just told us it was Betty's body.'

'It's a freaking weird thing not to mention, right? A gold room and gold bones?'

Rolly nodded.

'We wouldn't have known about it without you playing that vibrator thing so the lights would go on.'

'No. I guess not.'

'How much do you think all that stuff is worth?'

'No idea. I'm not sure how you get it all out of there.'

'Remember that guy, Leonard, I told you about?' said Macy.

'Who?'

'The guy that built Salvation Mountain.'

'Oh, yeah.'

'You remember how I thought it was cool, when someone goes crazy and spends their whole life on something that's not all about money.'

Rolly nodded.

'My dad was like that, wasn't he?' said Macy. 'He could've kept all that gold for himself, retired down to Puerto Vallarta or something. That's what the others would've done – Gibbons or Randy or that Dotty lady. My dad must've spent a lot of time working on that room, the gold rocket ship or whatever it is. How many years you think he spent doing that? Just to help those people out, make sure they connected with the aliens, hitching a ride to the planets or whatever it was. That's what it was about, wasn't it?'

'Sounds about right.'

Macy slid out of the booth. She walked to the rear of the trailer then walked back.

'I want to go back there,' she said, 'when I get the body. I'll cremate him and take his ashes there. Put him back with my mom. That's where he belongs. I want to seal the place up.'

'How are you going to do that?'

'I'll get some cement or something, maybe some boards and rebar, get rid of that ladder and seal up the hole. I don't want any spelunkers or gold bugs or aliens finding the place. I want it to stay like that, forever. At least until that Conjoinment thing comes along again. I'm the only one left now who was there with the UVTs. I'm the Sachem. I'm in charge. It's my responsibility now.'

'I guess you could look at it that way.'

'It's a real word, you know. I looked it up.'
'Sachem? What's it mean?'
'It's an Indian word. The chief. That little gold baby is now the chief.'
'Hail to the chief.'
'So, are you in, Waters?'
'What?'
'I need your help.'
'With what?'
'I want you to go with me,' said Macy. 'I want you to play that diddley bow again, like you did before. So I can see it one last time. Then we'll leave him inside, with my mom, and seal the place up. They'll be together. I'll be free. That's what I want, Waters.'

Rolly blinked and looked out at the audience. Someone was calling his name. Cool Bob stood at the microphone, beckoning Rolly on to the center stage. The audience cheered as he stepped out from the wings. He waved and connected his guitar cord into the amplifier. He wondered if he could ever plug a guitar into an amplifier again without thinking of the Astral Vibrator and the golden room, a room in a cave in the mountains, a room that lit up when you played the right notes, golden notes for the gold-blooded aliens. He wouldn't play any golden notes tonight. He would only play notes that were dirty and rough, bent notes and blue notes and slide notes. He would play imperfect frequencies for all the flawed earthlings he knew. He would play for the heretic citizens of Slab City, his own dishonored father and the eccentric orphan girl Macy Starr, for everyone who was going to die. As they all would. Someday.

The drummer counted to four. The band launched into the song. He joined them. The sound they made was like a beautiful rocket ship, breaking through gravity and arcing into an uncertain universe, full of bright stars.